WHERE RIVERS PART

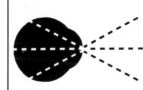

This Large Print Book carries the
Seal of Approval of N.A.V.H.

A TEXAS GOLD NOVEL, BOOK 2

WHERE RIVERS PART

KELLIE COATES GILBERT

THORNDIKE PRESS

A part of Gale, Cengage Learning

GALE
CENGAGE Learning·

Farmington Hills, Mich • San Francisco • New York • Waterville, Maine
Meriden, Conn • Mason, Ohio • Chicago

GALE
CENGAGE Learning·

LIBRARY OF CONGRESS CATALOGING-IN-PUBLICATION DATA

Gilbert, Kellie Coates.
    Where rivers part / by Kellie Coates Gilbert. — Large print edition.
        pages cm. — (Thorndike Press large print Christian fiction) (A Texas gold novel ; #2)
    ISBN 978-1-4104-7874-0 (hardcover) — ISBN 1-4104-7874-2 (hardcover)
    1. Large type books. I. Title.
PS3607.I42323W48 2015b
813'.6—dc23   2015001028

Published in 2015 by arrangement with Revell Books, a division of Baker Publishing Group

Printed in Mexico
1 2 3 4 5 6 7 19 18 17 16 15

To Eric and Jordan Gilbert
My heart's treasures — my sons.

When you pass through the waters,
I will be with you;
and when you pass through the rivers,
they will not sweep over you. . . .
For I am the LORD your God,
the Holy One of Israel, your Savior.

Isaiah 43:2–3 NIV

1

Conference hotels all look the same.

This is what Juliet Ryan thought as she stepped into the lobby of the Renaissance Marriott Convention Center, with its enormous floral arrangements and lengthy granite-topped counter lined with check-in clerks and their pasted smiles.

Even though she'd given up the secret vice months ago, Juliet found herself wanting a cigarette. Especially today, when the need to calm her nerves with a few quick puffs tugged at her like a leash.

She mentally shook off the craving and gave herself a pep talk. She had no reason to feel this anxious. Not really.

Then why was she letting him back in her head?

In quality control circles, the North American Food Safety Symposium (NAFSS) was the pinnacle in a very high stack of conferences held across the nation each year. Even her father would have to admit her inclusion signaled a grand recognition among her peers that she'd finally made it. This conference featured only the elite candidates in the food safety field, and she was one of them. She had every reason to feel confident.

After fishing a schedule from the leather attaché hanging from her shoulder, she quickly located the Grand Ballroom on the map and made her way down a long hall in that direction. Midway, she stopped to check her lipstick in a mirror that reflected an image of exactly what she hoped to portray — an educated, accomplished young woman who had earned the respect of her colleagues, not an easy feat in a field overrun with testosterone and gray hair.

Her spot on the dais was third from the end on a row of tables seating nine — not exactly the first order of prestige, but nonetheless a position of some cachet. After her presentation today, no doubt she'd cement a spot closer to the head of the table, even if she were the only woman presenter again next year.

On stage, Dr. Keller Thatcher, director of NAFSS, read off the impressive credentials of each of the panel members, while an audience of bobbleheads nodded their collective approval.

The first to take the podium was Leonard Paternoster, a plaintiffs' attorney who had carefully cultivated his notoriety after winning several highly publicized landmark awards — all delineated in the brochure Juliet nervously folded in her hands.

Mr. Paternoster gripped the podium. "Good morning, everyone. I am an attorney specializing in foodborne illness cases. Before I go any further, I need to disclose that I am here for one reason alone — and that is to help you put me out of business."

Juliet listened to the spiel she'd heard many times before, knowing the somberfaced attorney had been positioned to go first for good reason. The threat of a lawsuit always made people in the food industry sit up and pay attention. No one wanted another deadly restaurant outbreak like the Jack in the Box situation in the nineties.

She'd been in junior high when a silverhaired talk show personality named Phil Donahue interviewed those affected by the outbreak. Juliet's father wanted to take credit for her career choice, but really, the moment Juliet knew she wanted to spend her professional life pursuing food safety was triggered by that television program and the look in Vicki Detwiler's eyes as she described how her seventeen-month-old son tested positive for E. coli, and his agonizing last hours.

Of course, her career choice came with a few drawbacks. A person trained to ensure safety and wholesomeness of food products was rarely at the top of any dinner party guest list. She also hadn't counted on the bleak disinterest in men's eyes when they discovered how many hours she devoted to pathogens and coliforms.

Still, for all the disadvantages, Juliet loved her profession. Her work mattered.

She held on to this satisfying thought as she took her turn at the podium.

"Good morning. My name is Dr. Juliet Ryan, quality assurance director for Larimar Springs Corporation. I'm here to bring an added perspective to what my esteemed colleagues have shared this morning, and look at these issues from inside the walls of the food producer." Duplicating her father's calculated method for creating impact, she leaned forward ever so slightly and made eye contact with the audience. "We are on the front line, charged with keeping America's food products safe."

Over the next hour, Juliet communicated her carefully memorized points, all constructed to balance the often skewed belief that food corporations only thought in terms of the financial bottom line, then moved to her closing statements.

"Companies across America are using the most sophisticated scientific techniques available to refine the processes used to kill pathogens." She paused for emphasis, appreciating that every eye was focused on her and what she had to say. Her message had hit its mark with the distinguished audience. This was her moment in the spotlight, and she'd satisfactorily shone.

Relieved, she took a deep breath and concluded, "Consumer health and safety are at the very core of what we do every day, and because of the collective efforts of dedicated food scientists and quality assurance directors in companies across America, outbreaks are now rare, with fewer reported each year than ever before." She let her lips part in a wide smile, showing off gleaming (and costly) white teeth. "Thank you."

Juliet waited until the applause faded before extending appreciation to the directors of the symposium for inviting her to speak. She straightened her notes at the podium and prepared to return to her seat when a hand shot up in the back of the auditorium. "Uh, excuse me. I have a couple of questions."

11

Juliet froze. Her eyes darted to the owner of the familiar voice.

"Isn't it true that as recent as two months ago, twenty-four people in Kansas were sickened with cyclospora linked to honey? And only weeks before that, in California, over a hundred fell ill after eating frozen strawberries tainted with salmonella? I could name a dozen more such incidents, all in the last twelve months. I hope no one in this room lets down their guard, believing we've done even near enough."

Hundreds of heads turned to face the voice, likely wondering who would be bold enough to challenge her assertions. But Juliet knew . . .

The voice belonged to her father.

Juliet scrambled for the elevator. She crammed her finger against the call button, then buried her hands in her attaché, feeling around for the pack of cigarettes she no longer carried. Frustrated, she pulled out a half-eaten package of antacids instead, popped two tablets, and chewed furiously.

Like a wrecking ball, her father had nearly crumbled her success on that stage.

She thought she would die of embarrassment, that the audience would be forced to watch her melt into a woman-shaped

12

puddle. Thankfully, she'd pulled herself to-gether.

"Oh, I think we all agree we must remain vigilant," she'd countered. "That's why hundreds of us are here in this auditorium, when we could be out on a golf course somewhere enjoying this gorgeous day."

The remark drew a laugh and took the edge off the tension in the room. She'd successfully deflected what could have been a disaster.

A ding sounded as the doors opened to an already crowded elevator. Juliet shuffled inside and quickly moved to the rear, despite her tendency to feel claustrophobic. A man she recognized from the audience stepped aside, making room for her. "Appreciated your perspective this morning, Dr. Ryan."

"Thank you," she said.

The pedantic man nodded in her direction before turning to her father, whom she'd failed to notice earlier. He wore a slightly rumpled suit, and black frames were perched atop his fading brown hair with a mind of its own.

"Dr. Ryan, I admire your work. I read all your books. I especially appreciated *The Great Hunt for a Sustainable Food System.*"

Juliet's face bloomed red as she realized

his compliment had not been meant for her.

Her father thanked his fan, having the decency to give her an embarrassed smile first. Still, her mouth went dry, her palms instantly sweaty.

They rode in uncomfortable silence, stopping at each level to let passengers out. When the doors opened on the tenth floor, her father held the door with his hand to keep it from closing. He waited for an elderly woman with thinning hair to board, then hesitated only briefly before looking back at Juliet. "Well, this is my floor." He gave her an uneasy smile. "Uh, you did a nice job today, JuJu. Your mother will be proud when I tell her."

Juliet raised her chin, locking his gaze with her own. "Traveling without a pretty assistant? That's not like you."

His eyes steeled, his expression somewhere between sad and furious. He opened his mouth to respond but seemed to think better of it. After looking at her for several long seconds, he turned and stepped from the elevator.

The doors closed behind him, leaving Juliet alone with the woman inside the elevator. Juliet responded to her frown with a raw look. "Oh, don't worry. That was nothing. We didn't even draw blood this time."

Before the elevator could resume its upward chug, Juliet pounded the button to the lobby. With any luck, the hotel gift shop she'd passed earlier sold cigarettes.

2

As the sun toppled full over the San Antonio horizon, Juliet tucked her head and pounded her running shoes against the paved trail, pushing to pick up speed around the final corner. Her lungs burned against the already hot morning air, meting out punishment for every stolen puff she'd given in to yesterday. She'd been weak and must renew her determination to end the nasty habit — one she'd taken up to counter the stress of finishing her doctorate.

The encounter with her father had caught her off guard. After their tense exchange, she had two choices — head to the restaurant for a pile of onion rings or to the designated smoking area to the right of the pool. The way she figured things, her nicotine breath could be covered up with gum, but as she'd experienced for most of her childhood and early teen years, giving in to comfort food proved more difficult to hide, even though you wouldn't know it to look at her now.

Juliet finished her run, wiped her face with a towel, and stretched one slender leg out on the park bench, then the other, each time bending her forehead to her thigh, letting the motion pull her calf muscles taut.

Frankly, she was exhausted and wished she could curl up on that bench and catch a quick nap. The conference had taken a toll. Even at age thirty-three and despite her mostly healthy lifestyle, she felt herself getting older by the minute. Last month, the mirror revealed tiny lines at the corners of her eyes, which prompted a quick appointment at the exclusive Elian Spa for a very expensive laser treatment.

She'd finally attained an age where she'd be taken seriously in her line of work, but with it came a related set of issues. She couldn't afford to let her looks go.

After glancing at her watch, she cut her stretching routine short and headed for the parking lot, finishing off a bottle of water on the way — Larimar Springs water, a label she was proud of.

Several highly qualified candidates had vied for the quality assurance director position, but she'd learned the position was hers from the minute her résumé crossed the desk of the CEO.

During their initial meeting, Juliet found Alexa Carmichael's handshake firm and her no-nonsense approach even more unwavering. The woman was a walking advertisement for what women in business could achieve.

Juliet could tell from one quick glance that Alexa's suit was a Donna Karan. She'd seen the olive-colored jacket and pencil skirt at Neiman Marcus in Dallas last month. A bit out of her price range.

Most of her own designer apparel was snagged at off-the-rack stores. Only one item had been purchased at retail, and she'd agonized over paying that kind of money. But when Alexa Carmichael turned her pearl-laden neck and glanced with approval at Juliet's black patent Louboutins, she knew she'd spent well.

Both women shared a certain knowledge — ability mattered, but image was everything.

Twenty minutes into the interview, Juliet sensed she'd created a bond with the blonde executive, whose own sharp-edged style earned respect from those inside and outside the corporation. Who knew? Perhaps Alexa saw her younger self reflected in Juliet's confidence and credentials.

"We'll be in touch soon," Alexa promised with a smile, ending the interview in under an hour. "The role of the quality assurance director is critical, and we'll want to integrate you into the team as quickly as possible."

Her mother had been delighted, as expected. "Oh, honey. I knew you'd do well. You are so smart." Then, as if the idea just popped into her head at that moment, her mom's face broke into a delighted grin. "Now you'll get to move back to San Antonio. My girl will be home again."

Juliet's father, on the other hand, peered over top his magazine from across the table. He frowned, his broad forehead creasing. "So the devil enticed you to the dark side, huh?"

"Oh, Bennett. Stop." Her mother waved him off. "Ignore him, honey. We're both proud of you."

Unlike her dad, her mother had always been in her corner.

Not wanting to ruin a good run, Juliet pushed thoughts of her father from her mind and crossed the now crowded parking lot. Inside her car, she shoved her key into the ignition and started the engine, then quickly pushed the air-conditioning on high and waited for it to blow cool. Even this

19

early in the day, the morning air seemed weighted with heat. Outside the driver's side window, two women passed by in running clothes, each drenched in sweat and carrying a bottle of Larimar Springs water.

Perhaps she'd joined with the devil. But nothing quenched the heat like water.

"Morning, Dr. Ryan. How's it going?" Juliet's assistant jumped up from her desk and followed as Juliet made her way into her office.

"Good morning, Tavina." She opened her attaché and removed the contents — among them her travel itinerary, the invoice from the hotel, and the conference program — and placed them in Tavina's hand. "What's on the agenda for today?" She slipped into her desk chair and lifted the screen on her Mac.

"Alexa called some big meeting this morning. The large conference room at eleven. She said to tell you it would run over lunch." Tavina shuffled through the papers, immediately putting her hand on the documents she'd need for the expense report. "How was the conference? Sorry about the late-night route, but that flight was the only one available."

She opened her email folder and groaned

at the volume. She knew better than to let her inbox pile up while she was away. "Don't worry. The travel arrangements were fine," she said, looking up at Tavina. "Did Alexa say what the meeting was about?"

Tavina shook her head. "No. Just said to make sure you were there." Her assistant glanced back at the open door, then leaned forward and lowered her voice. "But word has it, there's some big announcement coming."

She rewarded Tavina with an appreciative nod.

No classroom instructor ever revealed what Juliet learned very early in her career — administrative assistants were one of your most valuable resources. Sure, a good one performed their job duties well, but the real gold was tapping into the stream of information that flowed from the administrative network — which is why she'd taken Tavina Mosely to lunch that first week on the job.

Juliet had wanted to treat her new assistant to an elegant lunch at the Colonial Room in the historic Menger Hotel, but Tavina widened her gorgeous deep brown eyes and said, "Oh no, huh-uh. That place is haunted. I appreciate the offer and all, but ghosts just ain't my thing."

So instead, they parked themselves at a

rustic thick wooden table in the trendy Boiler House located in the Pearl. Over spinach salads and grilled pineapple pound cake, she learned Tavina had grown up on the west side of San Antonio, in a condominium project known as Casiano Court, built in the fifties by the San Antonio Housing Authority. Not exactly a great neighborhood.

Both Tavina and her brothers attended community college, thanks to a mother who kept her children at the kitchen table with their studies and out of the streets where most of their friends hung out. "Mama used to tell us we could do things her way, or her way — but no matter what, we were going to do things her way." Her assistant laughed and dabbed the linen napkin at the corners of her mouth.

It was Tavina who clued her in to the fact Alexa was not a morning person — the result of working until the wee hours from home — and to never approach her with anything requiring a decision before she'd had at least two cups of coffee. The comptroller, Fred Macklin, had a penchant for issuing reports, and if your inbox filled with large stapled documents, he was the likely culprit. His secretary, a wiry little woman in her sixties, might go through your desk drawers if you didn't lock them.

"Alva Jacobs is the worse kind of snoop," Tavina warned. "I mean, really, what does the ol' bat think she'll find?"

Juliet was amazed. "She goes through people's desk drawers?"

"Yup, we all know to lock 'em before heading to lunch." Tavina finished off her cake and placed her fork neatly by the side of her plate. "And never wander around the plant alone during the evening shift."

Juliet lifted her brow. "Why not?"

Tavina's face took on a knowing look. "Well, the ugly girls can."

Juliet nodded slowly, hating that women in corporate America still faced obstacles of that nature. Tavina would be especially vulnerable, with her big brown doe-like eyes rimmed with thick black lashes and skin the color of milk chocolate — the expensive kind that melts in your mouth like silk. The girl could easily be a model, and a stunning one at that. Sadly, raising a small son on her own limited those options. But Tavina didn't seem to mind. She really liked her job.

Juliet was most interested in what Tavina had to say about Greer Latham, the vice president of marketing and sales. "All the girls definitely agree that dude is some fine eye candy," her assistant confided.

Juliet hesitated, not sure how to react to what she knew was dangerous territory. Tavina picked up on her concern and waved her off. "Oh, I know, I know. But it works both ways. The ladies look too, and you *know* that's so, girl."

To her credit, Tavina wasn't afraid to speak her mind, a fact that had benefited Juliet often in the early weeks of her new position.

From the frown now on her assistant's face, Juliet knew to brace herself for another round of candor. "What?"

Tavina sniffed at the papers in her hand. "Don't tell me you've been smoking again? You said you was quitting?"

"I know, I know. I only had one." Juliet swallowed her little white lie and waved Tavina out the door. "Now, let me get through these emails before that meeting."

Promptly at eleven o'clock, the executive board members and department heads gathered in the large conference room. Juliet took a seat sandwiched between the head of human resources and the extraction manager. Across the massive granite table, Greer Latham sat looking as perfectly GQ as Tavina had described in that first lunch,

24

with his precision haircut and expensive gray suit. Their eyes met only briefly before Alexa Carmichael strode into the room.

Alexa glanced around, quickly surveying those gathered in the conference room, then made her way to her designated spot at the head of the table. Above, a large gilded frame hung on the wall with the company logo: LARIMAR SPRINGS — PURE QUALITY, GREAT TASTE.

"Okay, people. We have a lot to cover this morning. So let's get started." She slid into a high-backed leather chair and opened a monogrammed leather portfolio, then gave a quick nod to Fred Macklin. The prematurely white-haired comptroller stood. With a wide smile, he passed out thick, stapled reports.

Alexa crossed her arms on the table. "As you know, Larimar Springs has enjoyed record profits over the past decade. Together, we've achieved much. Fundamentally, I believe this company is poised to do even more." Her face lit with excitement. "That is why it is my pleasure to announce that, as of eight o'clock this morning, Larimar Springs joined with a new equity partner, Montavan International, headquartered in Milan, Italy."

Alarm sprouted on the faces in the room.

Juliet felt her own heart flutter. Mergers often meant consolidation, and consolidation often meant layoffs. Even at the executive levels.

Alexa held up her hand and smiled. "Let me quickly assure you — this is a good thing. First, Montavan International will remain a silent partner. The day-to-day operations will remain firmly under my direction. You will see very little change in the way this company does business from a practical standpoint."

Juliet noted a catlike smile hinting at the corners of Fred Macklin's mouth. Obviously, he'd known this news before the meeting. And from the unruffled look on Greer's face, the announcement came as no surprise to him as well. She, along with the others, had been kept in the proverbial "only those who need to know" dark.

Juliet rationalized she was the newest executive team member — only on board a little over a month. It would stand to reason she'd been kept out of Alexa's inner circle on this one. Still, she felt unsettled somehow. Like she'd been late for the big game and wasn't quite up to speed on the playbook.

Alexa straightened with confidence. "The bottled water market is still highly untapped.

This strategic liaison will provide additional capital, access to European markets, and growth that will not only spur opportunity for us as a company but also for individuals, both at the executive and the employee levels."

Over the next hours, Juliet and her peers scribbled copious notes as Alexa fielded questions and reassured everyone in the meeting that the company integration with Montavan International was a smart business maneuver. The days ahead were bright, she claimed.

By the end of the meeting, Juliet found herself listening intently, believing it.

3

"Your company is merging? What will that mean?" Juliet's mother bent and peered into the open oven. A distracted scowl broke across her face. "I knew the temperature in that recipe was too high," she said under her breath. She reached with mitted hands and slid the onion tart out of the oven and onto the waiting baker's rack, then peered back at the *Bon Appétit* magazine lying open on the counter.

Juliet swiveled her barstool and faced her mom. "Nothing from a practical standpoint. Larimar Springs will continue to run as an independent company, and the executives, including me, will move forward with our responsibilities, same as before."

"Oh, that's good, honey." Her mother removed the mitts and tossed them on the counter. Her forefinger poked at the tart.

Her father entered the kitchen, his feet wrapped in ratty worn slippers her mother had given him for Christmas more than ten years ago. "What's good?" Before anyone had a chance to respond, he wrapped his arms around his apron-clad wife and kissed the back of her neck.

Juliet's mom grinned and slapped him away. "Not in front of the children," she teased. She tweaked his stubbled chin in a tender exchange, one that irked Juliet.

In college, Juliet was one of the rare few who did not have a stepmother or step-father. At that time, her parents had been married over twenty-five years. "You don't know how lucky you are," she was told over and over.

Marcy Elliott, a girl in her freshman bio-chem class, complained her own mother had cycled through four marriages, leaving a string of step-siblings trailing behind. "Holidays are a nightmare," she'd confided. Another complained she had to be the maid of honor at her dad's remarriage to a plastic-faced woman with a love for the plastic in her father's wallet.

Yes, everyone considered Juliet one of the lucky ones. But luck had many sides.

Juliet's mom moved to the cupboard and pulled down three white plates. "Bennett, be a dear and help me set the table." Her dad smiled and took the plates, but not before he snuck an annoying wink in her direction.

As soon as he'd left the room, her mom turned to Juliet. "I'll be glad when his classes start up again next month. Your father works nearly full-time at the institute and still has too much time on his hands every summer. Heaven help me if the university ever forces him to retire from his teaching post."

Juliet tried to fathom her father in retirement. Like her mother, she couldn't imagine Dr. Bennett Ryan letting go of the world that so defined him, even if leaving his position allowed for spending more time with his wife.

Juliet's parents had met at a Foreigner concert in Portland, Oregon. As the story went, he took one look at Carol and knew she was "the one." Her mother, on the other hand, claimed she hadn't been so sure at first, admitting she was attracted to the guy with rumpled light brown hair and a warm smile, but didn't quite know what to think when he stood next to her singing at the top of his lungs "I Wanna Know What Love Is" — off-key, she added.

Later, she learned his name was Bennett Ryan, he was from Texas, and they both attended the University of Oregon in nearby

Eugene, where she'd grown up. Despite his scattered appearance (she said he looked a lot like a young Harrison Ford), he was incredibly intelligent, an attribute she found very attractive.

Bennett had gazed at Carol's auburn hair and dimples and claimed he knew at that moment *exactly* what love was. After the concert, she ditched her friends, and she and Bennett headed to a little bakery nestled a half block from the Sellwood Bridge, discovering they shared a love of coconut cream pie and the popular television show *M*A*S*H,* and a disdain for all things Nixon and Watergate related. Juliet's mom was surprised to learn her dad didn't drive a truck (didn't all guys from Texas drive pickups?) but instead a Chevy Nova, the Spirit of America commemorative model made in 1976, our country's two hundredth birthday. And, she'd secretly confided, she loved his Old Spice aftershave.

Juliet had heard the story many times growing up.

Her mother picked up the tart and headed for the dining room. "Honey, grab the salad, would you?"

She slipped from the barstool and moved for the refrigerator.

Her mother had gotten her degree in

social work and left her fondness for Mount Hood, the Oregon coast, and misty forests filled with flowering rhododendrons to follow her father back to Texas, embracing the arid environment with the same enthusiasm she had for life. "Yuccas and aloe have their own kind of lovely," her mother reminded anyone who wondered why she'd left the beautiful Pacific Northwest.

Juliet followed her mom into the dining room, carrying a quinoa salad made with Kalamata olives and feta cheese. Her mother was a great cook and could often be found in the kitchen experimenting with a new recipe she'd seen on the Food Network. She seemed to always be looking for ways to stuff something healthy down Juliet's father, but every once in a while she folded to his pressure and made fried chicken and mashed potatoes with her signature cream gravy.

Unfortunately, Juliet had not inherited domesticity from her predecessors. Her gravy always ended up lumpy, or too thin, or too salty. "Don't feel bad," her dad would say. "Few women can cook like your mother."

Of course, he was also prone to point out other ways Juliet fell short. "JuJu, why try out for the track team? Running is not your strong suit." Or this classic: "Don't be so hard on yourself, microbial cytology concepts are tough to comprehend. Some never manage to absorb the underlying theories. If you want to excel, you'll just have to buckle down and apply yourself."

So when they all sat down for dinner and her father launched another judgment grenade across the table, she shouldn't have been surprised.

"I think your presentation in Chicago caught the attention of many in the audience." He dished a generous portion of the salad onto his plate.

Many, but not my father, Juliet thought. She stabbed a piece of poached tilapia with her fork and slid it onto her plate. "I agree. Of course, some will always be dissuaded by a vocal minority." Juliet moved on to the onion tart, challenging him with her eyes.

Her mother glanced nervously between the two of them. "Okay, you two. No work talk at the table. Besides, I'm dying to tell you both about what's happening with the birthing center."

Her father's gaze lingered briefly before he caved and shifted his attention to her mother. "Oh? What's going on with the center, Carol?"

"Well, donations from that last golf fundraiser we held here at the Quarry netted enough for us to open the center two months ahead of schedule." Her face filled with enthusiasm. "And I think we finally settled on a name. What do you both think of New Beginnings?" Juliet stared at her plate in silence while her mom chattered on. "I like the simplicity of the name. With the proper logo design, it would be perfect, I think. This center fills such a need here in San Antonio. When we finally open, *all* women, no matter their financial means, will have access to the best in birthing care."

True to her conciliatory nature, Juliet's mom had rallied forces to bridge a gap in medical services. Not only between the haves and have-nots, but more to her credit, she'd headed an effort to bring those with two normally opposing points of view — midwives and obstetricians — together for one purpose. She believed extracting the best from both worlds would ultimately serve women and newborns much better. She was often heard saying, "Both sides can learn from each other if they'll climb off their soapboxes and decide they don't have *all* the answers."

Carol Ryan felt much the same about politics and religion. "We all can see things differently and still treat one another with respect."

Of course, some years ago her mom had become a Christian, and lucky for Juliet's father, his wife had embraced the whole love and forgiveness thing.

Juliet slid her fish aside on her plate, no longer hungry.

Across the table, her father smiled at her mom, told her how proud he was of her work to fund the birthing center. Her mother let out a soft giggle when he suggested she was never more beautiful than when she'd been pregnant.

Her mom covered Juliet's hand with her own. "I remember when you were born. That was such a special night, sweetheart. I tried to keep my eyes on my focal point and breathe through the contractions, but your father distracted me. He'd pace, then kneel down and risk a peek at the action — like he was a baseball catcher or something." She laughed.

"Truth was, I was scared to death," her father confided. "Your mother dragged me to classes for months, but nothing prepared me for the actual birth." His voice filled with emotion, and he looked at her. "No classroom instructor can tell you what that moment is really like — how it feels to see your daughter enter the world."

Was he tearing up? Really?

Juliet quickly glanced at her watch. She cleared her throat. "Um — the news is on in five minutes. Mind if I turn on the television? There's supposed to be an announcement about the merger, and I don't want to miss it."

Her mother gently squeezed her hand. "Sure, honey." She glanced across the table and gave her husband an empathetic smile. "Bennett, let's move into the study and I'll serve dessert on the TV trays."

Her father went for the trays while she followed her mom into the kitchen, both of their arms loaded with dirty dishes. Her mother deposited her load onto the counter, then wiped her hands on a towel. "Honey, he loves you, you know."

She leaned and kissed her mother's cheek, caught the sweet fragrance of her patchouli-scented perfume. "Yes, I know," she lied.

Everything in her wanted to please her mom. Certainly, everything would be simpler if she could embrace the notion that love and forgiveness conquered all. Unfortunately, Juliet had drawn a line in her own heart.

Some things she would never forgive.

4

Before her father was the director of the North American Food Safety Institute (NAFSI), before he taught full-time at the University of Texas, and prior to becoming Dr. Bennett Ryan, Juliet bragged to her third-grade class that he was her father.

It was a Friday, if she remembered correctly, and all week the kids had anticipated Career Day, when parents would show up and give presentations and tell about their professions.

Susie Beckler's mom was a nurse, and she brought her stethoscope and let the students listen to each other's heartbeats. Mrs. Myers paired them up, and when it was her turn, Juliet pressed the little silver cup against Sam Carter's chest. She found the thumping rhythm fascinating until he silently passed gas, causing her to gag. She tried to stop by placing her hand over her mouth, and for some strange reason, her retching made Sam laugh. Mrs. Myers sternly made both of them return to their seats.

Janice Kirkland's dad was a weatherman at KENS-5 TV, and Juliet pouted clear through his presentation on how a tornado formed. She squeezed her eyes shut, refusing to participate, when Ellen Shaffer's dad, who owned his own publicity firm, brought a teleprompter and let the students try reading the visual text of a speech he'd written for the mayor, welcoming Shamu and announcing the opening of Water Circus in San Antonio. She remembered how smug Ellen acted, and how jealous she felt when all the kids applauded at the end as Ellen's dad passed out discounted tickets to Water Circus.

The entire afternoon was nearly a bust until her own dad showed up at his scheduled time, the last presentation of the day. Mrs. Myers finally excused her from sitting in her desk, allowing her to join him up front.

"I'll need a lab assistant," he explained, and handed her a white lab coat to wear — surprisingly, in just her size and with her full name embroidered above the pocket. Together they prepared to show her classmates a chemistry demonstration.

Her father looked out at the students. "Okay, everyone. How many of you know that the little bubbles in hydrogen peroxide are made of oxygen?" Hands shot up across the room as he pulled a bottle from his bag, opened the lid, and measured an amount into the waiting glass beaker on the corner of Mrs. Myers's desk. "Very good. I knew you were a smart bunch of kids."

He turned to Juliet. "Okay, carefully add the food coloring." She followed his instruction and squeezed out four drops of red into the container, just like they'd practiced.

"Now, what's next?" he prompted, encouraging her with a wide smile.

She dug in his bag and pulled a bottle of Joy dish soap from the bottom. Juliet held the little plastic bottle up like a prize.

Her father nodded. "That's right. Go ahead."

Juliet looked out over the classroom. All eyes were watching, waiting to see what she would do next. She carefully squeezed an amount of liquid soap until the level reached the designated line marker. At the same time, her father opened a small envelope of Fleischmann's yeast. He emptied the sandy-colored grains into a bowl and poured warm water from a thermos, then gently stirred the mixture with a popsicle stick.

Next (and this was her favorite part), he handed the bowl carefully to her. She held it tight, watching for his cue.

"Is everyone watching? You don't want to miss this," he warned. He gave the nod and Juliet poured the yeast mixture from the bowl into the beaker, never spilling a drop. She grinned and felt all tingly inside waiting for the chemical reaction.

All of a sudden, the mixture foamed up like a fat snake out of the glass container. The red mass kept growing and slithered onto Mrs. Myers's desk and onto the floor.

"Awesome!" seemed to be the collective response from the crowd of classmates all looking at the mess (and her) with amazement. "That is so cool!"

Ignoring the frown on Mrs. Myers's face as she scowled at the floor, Juliet's father bumped her elbow with his own before turning back to the class. "The foam we made is special because each tiny bubble is filled with oxygen," he explained. "The yeast acted as a catalyst to remove the oxygen from the hydrogen peroxide. Since it did this very fast, it created lots and lots of bubbles." Her father looked in her direction. "Juliet, did you notice the bottle got warm?"

She nodded with enthusiasm.

"Our experiment created what's called an exothermic reaction. That means it not only created foam, it created heat." Again, he turned to her. "And what do we call this experiment?"

She beamed. "We just made elephant toothpaste!"

The kids were invited to leave their desks and come take a closer look. As her classmates gathered up front, Juliet's eyes scanned their faces for Stinky Sam. And when no one was looking, she stuck her tongue out at him. She also gave a smug grin in Ellen's direction.

It'd been years since she'd thought back to that afternoon, and why the memory echoed in her head now, she couldn't say.

Juliet leaned back in her office chair.

For some reason, she couldn't seem to maintain focus on the stack of chem analysis reports because she kept hearing her mother's words from yesterday.

He loves you, you know.

Yes, she supposed her father loved her. But he'd made his own bed, and if he found it hard or lumpy, it was no one's fault but his own.

Juliet tucked her iPhone into her pocket, donned her white lab coat hanging on the back of her office door, and made her way through the front lobby, her heels clicking against the shiny tiled marble floor.

Tavina was filling in while the receptionist was at lunch. "I'm heading out to the lab, if you need me," Juliet told her.

"You're taking your iPhone?"

Juliet nodded. As proof, she pulled the electronic device from her pocket and held it high over her head as she walked toward the door leading to the east wing.

QA was located at the end of a long maze of cubicles, home to the accounting, logistics, and human resources folks. At the break room, Juliet turned right and continued down a narrow hallway to an entry posted with a large red and white sign that read AUTHORIZED PERSONNEL ONLY.

Juliet slid her security card through the reader and waited. When the lock beeped, she pushed through the heavy double doors leading to the lab. Just inside, her hands pulled a set of protective gear wrapped in sealed plastic from the shelf. She opened the package and slipped on the blue paper gown, shoe covers, and hair cap, then washed her hands at a large white basin, using soap that smelled of disinfectant. With her elbow, she pressed a red button on the wall next to another door with a tiny oblong window. The door buzzed and released, and

Juliet pushed with her shoulder and entered.

She stepped into a large room, kept several degrees colder than the outer offices. Stainless steel counters and lab stools lined the walls, with white cabinets above. In the center of the floor stood a compounding isolator and a polypropylene table, the surface scattered with glass beakers and funnels.

Malcolm Stanford, her QA supervisor, stood at the rear of the room near the incubator along with two women techs all dressed in sanitary gear. He looked up as Juliet approached. "Good morning, Dr. Ryan."

"Good morning, Malcolm." He had a petite build, small black eyes, and often a chilly personality that matched the lab's room temperature. "Malcolm, I noticed the nitrate levels were up on the last batch of reports."

He slid a stack of lab trays into a cupboard and closed the door. "I noticed that as well. But we're well below the requisite MCL standards."

Juliet nodded. "Still, I'd like to know why the levels increased."

"Probably the storms coming in off the gulf. Climate changes can affect the levels." He picked up a half-filled beaker from the counter.

Juliet set her jaw. While nitrates are naturally present in all sources of water, higher levels could indicate contamination. "All the more reason to run the samples through the spectrophotometer and get a second reading, which I believe is in line with the SOP revisions I issued," she reminded him, wondering why it was necessary to explain herself. Wasn't she the boss?

The supervisor glanced between the lab techs. "Uh, sure. We'll get right on it." He placed the beaker in a nearby sink. "I should have the results by morning."

Before Juliet could thank him, her cell phone buzzed. She excused herself and stepped away to take the call, pulling her iPhone from her pocket.

"Tavina? What's up?"

"Hey, Dr. Ryan. Alexa Carmichael wants to see you in a half hour. Her office."

"I'll be there. Thanks for letting me know." She clicked off her phone and turned back to Malcolm. "Now, let's take a look at the calibration schedules."

Twenty minutes later, Juliet headed for the lobby. She checked her watch as she passed the break room and the smell of microwaved pizza, wishing she'd eaten breakfast now that it looked like she'd be working through lunch.

In her short time here, Juliet had learned Alexa worked on two modes — high gear and higher gear. The woman often pulled an energy bar from her office drawer, which she ate in place of meals. On her desk were photos of a boy who looked to be around sixteen or seventeen.

"Your son?" Juliet once asked, pointing to a frame on Alexa's credenza.

"Yes," she'd replied, her face softening. In a rare moment, she shared something about her personal life. "Adam plays soccer. A forward. He's very good."

Most of what she knew of Alexa Carmichael, Juliet learned from surfing the web. Her husband was a doctor — a plastic surgeon, to be exact, which explained her boss's flawless face. She'd also seen Alexa pull into the parking lot driving an Aston Martin, which likely cost more than Juliet's condo. So the couple didn't want for money.

Juliet passed through the lobby with its shiny tiled floors and tastefully decorated waiting area. To the left of the receptionist counter, a wide corridor led to the executive offices.

She walked past her own office and briskly headed toward the door leading into Alexa's office suite. As her hand reached for the brass handle, a set of masculine fingers covered her own.

"Allow me."

Juliet's gaze lingered on the bit of hair on the knuckles before glancing up.

Greer Latham's face drew into a slow smile, one that left Juliet feeling a little unsettled. After a tentative nod, she pulled her hand away and took a step back, admiring his thick sandy-colored hair, cut to precision. He wore a charcoal tailored suit and a crisp white button-down with a striped tie in shades of gray. His eyes never left hers as he eased the door open.

"We're here for a one o'clock," he told the assistant perched at her desk outside Alexa's door.

Muriel Parke, an older woman with bulldog features, harnessed the respect her position provided and wore it like a winner's garland. No one got to Alexa without first going through Muriel. "She's waiting," came her reply.

Juliet followed Greer into Alexa's office, a showplace with ceiling-to-floor windows overlooking a courtyard featuring a waterfall and lush greenery. Her furniture was old-world style, with dark woods and intricate molding. The plush carpet was a leaf design in shades of teal and cream.

Alexa immediately waved them over to a round granite-topped conference table in the corner. "Thank you for coming on such short notice," she said.

Juliet took a seat opposite Greer, next to Dale Frissom, vice president of operations, while Alexa announced she had extremely good news. "We're about to close a deal with Water Circus," she reported. With her pen, she pointed at Greer. "Your team did an excellent job putting together the proposal and making the pitch."

A slight smile broke at the corners of Greer's mouth. "Thank you." He pulled at his right cuff. "The deal was a bit tricky. We worked hard to put this one in the bag." A smug assurance played across his face.

Alexa rewarded him with a wide smile. "The prospect of this deal clinched our merger with Montavan. But Greer's right. The negotiations have been tricky." She tapped her pen against her open palm and turned to Dale and Juliet. "Surprisingly, Water Circus wants to increase volume immediately to levels far greater than we anticipated. If we can meet the demand, they have agreed to give us exclusive retail rights for all the bottled water at the park." As she said this, her eyes took on an excited shine. "All of it . . . Do you have any idea what that means?"

Greer chimed in. "A bottom-line increase of over twelve million dollars annually."

Dale rubbed his cheek. "And a pretty fair strain on production resources. We're not at capacity yet, but what are we talking here?"

Alexa explained what would be required, adding that she'd make sure he had the equipment and personnel needed to accomplish the job.

Dale slowly nodded. "Well, if necessary, we can lease an additional facility. There's plenty of vacant warehouse space nearby." His face broke into a grin. "I'm in."

Alexa clapped her manicured hands. "Excellent. We can look to an outside staffing agency for any administrative support. Now, we need a commitment from the quality assurance area as well."

All eyes turned to Juliet.

She swallowed, wondering if the people sitting at the table could hear her pounding heart. In her short time with Larimar Springs, she'd worked hard to upgrade the lab and establish expanded protocols. She still had much she wanted to address in terms of developing an audit plan and staff training. A substantial increase in production would slow these critical plans.

As if reading her thoughts, Alexa lifted

her chin and pressed for an answer. "Is there a problem, Dr. Ryan?"

"No — no, of course QA will make that commitment," she assured everyone around the table, willing her confidence to match their own. "Provided we are allowed enough time to maintain our sampling protocols."

Alexa's eyes narrowed. "Be specific."

"We can work harder and faster, but incubation periods cannot be rushed."

"We expect the need to be great and grow rapidly. I can't stress enough how critical it is for every area to fully support this opportunity." Greer turned to Alexa, not bothering to stifle his concern. "Dr. Ryan has only been on board a short time. Perhaps we need —"

"Are you suggesting you can't handle the increase?" Alexa asked Juliet.

"I hope that's not what you're saying," Greer injected. "Because there is an awful lot riding on this deal. For everyone."

"We'll handle it." Juliet took a deep breath and glared across the table in his direction. "I assure you, my department will do whatever it takes."

5

Juliet stepped from the shower and dried off. Still feeling a bit cranky, she wiped steam from the mirror and wrapped her hair in the towel before moving to the walk-in closet. While reaching for her yoga pants, she tried not to look at the unpacked boxes still on the floor. Somehow her mother's organization gene had not gotten passed down. More importantly, she just hadn't had time.

No matter how hard she worked, she never seemed to be able to get ahead of the long list of items needing her attention. And now her workload had just increased exponentially. If that didn't create enough stress, she faced office politics — a QA supervisor who seemed to resent the changes she implemented, and self-serving comments from Mr. GQ in the meeting, casting doubt on her ability.

She shoved her arms into the sleeves of

the matching robe and yanked the belt closed, tying it tightly around her waist.

Her only consolation was that no doubt Alexa Carmichael had been kicked around on her way to the top as well and knew just how things were. She'd no doubt faced all this and more before attaining her level of respect.

There would always be men like Greer Latham, friendly in the parking lot and vicious in the boardroom. Thanks to her father, she'd learned to watch for men with ulterior motives whose only loyalty was to themselves. She dealt with these situations head-on, training herself to use before she got used.

The world was dog-eat-dog and she was nobody's puppy chow.

Of course, the increase in production could be her chance to shine, she supposed. The effort required to keep on top of everything would be exhausting, but she'd move heaven and earth to pull it off.

She'd finished dressing and was lotioning her arms when the doorbell rang. Juliet scowled and flipped the lid closed on the Neutrogena bottle. Who could possibly be at her door this time of night?

She made her way down the hall and to the front door of her condo. Leaning forward, she peeked through the tiny security lens. *Oh, great.*

She clicked the lock and opened the door. "What are *you* doing here?"

"Well, that's some greeting."

"After today, what would you expect?"

"Oh, c'mon. May I come in?"

Juliet stepped aside, allowing Greer entrance. He was wearing jeans, a light-blue button-down, and a remorseful look. "Look, I'm sorry. Really. I only wanted to make sure you carefully considered everything that was at stake while in that meeting."

Juliet pulled the towel from her head and shook out her wet hair. "You could have warned me that was coming. The deal points, I mean."

"You know I couldn't," he explained in a tone Juliet considered dangerously close to what a person would use with a child. He followed her into the open kitchen area.

"I was about to make tea." She grabbed the teapot from the stainless steel stove. "Want some?" She moved to the sink and turned on the faucet. "And I'm fully aware of the implications at work, thank you."

Greer held up both hands. "Hey, I'm not the enemy, babe. I'm the one who told you about the job opening and arranged for that interview. Remember?"

Her hand slammed the faucet off. She turned. "I landed that position because I was qualified."

Greer shook his head. "I know that. And let me remind you I'm not the one who decided to hide our relationship from everyone."

"I told you. I'm not ready to go public."

He looked at her dubiously. "Who cares what Alexa and everybody else thinks?"

Irritation swelled, causing her to choose her next words carefully. "It's different for a woman at work. I don't want anyone doubting my credentials because of our personal relationship. But that's off point and doesn't excuse your raising doubts about my ability to handle the increased production."

Greer moved forward and placed his hands at her waist. "What do I have to do to convince you I'm your biggest fan? There's no doubt in my mind you can hold your own at Larimar Springs — which is why I treated you no differently in that meeting than I would've any other person in that position."

Juliet stared into his steel-blue eyes. Should she remind him he hadn't put the vice president of operations through the wringer?

Greer's fingers laced through her damp

hair. "I'm not your father. You can trust me."

She ignored the fact he smelled like soft leather and spice, and warm male skin. "This isn't about my father."

He leaned closer. She could feel his breath against her cheek, his chiseled chest against her own. He paused, slipped the teapot from her hand, and placed it on the counter.

Time seemed to slow down. Her legs trembled beneath her.

Outside the windows of her condominium, the lights of downtown San Antonio shimmered in the far distance. "You can trust me," he whispered, taking her face in his hands.

As Greer's lips melted into her own, Juliet shut her eyes and tried to remember why she'd ever doubted.

6

Autumn in San Antonio barely differed from any other season. Sure, the grass color faded and the leaves on the oaks grew thinner, but unlike the golden-leafed months she'd spent up north while in college, often the only real sign of fall in Texas was shorter days.

Juliet drove north on 287, past the Pearl and across the San Antonio River. Out her passenger window, the sky turned dusk and she could barely make out the trees in Brackenridge Park. Traffic at this time of night was often heavy, with downtown workers migrating home to the suburbs, a fact that should've prompted Juliet to leave earlier, had she not been so slammed at work. She glanced at the digital clock on the dash. No doubt she'd be late to her mother's birthday party.

Last week she'd been out for a quick dinner with friends when her iPhone buzzed.

She'd been startled seeing her father's name appear. Rarely did she talk to him over the phone, and she couldn't recall a time when they'd texted.

Throwing a birthday party for your mom at the Quarry. Fri 6:00. Hope you'll come help celebrate her 57th.

Juliet's face immediately tightened. She worked her thumbs across the screen, typing out a quick response.

I'll be there. And she's turning 58.

She muted her phone and tossed it in her purse.

One of her friends shouted over the noise in the restaurant. "Who was that?"

Juliet shook her head. "No one important," she'd answered, and zipped the bag closed.

The exit leading to Alamo Heights loomed ahead. Juliet turned on her blinker and cut into the right-hand lane, then pulled off the freeway. The Quarry Golf Club was located on Basse Road, not far from the Alamo Quarry Marketplace with its landmark smoke stacks.

Her parents had moved to this neighborhood seven years ago. Here locals were known as "oh-niners," representing the trendy zip code with its upscale shopping and eclectic restaurants.

When Juliet visited, she'd often join her mother for her weekly shopping at Central Market, where the two of them would lunch on samples handed out at the end of nearly every aisle. Sometimes they would circle back to the deli twice when the bald-headed deli manager offered up a sampling of his olive selection — Arbequinas, Cerignolas, and Kalamatas. Her mother's favorites were the small, tart-flavored Picholines. "They taste just like Granny Smith apples," she often claimed, her eyes twinkling with satisfaction.

Juliet pulled into the already crowded parking lot, relieved to be late by only twenty minutes. Inside, she was greeted by the restaurant manager, a friend of her mother's who pointed to where the birthday girl stood in the corner of the room surrounded by friends, laughing and talking. Above their heads, a massive banner lined the wall: CAROL RYAN — BIRTHDAY GIRL! When her mom looked up, Juliet smiled and gave a little wave.

The room was packed, with the crowd spilling out onto the large patio overlooking the abandoned limestone quarry that had been transformed by savvy investors into a top-rated golf course. Through the windows, Juliet spotted several members of her mother's church standing out on the patio near large terra-cotta pots filled with yellow and rust-colored mums and cascading bright green potato vine.

Just inside the door, Frank Warren from their old neighborhood grabbed two chicken wings from a server passing a platter of hors d'oeuvres. Frank's wife elbowed him as he slid a quick third before the server moved on.

On the other side of the room, her mom's best friend chatted at a table with two women who were on the board of the new birthing center. Sandy looked in Juliet's direction, smiled, and wiggled her fingers.

Juliet waved back, then turned and headed for the bar. "Hi, Clarence. I'll have a club soda with lime, please."

Despite the noise, she could hear her father's laughter. He remained out of sight, hidden in part by an enormous platter of cheese and fruit sitting on the corner of the bar. Juliet waited for her drink, then stepped back and stole a glance in that direction.

Her father sat on a stool, surrounded by three women, one with her arm casually placed on his shoulder. He said something, his hands waving wildly, and they all laughed.

Her father noticed her then.

Juliet gave him a hard look, one he'd seen from her before.

Her father scrambled up, excused himself, and quickly moved in her direction. "JuJu, I'm glad you could make it."

Words piled up in her mouth, colliding with disgust. "Nice party," she hissed.

Looking confused, her father glanced at the women, then quickly focused back on Juliet, his eyes raw with emotion. "You've got it wrong." When she said nothing, he gripped her elbow, nearly causing her drink to splash from the glass, and guided her to where the women stood.

"Ladies, I'd like you to meet my daughter, Dr. Juliet Ryan." He forced a smile. "Honey, this is Carla Montgomery, Patty Blake, and Janice O'Brien."

The woman with the wandering arm grinned. "We've been held captive to your father's awful jokes."

Her father stubbornly lifted his chin. "These women are on the board at the institute. We work together." He pointed his glass toward a group of men approaching. "And these gentlemen are their husbands."

"Juliet, sweetheart." Her mother walked up then, open arms extended, but not before quickly glancing between her husband and daughter.

Juliet moved into her mother's embrace, giving her a tight hug. "Happy birthday, Mom."

Outside on the patio, a band warmed up. The lead singer tapped on the microphone a couple of times. "Testing, testing. One, two."

A couple of chords drifted through the open double doors leading outside, where strings of lights hung in the air, gently swaying in the breeze coming off the golf course. "We're going to play a little song dedicated to the birthday girl."

Juliet's mom laughed and covered her mouth with her hand. She shook her head in tickled disbelief as the lead singer leaned close to the microphone. "Carol Ryan, this is for you . . . WILD thing, pum, pum . . . You make Bennett's heart sing, pum, pum . . ."

The crowd broke out in laughter. Juliet's father stood and scooped his wife close with his arm. He led her to the patio, and Juliet watched through the glass windows as he swung her around to the music.

Juliet smiled despite herself. Her mother was beautiful tonight. And she looked radiantly happy.

When the music finally died down, Juliet

shifted through the crowd and returned to the bar.

"Another club soda?" Clarence asked, drying a glass with a towel.

She nodded before glancing up at the television mounted on the wall. On the screen, two attendants in white coats pulled a gurney from an ambulance and wheeled a young child into a hospital emergency department. A silent ticker slowly scrolled across the bottom of the television.

Child taken to Children's Hospital with severe diarrhea, abdominal cramping, and vomiting.

A graphic flashed onscreen listing E. coli symptoms, while the ticker below continued.

Undercooked hamburgers at backyard barbecue suspected.

Juliet's heart sank. "When will people learn to fully cook their ground beef?" she muttered, angry that someone's carelessness had sickened another child.

"Dr. Ryan?"

She turned to find Dr. O'Brien standing beside her. "I'm afraid we got off to a bad start." Her father's friend extended her hand. A collection of gold bracelets dangled against a petite gold Rolex.

Juliet took her refreshed drink from Clarence, thanked him, then turned and shook the woman's hand. Not knowing what else to say, she let the notion that she may have misread the earlier situation temper her response. "It's nice of you to join in celebrating my mother's birthday."

"Glad to be invited. This is some party." Dr. O'Brien's brightly colored lips broke into a smile, showing off a perfect set of white teeth. "Your father thinks very highly of you. He brags regularly about his daughter the scientist."

Her father joined them, still breathless from dancing. "That's right," he said. He lifted his finger to Clarence, indicating he needed another drink. Clarence nodded, wiped his hands on a towel, and grabbed a glass from the shelf behind the bar.

Her father slid onto a barstool. "I keep telling everybody how hard I try to convince you to come work at the institute."

"I have a job." Juliet reached for the nearby tray on the counter, lifted a toothpicked cube of cheese, and slid it in her mouth.

"At Larimar Springs? NAFSI filed two formal requests for an independent audit of their QA facilities last year. Refused us both times." He turned to Dr. O'Brien. "Alexa Carmichael hired Juliet, likely figuring I won't take my own daughter to task."

Juliet felt her whole body heat up. "Did it ever occur to you I'm a highly qualified microbiologist? And a respected quality assurance director?"

He swished the liquid in his glass. "You should be — I raised you." He lifted the drink to his lips.

"No, Mother raised me." She glanced in Dr. O'Brien's direction, then back. "You were always far too busy."

Carol Ryan looked across the car seat at her husband. "For goodness' sake, Bennett. Whose side are you on?"

Bennett gripped the steering wheel a little tighter. "She hates me."

"She doesn't hate you," Carol argued. "She's angry. There's a difference."

Bennett shook his head. "I'm telling you, I've met that Carmichael woman she's working for, and I don't like her. Companies driven by the almighty dollar always put safety in the backseat."

Carol pressed her head against the headrest in frustration. "I love you, but you are a self-righteous man."

"So I'm the bad guy?" He checked the side mirror before switching lanes.

She glared in his direction. "And you

think our brilliant daughter won't uncover a problem if there is one? Bennett, that isn't what this is about, and you know it." She rubbed at her forehead. "I prayed in time you'd both come to your senses and quit acting like two bickering children. I should have locked the two of you in a room long ago . . . made you work this out."

"I've tried to work things out with our daughter. Many times."

Carol shook her head. "Yes, and then you go and stir up the pot again. Like you did tonight. When will you ever learn, Bennett?"

They rode in silence for several minutes.

Finally, he reached and stroked her cheek with the back of his fingers. "I can't believe a pretty girl like you still hangs around an old poop like me."

Carol covered his hand with her own. "Please, Bennett. I'm asking you again. For all our sakes — please back off."

7

Juliet pulled into the small parking lot of the New Beginnings birthing center, located on a lot next to the campus of the Talavera Community Church, a multibuilding complex off Bandera Road. According to Juliet's mother, the elder board had generously donated the land at her request, a fact that brought her mother a lot of personal pride.

TCC, as her mother referred to it, was a megachurch by anyone's standards, with members numbering in the thousands. The pastor's messages were broadcast via a weekly television program with a national following that rivaled Oprah. Well, maybe not that big . . . but he did have more books on the front tables of their local bookstores than James Patterson and Lisa Scottoline combined.

Juliet had been seventeen when her mother claimed she'd "accepted Jesus."

She'd been sitting at the kitchen counter

with a bag of Fritos and an open biology textbook when her mother appeared dressed in cream-colored slacks and a navy blouse and told her she was going out with Sandy. "Honey, I probably won't be home until late. I left a chicken and rice casserole." She dug in her bag for her car keys. "In a half hour, turn the oven to 350 degrees, and make a salad for you and your father," she added before heading for the door.

Juliet remembered thinking her mother was far too optimistic, given her father hadn't made it home for dinner in over a month. As if reading her mind, her mom stopped and looked back in her direction. "If he's not home by seven, put the remaining casserole in some Tupperware and store it in the fridge."

Later Juliet learned Sandy and her mother had attended a Billy Graham crusade that night. Local newspapers reported the four-day event drew nearly two hundred fifty thousand people and filled the Alamodome for the first time in its three-year history. On the last night, some even watched from nearby Hemisfair Park, including her mom, who in the days following traded her weekly martini night with the girls for a fellowship group, which met in various homes for Bible study.

Juliet had watched with amusement as her father's face drew into a puzzled frown. "What do you mean you're *born again?*" To his credit, he tried to talk his wife out of it. "Carol, what sense does it make that a man died and then three days later he came alive again? That's scientifically impossible."

Her mother remained unmoved by his logic. "Faith is the substance of things hoped for, the evidence of things not seen," she quietly responded. "I don't need physical proof. I believe what the Bible says."

In the end, Juliet's father accepted his wife's new faith. As had she. They didn't really have a choice. And it had seemed to help her . . . with everything.

Juliet parked next to her mom's Buick Enclave. After checking her iPhone for messages, she made her way inside, where she found her mother on a ladder painting what appeared to be some kind of quote on the front lobby wall.

"Hi, Mom."

Her mother turned, paintbrush in hand. "Oh, honey. What a surprise!" She pointed to her handiwork. "Do you like it? When I'm finished, it'll read, 'I am fearfully and wonderfully made.' " She grinned broadly and dipped her long-handled brush in the paint can nested on the top of the ladder.

"From Psalm 139."

"Mom, please be careful up there. You could fall."

"Oh, pooh. I'm fine." She motioned to an overstuffed chair next to the window. "Sit, sit. I'll be done in a couple of minutes."

Juliet nodded and sank into the chair to watch. Her mom returned to her task, finishing up the lettering. Her short red-haired bob was tied up in a cute scarf, and she wore a matching apron over her T-shirt and jeans.

To pass the time, she picked up a magazine on a nearby table. The pages were filled with photos of pregnant women and articles on caring for infants.

"That'll be you someday."

Juliet looked up at her mother, confused. "What do you mean?"

Her mother pointed at the magazine. "You," she said. "I can't wait to see you wearing maternity clothes and deciding what color to paint your nursery."

Juliet held up an ad. "And buying hemorrhoid cream? Uh, no thank you." No matter how much her mom pushed, motherhood was not a club she was anxious to join.

With one flowing stroke, her mom painted a perfect letter *F* in a calligraphy font. She leaned back to inspect her work. "You won't remember the bad parts, honey. Only the good."

Juliet closed the magazine and tossed it back on the table. "Well, that's a ways off. I have to find someone I'd want to marry first."

"Well, if you're having trouble in that department, there are some nice men at the church. I could introduce —"

"Uh, no," Juliet interrupted. "That's okay. I don't have time for any of that right now." Greer Latham flashed in her mind. Her mother would never approve of her casual relationship with a coworker. And Greer wasn't exactly marriage material. "To tell you the truth, Mom, I'm not sure I'd enjoy being someone's wife."

Her mom opened her mouth to argue when a woman with gray hair and bright red glasses peeked her head into the lobby from down the hallway. "Carol, the plumbers called. They'll be here Monday morning, as promised."

Juliet's mom nodded. "Okay, Jean. Thanks."

The woman wiggled her fingers at Juliet before retreating back down the hall.

Her mother placed the brush carefully across the top of the paint can and stepped down. She wiped her hands on a rag.

"Honey, take some advice from someone who loves you more than her own soul — life is so much better when shared with someone."

"Not always." Juliet felt the words escape before she had time to consider their impact.

Her mother dropped the rag onto a rung, nearly toppling the can off the top. "I know what you're implicating," she said.

"But —"

Her mother held up her hand, cutting her off. "But, nothing. Yes, your father made mistakes. He's human."

Juliet shook her head. "Mom — all those women."

"That's between us." Her mother gathered herself. "You never understood. I loved him. We got through it."

Juliet's throat went thick with unshed tears, and she sank deeper in the chair. "Well, someone had to fight. You didn't."

Her mom's face softened. She placed her hand on her daughter's shoulder, then knelt at her feet. "Sweetheart, I did fight. I fought *for* my marriage. I forgave him. That doesn't mean I placed a stamp of approval on what he did. It means I accepted his apology and released my husband from any grudge I might hang on to — so he could be free to choose a more honorable way of living." She took Juliet's hands in her own. "We are never more like God than when we forgive."

Juliet wanted to roll her eyes at the Christian cliché. Instead, she stared across the room at the freshly constructed admitting desk. Her mother was quick, smart, and well-read, but when it came to her father and issues of faith, Carol Ryan's mind remained rigid as that countertop.

"I got way more than I gave up. Consider what I'm telling you." Her mother patted her hand and stood. "Forgive him, Juliet."

Juliet answered quietly, "I'm sorry, Mom. I can't."

Her mother's eyes filled with sadness. She sighed and stood. "I swear you two are just alike. You even chose the same line of work."

"No, Mom. We have very different jobs. Dad talks about food safety . . . and I'm on the front line actually making sure food products are safe."

8

On Sunday morning, Juliet woke to chimes ringing from the San Fernando Cathedral, located only a half mile from Greer's downtown condominium. It took her a few disoriented minutes to remember where she was and why. She lifted from his sofa and opened her drowsy lids to bright sunlight streaming through the plate-glass windows no longer shaded by drapes, indicating Greer must already be up. That thought barely crossed her mind when he appeared at the doorway, a mug of hot steaming coffee in hand.

"Want some?" he asked.

She nodded, and he moved to the edge of the sofa and handed her the cup. He grinned. "I'd like to think I'm exciting enough not to put a woman to sleep by ten o'clock."

Juliet sat up. She smoothed her wrinkled shirt. "Sorry, I haven't been sleeping through the night lately. Guess I was exhausted."

He sat on the edge of the sofa next to her. "Forgiven. This time," he teased.

She wrapped her fingers around the mug, leaned against the pillows, and took a sip of the steaming liquid. "Normally, I take advantage of my insomnia and catch up on some reading I need to plow through."

He smiled, showing off a perfect set of white teeth. "You stay up and read in the middle of the night?"

Juliet nodded. "Better than television programming at that hour." She glanced at the clock on the side table. "How long did I —" She bolted up. "Is it really nine o'clock?"

Greer slid a finger down her arm. "Why so tense?"

Juliet stared across the sterile-looking room, decorated in monochromatic shades of gray with dark wood furniture and metal accents, trying to come up with an appropriate answer. "I'm not tense. I just —"

Her phone buzzed.

Greer leaned to pick it up. She quickly grabbed his arm. "No! Don't."

He gave her a puzzled look. "Okay." He slowly withdrew his hand, clearly confused.

"It's likely my mother," she explained. "She always calls on her way home from church." She checked the screen and confirmed it was indeed her mother calling and clicked off the phone. "I'll call her back later."

No doubt her mom had called her own house first, and when Juliet didn't pick up, she tried her cell. If Greer had answered, her mom could have easily put two and two together. She wasn't exactly pure as snow, but she didn't like the idea of pointing out that fact to her mother.

Greer scowled. "How old are you exactly?"

"I know, I know." Using her free hand, she pulled the afghan up and tucked it around her. Juliet barely understood her need to closet her relationship from everyone, especially her mother. How could she make him understand?

From the look on Greer's stubble-shadowed face, he knew what she was thinking. "I don't get it, Juliet. What is it with you and your parents?"

Her eyes followed his manicured nails as they made their way up her arm. She swallowed, not entirely comfortable with his question. "It's hard to explain." She pulled the mug to her lips and took a sip of coffee.

Greer tucked a stray lock of hair behind her ear. "Your father is a highly respected voice in your profession. From a purely business perspective, I would think you'd benefit from mending whatever is broken between the two of you."

She could tell by the way he looked at her he thought she was acting like a petulant teenager swept by her moods. "Think about it," he urged.

Irritation sparked in her gut. Why was everyone pushing her to play Chelsea Clinton?

It was time she took control.

With a sly grin, she slid her mug onto the table. "So . . . you want to spend our Sunday morning talking about my parents?" She locked her gaze with his.

He reached and clicked a remote, sending a light sax tune sifting through the speakers mounted in the ceiling. "I know what you're doing," he said.

Juliet raised her eyebrows. "Oh yeah? What's that?"

Greer moved closer. "You're avoiding this conversation you never want to have."

She buried her face against his neck, taking in the slight scent of Acqua di Gio cologne still clinging from the day before. *Guilty as charged,* she thought.

Juliet felt his fingers run through her hair. "Don't worry," she assured him. "I've got everything handled."

She lifted her face and waited for his lips to find her own, while outside, the church chimes rang yet again in the distance.

"Where are you going?"

Juliet slipped into her jacket and zipped up. She glanced over at Greer, propped up against the back of the sofa, his sandy-colored hair still perfectly in place. "I told you. I have to go back to the office."

He reached out. "C'mon, babe. What project is so important it can't wait until tomorrow?"

She raised her eyebrows. "Do I have to remind you about the workload my department is under, given the demands of the Water Circus deal?"

"At your level, you oversee the effort. Let Malcolm Stanford carry the ball when it comes to the lab operations. He's the supervisor. He's qualified." Greer turned and straightened a cushion. "In case I have to remind you, supervisors make a nice salary. Let him earn it."

Juliet pulled her loafers from the floor. "Can't." She bent and slipped them on.

Greer pulled her backward and moved to kiss her.

Juliet blocked him with her arm. "Now I know what *you're* doing."

He laughed. "Busted." He diverted and gave her a peck on the forehead. "Seriously though, Juliet. Take some advice. If you're going to score in the executive leagues, you're going to have to coach and let your quarterback run the ball into the end zone."

She gave him a look. "Are you really going to use a football analogy on me? You — a guy who doesn't even know a quarterback from a fullback?"

"True," he responded, "but if I played for the PGA, I'd be on the top of the leader board every time."

She rolled her eyes.

"Which is why . . ." He paused, trying to attract her full attention. When she failed to look at him, he gently took her chin and turned her to face him. "Which is why you are going to skip going to the office this afternoon so you can join me and Alexa on the back nine at Dominion."

He got her attention. "You're playing golf with Alexa?" She tried to sound nonchalant, but the fact he had a tee time set up with their boss and just now was mentioning that fact put her on edge.

"I was going to invite you earlier, but . . . well, I got a little distracted." He folded his arms behind that perfect head of hair.

"What time?" she asked, mentally calculating how she might juggle her work to fit in a round of golf. With everything she had on her plate, she'd have to work through the night to make up for it, but she wasn't about to pass up a whole afternoon of face time with Alexa Carmichael. She especially wasn't going to forfeit and let Greer continue to position himself with the CEO of Larimar Springs.

Call it jealousy if you want, but Juliet was already thinking Greer had grown a little too arrogant when it came to work, and somebody needed to mow him down a little. Professionally speaking, of course.

Besides, who was he to suggest she needed to coach her lab supervisor? A good leader never failed to get their hands dirty in the everyday. She'd stay in the trenches with the troops. That way, when the grenades hit, she'd know exactly how to take cover.

Sure, Malcolm Stanford could be a real pain. She wouldn't argue that. But she didn't need Greer Latham, or any man for that matter, telling her how to do her job — or how to relate to her father.

"What time are you teeing off?" she repeated, a little more harshly than she'd intended.

A slight grin broke on Greer's face. "One o'clock."

■ ■ ■ ■

After racing home for a quick shower, Juliet grabbed her Calloways and tossed her bag in the hatch of her Jeep Grand Cherokee.

Greer Latham might be a scratch golfer, but her own handicap wasn't shabby. She could hold her own — behind a desk and on the greens, a fact she'd bragged about the first time she met Greer.

She'd been home for Fiesta last spring, and some girlfriends from high school prodded her to join in an afternoon of fun. Feeling more than festive, the four of them took a cab out to Brackenridge Park — known by the locals as Old Brack — and rented clubs. After a less-than-stellar nine-hole round, she followed the girls into the clubhouse for a refresher. Patty Jo spotted him first, sitting at the bar pouring a can of cola into his glass, followed by a healthy squeeze of lime. "Oh my heavens, look at *him*," her friend said in a low voice filled with admiration. "He couldn't have even broken a sweat out there — not and look like that."

True, the man in the light blue polo and pressed chinos ranked pretty high on the gorgeous meter. Even before he turned around, she could tell he was model perfect, like he'd stepped out of a magazine — hence the nickname Mr. GQ.

He turned and their eyes met.

Like most women, she was attracted to his chiseled jawline and the way his cheeks dimpled slightly when he smiled. But his eyes — his eyes were a magical blend of blue, as deep and stirring as the ocean water that had captivated her attention on a road trip along the Oregon coast, near a place called Devil's Cauldron.

Despite the admiration heaped on him by her friends, Greer's attention that afternoon focused solely on her. Nothing about Greer Latham was subtle. He unashamedly targeted his frequent glances in her direction, and later his conversation.

Juliet ditched her friends and let him drive her home. Despite what had originally appeared a chilly exterior, she found him warm and engaging. In no time, she discovered herself opening up, telling him about her family and her job, and eventually, when he asked about her father, she let her guard drop a bit. Without disclosing details, she revealed the tension between them.

"Well, he raised you. He's got that going for him," he'd responded, cementing her budding affection.

She spent several evenings out with Greer

before returning to New York, and many more evenings last spring with her eyes glued to her phone app as they exchanged tweets. When she saw his hashtag #MoveHome4JobIFound4U, she let herself take a ride on the wild side. She bought a ticket, met with Alexa Carmichael, and soon became quality assurance director for Larimar Springs.

Greer was vice president of marketing and sales, which she admitted caused her great pause. "It's never a good idea to consort with co-workers," she told herself, while in the back of her mind she knew the position was perfect and that she'd not likely duplicate another in the San Antonio market anytime soon.

In the end, and after much encouragement from Greer, she'd thrown caution aside and accepted the job, with the proviso that their relationship remain their private business and not be disclosed to anyone at Larimar Springs.

Without really deciding, she'd also never introduced Greer to her mom — unsure why exactly, other than dating relationships seemed to have a shelf life of no more than two years, it seemed. When relationships hit that mark, a couple often faced a crossroads — you'd either head for marriage or drift apart like ships without any navigation tools on board.

She had no reason to believe her connection with Greer would turn out any different. She wasn't interested in marriage, so why invite pressure from her mother to reconsider?

And why risk any discrimination in the minds of their co-workers, who might believe Greer had pulled strings to get his girlfriend hired on at an executive level? Never mind she'd completed her doctorate, making her far more qualified than other candidates.

No doubt, working together under these circumstances would require a calculated mind-set, but both she and Greer were professionals. They would handle it.

Juliet pulled through the country club gates and into the parking lot twenty minutes before the scheduled tee time. Across the sculpted drive, near a clump of towering banana palms, she spotted Greer's silver Jaguar parked next to Alexa Carmichael's black Aston Martin.

She needled into a spot near the gate that led to the tennis courts and swimming area. After collecting her gear, she made her way to the entrance, where terra-cotta pots filled with glossy green sego palms secured each side of massive oak doors framed in intricate wrought iron.

Inside the clubhouse, Greer and Alexa stood at the counter, dressed in golf attire. "Juliet, I'm so glad you could join us." Alexa gave her arm an affectionate squeeze.

The man behind the counter handed Greer two sets of keys. "Your carts will be waiting on the portico, sir."

Only then did she notice another man standing on the other side of Greer, several feet away. He seemed vaguely familiar.

Suddenly, recognition dawned and her gut filled with trepidation. Once again, it seemed Greer had played her and she'd been caught off guard.

Alexa's bright coral lips parted into a wide smile. "Juliet, you've not had a chance to meet Cyril Montavan." She motioned with her open hand. "Of Montavan International — our new business partner."

Juliet nearly toppled her golf bag while extending to shake. "Yes, hello. So nice to meet you."

"Likewise." The charming man took her hand and gently squeezed, holding his palm against her own for several seconds before he released. Their new partner could have doubled for George Clooney, her mother's favorite Hollywood actor. Especially the way the corners of his eyes crinkled when he smiled.

Golf didn't seem to be the only kind of game Greer Latham was playing this afternoon. He should have given her a heads-up. She intended to punish him with an appropriate glare, but her gaze landed on the back of his polo as he rushed forward to open the door for Alexa.

Outside, the warm air smelled of freshly mown grass with a hint of cedar. Alexa pulled on her sunglasses and adjusted her visor. "I'll share a cart with Cyril. Juliet, you don't mind riding with Greer, do you?"

"No, of course not." She took a deep breath and handed over her bag to the attendant, watching as the fresh-faced young man fastened their clubs to the back of the cart. "So long as he doesn't drive us into any water hazards." She gave a brittle laugh and climbed into the passenger side of the cart.

"No guarantees," Greer joked as he took his place in the driver's seat next to her. He pressed his foot against the accelerator and followed Cyril and Alexa's cart to the first tee box.

In a casual manner, Greer rested his hand on the steering wheel as they drove in silence past a water feature surrounded by lush, manicured landscaping. As soon as he cut the engine, he leaned over. "You're acting like something's wrong."

Juliet stared out over the contoured green. "Why didn't you let me in on the fact we'd be playing with Cyril Montavan?"

"Because I didn't know either, until Alexa phoned me on the way over to tell me." He stepped from the cart. Not bothering to hide his irritation, Greer moved to the back of the cart and pulled his driver from the bag. With a light laugh, he slipped off the cover. "What are you accusing me of?"

Juliet kept her voice low. "I'm not accusing you of anything. I just —" She shook her head. "I don't like surprises, that's all."

Greer tucked his club under his arm and opened a box of balls with his free hand. "Wasn't intentional," he assured her. "I was as taken off guard as you."

Juliet retrieved her own driver, grabbed the ball Greer handed her, and followed him up the mound. She didn't believe him, not entirely, but for now no good purpose would be served in coming across as insecure.

Cyril stepped up to the tee box and prepared for his shot. Before lining up, he looked back in their direction. "Any point-ers?"

Greer pulled his glove from his back pocket. "This par four has a slight dogleg to the left. Watch that bunker. I normally try to favor the right center of the fairway."

At her turn, Juliet set her tee and ball and lined up. Despite her impressive twenty-eight handicap, her mouth went dry. She knew more than her golf game was on show today. Pushing aside her sudden nerves, she tucked her chin and pulled her arms back. Using measured force, she swung, making sure to follow through. Thankfully, she made a clean shot down the fairway. Satisfied, she let out the breath she'd been holding, tucked the shaft of her driver under her arm, and pulled off her glove.

"I can see we're playing with pros." Cyril gave Juliet a warm smile as Alexa stepped up to the mound.

"Juliet is a pro all the way around." Greer's eyes met hers as if to say, "I'm on your side here."

She decided to believe him. Until the seventh hole.

The drink cart pulled up as Juliet was enjoying the fact she'd birdied the sixth to Greer's double bogey, thanks to a rare pulled shot that landed him in the hidden bunker.

Greer stepped from the cart and motioned to Cyril. "Do you want a beer?"

Cyril shook his head. "No. Not for me. A soda would be fine. Thank you."

Alexa pulled a small jeweled case from her golf bag, opened the lid, and retrieved a wet wipe from inside. She swiped the back of her neck. "I'm dying for an iced coffee."

Greer looked to Juliet.

"That's good for me as well," she said, then drained the last of the bottle of water she'd been nursing.

While Alexa and Greer placed an order, Cyril joined Juliet at the rear of Alexa's cart, several yards away. "You have an impressive curriculum vitae," he said. "Yesterday, when Greer offered to host us as guests at his club, I was glad to hear you would be joining us so I could meet you personally."

Despite the compliment, Juliet's internal alarm rang. "Yesterday?"

"Yes," he confirmed. "When Alexa and Greer picked me up at the airport."

"Here you are." Greer approached with a can of soda in his hand. "Cyril, I hope you like Dr Pepper — also known as Texas nectar."

Her so-called boyfriend watched her,

proprietary and cool. But there was something else in his eyes too. Something calculating.

So her suspicions were well-founded. Greer had lied to her. What Juliet didn't understand was why.

Rolling the dimpled golf ball between her fingers, she smiled, realizing he must feel threatened by her to go to such an extreme to keep his professional edge. Not exactly a bad thing.

Some might wonder how she could compartmentalize competing at work while maintaining a romantic friendship. The answer was easy, really — she'd duplicate what many men did every day.

Her father proved you could live two separate lives with a smile pasted on your face.

Alexa pulled on her glove and stepped to the ladies' tee box. Like everything Alexa Carmichael did, her swing was perfectly smooth. She smacked the sweet spot, sending the ball into the air in a straight line two hundred yards down the fairway. "There you go. That's how it's done," she boasted.

Juliet made a decision. She'd keep what she'd discovered to herself. Tuck the tidbit away and use the revelation to her advantage. Clearly, Greer hadn't recognized the level of competence she'd bring to the mix, or that he'd be forced to share a little of that spotlight he often basked in.

She sauntered back to the cart and slid into the leather bench seat next to Mr. GQ, with his perfect hair and manicured nails.

Without Greer knowing, she'd turn the tables and continue to shine at work, no matter how nervous it made him feel. She wasn't the type to stand down in order to eliminate the risk of losing a man.

Juliet would score.

And not just on this golf course.

9

Juliet had been home from the golf course less than an hour when her cell phone rang.

"Hey, Juliet. It's me, Tavina. Sorry to call you at home on a Sunday night, but I just learned my extended family is arriving from New Orleans in the morning and we want to take them to Water Circus tomorrow. Would it be too much trouble if I took the day off?"

Juliet mentally scanned her calendar. "No, that should be fine. Thanks for letting me know."

"Really? Oh, thanks so much. I really wanted MD to get time with his little cousins."

To borrow from a popular cliché, Tavina believed the sun rose and set on her three-year-old boy, a cute little guy with big brown eyes and a dimpled smile. Tavina named him Marquis DeAndre Mosely. "That's the only way we're likely to have an MD in the family," she said with a laugh.

The few times Tavina had brought little MD to the office, he was surprisingly well-spoken for a toddler. He'd also been trained to use his manners. Juliet offered him an energy bar from her desk drawer, and he quickly said, "Thank you, ma'am." Then, to Juliet's delight, he added, "You're pretty."

Juliet reassured Tavina it was no trouble for her to take the day off and enjoy her family. "I can get by one Monday without you," she told her assistant.

"I'll call the temp service and arrange for a replacement," Tavina offered.

"No, don't worry about it. It's only one day. I can ask the receptionist to help out if I need anything."

Juliet hung up the phone and headed for the kitchen, where a can of Pacific Chai tea she'd found at Whole Foods last week was calling her name. Before she could put a pot of water on to boil, the phone rang a second time. This time it was her mother.

"Honey, I know it's late, but your dad and I are downtown and we're heading to the Riverwalk for dinner. Would you join us?"

Juliet groaned inside. She was pooped. The only thing she really wanted was to wrap her yoga pant–covered legs up on the couch and catch up on her DVR episodes of *The Good Wife.*

"Oh, Mom. I'm pretty tired . . ."

Silence.

"And I have an early morning," Juliet quickly added.

"Well, sure — I understand." Her mother paused. "Maybe another time."

Juliet sighed. She couldn't take the disappointment she heard in her mom's voice. "Look, okay — I'll go. But I really don't want to be out late. I have a big week ahead."

"No, no. I understand completely. We'll meet you in an hour at Casa Rio."

After slipping on a pair of jeans and boots, Juliet ran a brush through her hair and covered her lips in a light peach gloss. Before heading out the door for the car, she grabbed her leather jacket from the hall closet, not that she expected the night air to chill enough to wear one. But hey, the coat matched her boots. That counted for something.

Traffic would be light on a Sunday night. She would get downtown in plenty of time to meet her mother at the scheduled time. Juliet clicked on the radio. Using the designated button on her steering wheel, she scanned the stations, searching for some light jazz.

Suddenly, the term *E. coli* broadcast through the speakers. Juliet stopped the dial and turned up the volume.

"A six-year-old who fell sick late last week of suspected E. coli has died, and two more children have fallen victim to a deadly strain of O157:H7. A spokesman from Children's Hospital here in San Antonio has confirmed that the Centers for Disease Control out of Atlanta, Georgia, has been alerted and an investigation is now under way. While health officials are working to identify the source, at this juncture no one is able to confirm these incidents are related.

"People usually get sick two to eight days after ingesting contaminated food or water. Most people infected with the O157:H7 strain develop diarrhea — usually watery and often bloody — and abdominal cramps and recover within a week. But some develop more severe infection leading to hemolytic uremic syndrome, or HUS, a type of kidney failure and nervous system impairment, often deadly in children under six years old and the elderly. Listeners are strongly encouraged to take all proper precautions. More information about the symptoms of HUS and ways to prevent contracting this disease has been posted online at our website."

Juliet's stomach clenched. The ominous report suggested more than a simple under-cooked burger at a backyard barbecue. She knew many in her field would be working feverishly to identify the source and end the outbreak. Time was of the essence in these situations.

Tomorrow she'd put in some calls. See if she could help in any way.

She pulled into downtown, found a lot off Market Street, and parked her Jeep on the fourth level, next to an old green and white pickup with a bumper sticker proudly displayed in the back window that said, "I'm from Texas. What country are you from?"

Normally she would smile at the humor, but not today. Not after learning of a potential outbreak in their city.

She'd need to cut this dinner short. No doubt the scientific forums she followed on the internet would be buzzing tonight as everyone in her field closely monitored the developments.

She quickly made her way along the sidewalk and down the cement stairs to the path lining the murky black San Antonio River that snaked through downtown. The Riverwalk, lined with restaurants, hotels, and more, had long been known as Texas's number one tourist attraction. Just ahead,

Juliet spotted the brightly colored patio umbrellas lining the Casa Rio.

Her mother saw her and waved. As Juliet approached, the maître d' directed her to their table.

"There you are." Her mother placed her napkin on the table and lifted from her chair.

"No, sit." Juliet bent and kissed her mother's cheek.

"Your father was held up." Her mom scooted up to the table. "Something about an outbreak."

Juliet slid into a chair opposite hers. "I heard on the radio on the way here. Does Dad know anything?"

"Not that he's been able to tell me yet." Her mother handed her a menu. "But he promised he'd be here. We were doing a little shopping downtown when he got the call."

"It's awful. Those kids." Juliet shook her head. "And so unnecessary, what with everything the science community knows about food pathogens. Someone along the line clearly failed to utilize proper detection methods. Whoever is responsible should be hung by their toes from the top of the Tower of the Americas."

"Oh, Juliet!"

95

"I'm serious, Mom. There's no excuse." Her eyes scanned the entrée selections, although she didn't need to. Founded in 1946, Casa Rio was the first San Antonio business to open its doors to the river and take advantage of the unique waterfront setting. Her family had been coming here for years, and Juliet always ordered the same thing — pollo asado, with an extra side of chunky guacamole.

The waiter took their order.

"Gracias, amigo." Juliet handed him the menu. She looked across the table. "What's the matter, Mom? You look tired." She scooped salsa onto a chip and brought it to her mouth.

Her mother adjusted a pair of reading glasses nested in her thick bobbed hair. "Gee, thanks a lot."

Juliet's expression tightened with concern. "I'm serious. Maybe you're overdoing it a bit at the birthing center." She popped the chip in her mouth, savoring the strong bite of the finely chopped jalapeños mixed with chunks of tomato and onion, garlic, and cumin.

Her mom waved her off. "A little hard work never hurt anyone. If I look a bit haggard" — she straightened her fork on the table — "maybe it's because your father dragged me all over town today looking for hatch chilies. They're past season, but he insisted on searching every farmer's market in Bexar County until he found a batch."

"Hey, do I hear my name being taken in vain?"

Juliet glanced up. Her father appeared next to her mother. He planted a kiss on top of his wife's head and moved to take a seat next to her.

Her mother smiled at him. "I ordered the enchilada plate for you."

"With extra green sauce?"

She nodded. "Yes, with extra sauce."

He turned to Juliet. "Now, that's why your mama's a keeper."

Juliet gave him a weak smile, stifling a comment that in her opinion, he was lucky her mom kept *him* around.

Her father rustled a chip from the basket and dredged it through the bowl of salsa like he was trying to drown the thing. Her mother wet her fingers and tamed a strand of his hair.

He turned to Juliet. "So, did you hear about it?"

"About?" She played dumb, stubbornly refusing to play along.

He talked while he chewed. "The outbreak. Sorry situation if you ask me." He swore under his breath. "Today's corporations. Always cutting corners when it comes to safety."

"Bennett — language."

Juliet's father shrugged. "Sorry, Carol. But Juliet's hardly a little girl —"

"That's not what I'm talking about," her mother chided. "You know I don't care for foul language."

He slipped his hand over hers in a signaled apology.

Juliet reached for her glass of iced tea. "Why are you pinning the outbreak on some corporation? Could be a public pool for all we know, run by a municipality. Here in Texas, there were three reported cases just like that last year."

"Not likely." He popped another chip in his mouth and chewed noisily.

Juliet's mother held up both hands. "Look, you two, let's change the subject."

Juliet ignored her mom's admonition and pierced her father with a sharp glare. "What do you mean, not likely?"

Her father slowly leaned back in his chair. He lifted his eyebrows. "Surely you're not unaware that statistics show —"

Juliet threw her linen napkin to the table. "Oh, c'mon. Get over yourself, Dad. The laboratories in corporations across this country employ state-of-the-art mechanisms to detect even a hint of pathogens."

Her father smirked. "Yeah, so they don't get sued."

"Oh, here we go." Juliet grabbed her purse. "Look, Mom. I'm too tired for this tonight."

Her mother's arm reached across the table. "Honey, wait —"

Juliet shook her head. "I'm sorry. I've got a lot on my mind, and it's just better if I head out." She ignored the tears pooling in her mother's eyes. "Just have them box my dinner. You can eat it for lunch tomorrow." She glanced over at her father as she moved to kiss her mother's cheek.

"Carol, honey. I'm sorry." He too reached for Juliet, remorse clearly written on his face. "I'm sorry. Juliet, please stay."

Juliet lifted her chin and pulled her hand away. "Call me tomorrow, Mom." She turned and scurried away, brushing past the growing crowd mingling down the sidewalk path lining the river.

She'd walked about a quarter of a block when in the distance, she heard screams over the sound of the mariachi band playing on a nearby veranda.

The music stopped. Juliet froze.

"Someone call 911!"

She turned back toward the commotion.

Her father's voice rang out. "Carol!" he screamed. "Hurry, somebody! I need a doctor!"

Looking back, Juliet marveled at how everything raced and slowed at the same time. She knew she'd dropped her purse and ran back, her feet pounding the sidewalk like a drum. Her mind simultaneously blurred and absorbed details — clumps of variegated green hostas and lacey ferns sprouting from the edge of shimmering water that reflected the hanging lights overhead. Chattering tourists sitting in a boat floating by, and the mingled smells of grilled meat and onion drifting from the open-doored restaurants.

But the single sight she would never forget was that of her mother's face turning pale gray as she lay crumpled at the base of the table, while her father heaved compressions at her chest. Her eyes — open and sightless. His — frantic and filled with fear.

In her own — Juliet would never forget she was responsible.

10

The morning of the funeral dawned unusually blustery. Thick clouds, heavy with moisture, had rolled in the evening before, drifting up from a tropical storm in the gulf, while a cold front swept into central Texas from the west. Just as a hint of light showed up on the dark horizon, the two weather fronts collided and rain fell from the thunderous sky, as if heaven too might be overwrought with emotion.

Juliet didn't know what the angels had to cry about. The celestial beings should be rejoicing. They had her mother now.

She did not.

Despite the storm, cars crammed every space in the parking lots surrounding Talavera Community Church. Inside the door, strains from "Be Unto Your Name," her mom's favorite song, met people arriving, along with the scent of the floral bouquets spilling over the stage.

Neighbors, fellow church members, and staff from New Beginnings filled every inch of seating in the sanctuary where Carol had worshiped each Sunday. Juliet's mother lived in San Antonio for over thirty years, and it seemed every person she'd met was here to pay respects and bid a proper good-bye.

When the service got under way, Juliet stared at her lap and tore a tissue into tiny bits during the opening prayer, keenly aware her father sat next her.

Were his hands trembling?

First on the program were the musical selections, one by a young girl with an amazing voice and another sung by the youth choir. She knew the songs, the flowers, and the sympathetic looks were meant to comfort, but nothing about this formal service abated the pain she felt — the deep despair residing inside her soul. She wasn't comforted at all. In fact, she was more agitated by the minute.

What was the use of any of this, when the person you most loved and needed was no longer here?

Finally, Pastor Roper made his way to the front.

Juliet swallowed against the lump in her throat and stared ahead, trying to focus on the pastor and not on the shame building in her gut.

"Carol Ryan was a woman who didn't fear death," he began. "She knew where she'd live once she departed from this world. Not because of her good deeds, although there were certainly many, but because Carol trusted in Jesus. She never doubted his promises because he'd already proven she could count on him."

Her mind shifted back to that night on the Riverwalk. By the time Juliet made her way back to the table, the vacant look in her mother's eyes left no doubt her mother had already left her.

Who could blame her?

Juliet had acted like a spiteful prepubescent, stomping off in a fit. And now? Well, now she could never tell her mom she was sorry.

Not now. Not ever.

She watched the blue-suited pastor at the podium. His words echoed in her ears.

"Once, I overheard Carol counseling an unwed mother. The young girl was frightened, felt like she had nowhere to turn. She was out of options and dangerously close to making a decision she didn't really want to make. Carol told that mother-to-be she'd found that when you go through the deepest waters, the Lord goes with you. But giving counsel wasn't enough. Carol wrote the woman a generous personal check. Here at Talavera, we call that an example of Jesus with legs."

Pastor Roper gripped the edge of the podium and directed a quiet smile out over the audience. "That young woman is here with us today and serves as a board member of New Beginnings. Lord willing, she'll carry on Carol's vision to provide free resources to women who need help."

A woman sitting across the aisle lifted a handkerchief to her eyes.

Why had Juliet never heard that story about her mother?

She sniffed and bit at her lips. What else had she failed to learn about the woman who had spent her life loving and nurturing her only daughter?

Exhausted, she looked around at the walls of the church. Plain, and not at all like the gilded cathedrals portrayed in most movies. No stained-glass windows or soaring ceilings. No statuary or chords playing on an organ. No officiates in robes.

Her mother's church, although large, was sparsely decorated except for a massive wooden cross on the wall behind the stage.

Once, Juliet had boldly challenged her

mother. "How can you pray to someone who might not even be there?"

"Oh, he's here," her mom answered. "You just have to quiet your heart and listen for him."

Up front, the pastor slowly closed his Bible. "Carol Ryan loved Jesus and spent her life proving it. In the days ahead, every time she comes to mind, which will no doubt be often, I'll think of this quote from Proverbs 31." He looked directly at Juliet and her father. "I believe this scripture describes Carol Ryan perfectly. 'Her children rise up and call her blessed. Her husband also, and he praises her. Many daughters have done well, but you excel them all.' "

He sighed. "I know I join many here in saying I will miss her terribly."

The pastor left the podium, and Juliet felt her father lift from his seat. He stepped into the aisle and walked slowly forward, stopping at her mother's closed casket. Juliet noticed his shoulders sag as he touched the corner of the smooth, dark wood.

Her father trudged slowly up the two steps to the podium. After adjusting the microphone, he swiped his handkerchief across his eyes, then looked out over the audience.

"I met Carol Gandiaga on a fall day much

like this one over thirty-four years ago. In a crowd of hundreds, I spotted this red-headed fiery gal dancing like she didn't care who was watching." He paused and looked up at the ceiling. "Uh, sorry, honey. She'd say her hair was *auburn*," he corrected, giving everyone a crinkled-eyed smile. "Anyway, I wasn't the only guy noticing her that night. The luckiest moment of my life was when she looked over and caught me staring. She smiled back, with one of those looks that sends your heart racing."

Juliet's father rubbed his hand against his chin, his eyes glazed with a faraway look. "I didn't deserve a woman like that pretty redhead. Not even close."

Juliet nervously picked at her thumbnail and swallowed the knot tied up in her throat.

Her father cleared his throat with a slight cough and blinked several times before looking back out at the crowd. "Carol stood me up on our third date. Liked to have scared me to death. I thought she'd finally wised up and ditched a poop like me. Turns out she was handing out freshly baked cinnamon rolls to people who lived in tents down by the river. That was before cell phones, mind you. Not exactly a safe thing to do — especially by herself. When I chastised her, she simply said, 'Oh, Bennett, you worry too much.' Months later, after she agreed to become Carol Ryan, those folks from the river showed up to help load the moving truck. When she bid that tattered group goodbye, their eyes clearly revealed they'd joined the rest of us who were completely and forever smitten."

Her father ran his hand through his hair. He swallowed as if trying to keep his composure. "My Carol's no doubt up there now with twelve guys better than me chasing her around." He paused and looked up to the ceiling again, tears pooling.

"Always remember, Mrs. Ryan, . . . how very much I love you."

After the service, family friends gathered at her parents' house, arriving with arms laden with casseroles, platters of turkey and sliced ham, rolls, and gelatin salads in a rainbow of colors. Added to the collection of pies and homemade cakes already parading down the kitchen counter, and a person could think today was some sort of celebration, not the end of Juliet's world.

She couldn't stomach calorie one, which is why when everyone else heaped mounds of funeral food onto sturdy white Chinet plates, she hid out in the study, wondering how a person could be in a crowd of people and feel this alone.

The luxury of a cigarette might dull this pain. For reasons she didn't understand, and perhaps only years of counseling would reveal, hot acrid smoke filling her lungs would provide a temporary respite from the severe isolation of soul she carried around like ashes inside her chest.

Juliet resisted giving in. She knew she'd go outside and stand near her mother's terra-cotta water fountain in the backyard, ready to light up, and she'd hear her mother's voice. "Honey, don't fill your lungs with that poison. Instead, breathe! Isn't the air delicious this afternoon? Even in the rain?"

Her mother seemed to be everywhere. Her voice, her presence. At times, even her smell.

Especially in this room.

Her parents' rim home overlooking the golf course was nicely decorated in a Santa Fe style — oh, not the magazine layout kind, but upon entering, a feeling of home greeted you. Her mother had a certain knack for placing comfortable sofas with interesting tables in a pattern that invited you to kick off your shoes, pull your feet up, and settle in for a chat.

Who would Juliet bare her soul to now

that her mom — her best friend — was gone?

Juliet stepped to the bookcases lining the wall and dragged her finger across the spines of her mother's books while listening to the chatter filtering through the door wedged partly open.

One Flew Over the Cuckoo's Nest rested comfortably in the first spot on the middle shelf, authored by Ken Kesey, who had lived just outside Eugene, her mother's hometown in Oregon. Next, her fingers slid across a tattered paperback copy of *The Thorn Birds* by Colleen McCullough.

The books on the top shelf generated the most familiarity. The entire Nancy Drew mystery collection lined the bookcase.

Juliet closed her eyes, imagining leaning against her mother's chest and the sound of her mom's voice as she read to her before bed.

"Juliet? Are you okay, honey?"

Juliet startled. She turned to an apologetic Sandy LeCroix holding a steaming mug. "I thought you'd like this," she offered.

She didn't. To be polite, she took the coffee. "Thanks, Sandy."

"You've got to quit beating yourself up over this." Mimicking something her mother would do, Sandy brushed Juliet's hair off her face. The gesture made the skin on the back of her neck tighten.

She looked at her mother's best friend, all else fading in the bright light of one soul-piercing fact. "It's my fault, Sandy. The one time she asked me for something, I told her no. Our bickering killed her."

"No one is to blame. You heard the doctors. A clot . . ."

Juliet shook her head. "But the last thing my mother saw . . . was her daughter walking away from her." Tears burned at the back of her eyelids. "Not after saying 'I love you, Mom' — but in anger."

Sandy reached for Juliet's arm. "Carol wouldn't want —"

Juliet pulled back, glancing frantically out the window where her mother's carefully tended knockout roses mocked her, the blooms stripped of petals from the pouring rain.

Outside the door, her father's voice mingled with laughter. She placed the mug on the bookshelf. "Look, I've got to go."

"No, Juliet. Please stay," Sandy implored. "He needs you. You need each other."

Juliet's throat grew thick. "I can't. Besides, he seems to be doing okay. Won't be any time and he'll land in some pretty girl's lap," she argued. She pointed her finger at her mother's friend. "You wait and see."

Sandy stood her ground. "Do it for her."

Juliet rubbed her forehead. The pounding had returned. She looked up. "That's not fair."

"I agree. If life were fair, my best friend would be here. We'd be laughing and placing bets on whether or not Judith Montgomery would show up with her famous green Jell-O mold, gelled with that awful cottage cheese and pineapple." Sandy's voice choked. She swallowed, her lips quivering. "Just — do it for her."

Stubbornness had never been her crowning glory. Seeing Sandy's pain chipped at the cold chunk in Juliet's chest where her heart should've been for the past several years. There was no way she could make Sandy understand.

Juliet conceded. "Okay. Okay. I'll stay. At least tonight." She folded her mom's friend into her arms. The warmth of Sandy's cheek against her own reminded Juliet she'd never again feel her mother's embrace. "But no promises after that."

By the time her father bid farewell to the last guest at the door, Juliet had escaped to the kitchen and busied herself cleaning up the dishes. She grabbed a long-handled plastic tool filled with dish soap and a sponge attached at the end — her mother would know the name, but Juliet had no idea what the cleaning gadget was called — and jabbed at a lasagna-crusted pan, trying to remove the hardened cheese clinging to the sides. Only partially winning the battle, she dipped the oblong glass casserole dish into warm sudsy water before placing it in her mom's new Kenmore dishwasher. Her mother had bragged she'd haggled with the salesman over extended warranties, never realizing how little it would matter.

"Hey there."

Juliet looked up as her father joined her in the kitchen.

He kneaded the back of his neck. "You don't have to clean up, JuJu."

Juliet's hands dove back into the hot water. "Perhaps you've forgotten, the cleaning lady doesn't come until Friday." Immediately, she was sorry for her sarcasm. She regrouped and forced a weak smile. "Besides, I don't mind."

Her father nodded. He moved to the counter and scraped off the turkey platter into the garbage can. "The service. It was nice, don't you think."

"Yeah. Everything was really nice." She slid a couple of plates into the waiting racks. "Mom would've approved."

"So many people turned out." Her dad's voice sounded tired. Exhausted, really.

Juliet turned and pointed him to the door. "You're like the walking dead. Why don't you go in and watch the news?" Immediately, she cringed at her choice of words. "I mean, you must be pooped. Go sit down in front of the television and I'll finish up in here."

Her father looked dazed. Like a little boy, he complied with her order. "Okay." He moved for the doorway to the living room, then paused and turned. "The hydrangeas we had flown in from Oregon were beautiful on top of her casket. She would have been pleased." He swallowed hard as if something climbed up his throat. "Those were her favorites, you know. The blue ones."

Not knowing how to respond to the raw pain in her father's voice, Juliet opened the cupboard door to the left of the sink. "We need a bowl to store the olives —" She stopped talking and pulled a Barbie cereal bowl from the shelf. "She kept this?"

Her dad nodded. "There was about a year there where you wouldn't eat out of anything else." A slow smile lifted the corners of his mouth. "You were a very stubborn little girl. You championed the temper tantrum." His eyes brightened. "We didn't know what to do but give in."

For several seconds, they stood in the kitchen — looking at each other as if they didn't know what to say next.

Finally, her father shifted his attention to the refrigerator. His fingers lifted a tiny Alamo-shaped magnet from a small square piece of paper. He pulled his reading glasses from his head and positioned them, then leaned forward to read.

His breath audibly caught, immediately followed by a high-pitched groan. A noise sounding like a tiny animal caught in barbed wire.

Juliet didn't try to hide her alarm. "Dad — what is it?"

The slip of paper floated to the floor. "She — she had an appointment this afternoon," he muttered in a choked voice. "With a cardiologist." He stumbled against the refrigerator, his eyes wrecked with tears.

Juliet rushed and caught his shoulders as he folded. She shifted his weight against her own, fighting to hold him up. "Oh, Daddy —"

They went to the floor together. There was no stopping her own tears then.

Time stilled while Juliet held her sobbing father.

11

The next two days passed uneventfully, though Juliet felt jumpy and unable to concentrate. She busied herself over the weekend with morning runs, followed with thank-you cards and organizing the mountain of details her father would need to take care of after her mother's death.

First, he'd need to meet with the attorney to start the probate process. Social Security forms would have to be completed and mailed in, health insurance and credit cards canceled, automatic payments for the gym membership stopped, and bank accounts changed over. He should schedule a meeting with the accountant to reevaluate the retirement plan and tax strategies, and collect on her mother's life insurance policies.

Juliet hoped creating the list might satisfy the guilty ache in her gut.

It didn't.

So she turned to cleaning her condo.

Despite knowing the maid service would show up next Wednesday, she poured a generous amount of bleach into a bucket of soapy water and wiped down the shelves in her refrigerator. Using an old toothbrush, she scoured the baseboards. She shined the bathroom mirrors and scrubbed her toilets.

The smell of Comet and Windex reminded Juliet of her mother in rubber gloves, working out her frustrations on the bathroom sinks. Back then, it seemed her mother cleaned a lot of sinks.

With her toilets and showers sparkling, Juliet resorted to watching television. She turned the set on and clicked past the religious channels, even the one with Pastor Roper. She couldn't bear to hear any more about how God would get you through hard times. Religious platitudes could never minimize the vacancy she felt inside.

She had her mother's Bible — one of many keepsakes she'd secreted away as mementos. Juliet tucked the worn leather-bound book away in a drawer, not ready to scrutinize the underlined passages and read her mother's handwritten notes in the margins. Someday maybe, when her heart didn't feel so splintered.

Juliet nestled back against the sofa and scrolled past any program too serious. She lost herself in a couple of commercials, one for a new migraine pharmaceutical and another promoting flood insurance, then caught the last few minutes of an old *Gilligan's Island* rerun. Something felt appealing about the group of castaways who ran into a storm and got lost.

When the episode wrapped up, she moved on to a shopping channel, drawn to a tube of highlighter guaranteed to erase dark under-eye circles and make a person look less tired.

On impulse, she ordered.

Juliet looked up at the ceiling. "Okay, Mom. No laughing. It's been a really hard week."

Suddenly, tears formed. How could she spend a lifetime without her mother?

Using the back of her hand, she swiped her cheeks and clicked the remote again, this time stopping on a news channel.

"The nation's top disease detectives have gathered in central Texas tonight in search of the cause of a mysterious and deadly outbreak of E. coli. It is an especially virulent strain, with a number of victims already affected.

"There is concern that this outbreak will spread, extending past the nearly dozen cases known so far. Sadly, one child has died, and scientists are continuing their search for a possible link."

Juliet leaned forward and turned up the volume.

"Authorities acknowledge they are in a race against the clock to isolate the source and remove it from the market. Samples taken from those in the hospital reveal identical molecular and pathological structure, pointing to a centralized source. All known cases so far have been limited to San Antonio, giving officials reason to believe there is a local origin.

"Until the CDC officials determine the cause, the public is urged to take proper precautions. Thoroughly cook meat products, particularly ground beef and chicken. Clean fresh produce, and wash cooking utensils and hands after handling food items."

Juliet chewed at the inside of her cheek. With everything that had transpired in the last days, she'd nearly pushed the news item from her thoughts.

The heated exchange between Juliet and her father replayed in her mind — and how her explosive reaction to his denunciation of corporate food safety had ignited a weapon of mass destruction. Her mother the target.

Despite her good intentions, anger flared yet again.

This time, Juliet doused her emotions with a dose of reason. A toddler was dead. Somewhere in San Antonio, a mother grieved the loss. Another person with a gaping hole in her heart. A condition Juliet found far too familiar.

Her hand reached for her phone. She scrolled through her contact list and dialed.

"Hey, you've reached Greer Latham. I'm unable to take your call. Please leave a message."

Juliet scowled and waited for the beep. "It's Juliet. I know I'm scheduled to take another week, but I'm coming in tomorrow morning. I don't know if you've been listening to the news, but I think it's important I get back."

She clicked off and put the phone on the counter. That was the second time they'd failed to connect this weekend.

When she stepped from the shower a half hour later, she heard her phone ringing in the other room. Juliet pulled on her robe and dashed down the hall, scrambling to pick up, but too late. She'd missed Greer's call. Almost immediately, an alert sounded indicating he'd left a message.

"Hey, babe. Sorry I keep missing you. And

I wish I'd made the funeral on Friday. Things at work have been so crazy that I just couldn't get away. But hey, I heard your message and you don't have to rush back. Malcolm Stanford has the lab covered. Take the time you need. Call some girlfriends. Go shopping. You deserve it after . . . well, after everything. Besides, I'll call you if anything comes up. You know that."

The phone beeped, cutting him off.

Several seconds passed before Juliet pulled the phone from her ear and slowly returned it to the counter. She clutched her robe against her chilled skin and let her hand trail across the granite, giving his message time to incubate.

As a food safety professional, she'd learned to distill facts and come to a calculated and reasonable conclusion. But it didn't take a highly trained microbiologist to connect these dots.

In the middle of an outbreak in their city, Greer Latham wanted her to go shopping.

In that moment, she knew returning to work tomorrow was the right decision.

Juliet pulled her keys from her bag and unlocked her parents' front door. She gave a quick knock, then pushed the door open. "Dad?" she hollered.

"In here, JuJu." His voice came from the kitchen, where she found him wearing one of her mother's aprons. He stood in front of the stove with a pair of tongs in his hand.

Juliet placed her purse on the table, next to a bowl of half-eaten Cheerios.

"You're a little early," he said, and turned down the flame.

"Sorry, traffic was light on a Sunday night."

"Hope you're hungry." He grabbed the shaker and sprinkled salt across the food in the sizzling pan.

Stopping short of kissing him on his cheek, she tentatively placed her hand on his back and peeked over her dad's shoulder at the pan filled with chicken, fried crispy golden. "What's this? You don't cook."

He gave a halfhearted shrug. "I — I guess I just wanted some of her smell around."

She frowned, confused. "You think Mom smelled like fried chicken?"

"Ah, you know what I mean."

Juliet patted him, noticing how gray his hair had become at the temples. "Well, what can I do to help?"

He reached for the pepper. "You don't cook either."

She stepped back and rubbed her hands together. "Can't be that hard, can it?" She handed him the platter from the counter and watched as he pulled the chicken from the pan with the tongs. "What do you want me to do?"

"You can make the gravy," he said. "I'm no good at it."

Turned out neither was she. But neither of them mentioned the fact as they sat at the table, silently eating.

Juliet could tell her dad was struggling to cope. His face was stubbled with growth, and he hadn't bothered to put on his standard button-down, wearing only a white undershirt. She doubted he'd even taken a shower since Friday, from the looks of his hair.

After being so angry with him for all those years, Juliet barely knew how to comfort him. Only that she wanted to somehow.

"So, how do you like the gravy, Dad?"

He glanced up. "The gravy? It's good — really good."

"Liar," she teased. "It's as lumpy as an armadillo's back. But thanks for the compliment."

"Tastes just like your mother's." To prove his point, he scooped a large bite of potatoes and gravy from his plate and into his mouth.

"Like you often said, nobody could cook like Mom." Juliet reached for her glass of tea. "Least of all me."

He placed his fork down along his plate and looked across the table. "She lives on in you, you know." His eyes filled with emotion. "You have her pretty eyes, and your hands are identical. You're smart as a whip. Just like Carol."

Juliet savored the rare compliments. She found herself wondering what it would be like to reach across the table for his hand. No person on earth shared her pain and understood the depth of this loss except him. Likely he'd suffered the same guilt too — the remorse she battled in her mind over the role they'd both played in the fact her mother was no longer here.

Despite medical evidence that might prove otherwise, Juliet knew their verbal altercation that night had fatally wounded the person they both loved the most.

And so did he.

Later, as they sat on the couch going through some old family photos, Juliet draped her mother's afghan over her legs and ventured a compliment of her own. "You — uh, I can see why she was drawn to you . . . Well, what I mean is, you were a looker back then."

Her comment hit its mark, and her father grinned. "Oh, I don't know about that."

Their relationship sat atop a fault line. One wrong move by either of them and the foundation of this fragile relationship might crumble. Despite the risk, Juliet wanted to move ahead.

For her mother.

She pulled a snapshot from the box. "Remember this?"

Her dad took the photo of her and her mother running hand in hand toward a hillside covered in bluebonnets. "Yeah, I do," he said softly. "We took an extended weekend and headed to the Hill Country for a little getaway. Your mother had that station wagon crammed to the hilt. I suggested she might save some room for you."

Juliet nodded. "And she gave me a history lesson during the drive."

He rubbed his chin, smiling. "Ah yes. You leaned forward from the backseat and asked why there was a sign pointing to Lyndon Johnson's ranch."

Juliet laughed. "Which prompted an introduction to his presidency and the Kennedy shooting."

"And the whole conspiracy theory, from her very liberal Oregon point of view," he inserted. "I glanced in the rearview mirror and you rolled your eyes, bored to death." He fingered the photo. "So I diverted her attention by pointing out the bluebonnets, and she squealed and told me to pull over. You quickly took advantage of the opportunity and begged to get out for a closer look." Her father placed the photo back in the box. "One of the rare times you and I joined forces and pulled one over on your mom."

Juliet leaned back, enjoying the memory. She also remembered walking back to the car and seeing her parents walk with her dad's arm around her mother's shoulders. After they'd tucked her back inside the car, she looked out the open window. Her dad patted her mom's bottom and whispered in her ear. She'd laughed and slapped at his hand. Told him, "Later, Bennett, after Juliet is asleep."

Juliet shifted the box of photos onto the sofa and pulled the afghan from her lap. "You need a refill on your iced tea?"

He glanced at his nearly full glass and shook his head.

Juliet grabbed her glass and headed for the kitchen. When she returned, she slipped back into place next to him. "What's that one?"

He held up a photo of her in a little white lab coat. The one he'd taken of her that day he came to her classroom. "This is my favorite photo of you. Pretty, smart, and mouthy. But it was that fierce intensity I loved most."

Juliet stole a glance at him, puzzled. She wasn't used to this side of her father — the one generous with praise. Losing her mother had somehow softened his sharp edges. Despite feeling awkward, she reached out and squeezed his hand.

Their eyes locked, and a long overdue moment of understanding passed between them before they turned their attention back to the box.

"Who's this?" Her father extended a photograph of her with another little girl playing dress-up in her mother's nightgowns and high heels. Juliet took the snapshot, pulling it closer for examination.

She shook her head. "I don't know —" She stopped midsentence. "Oh," she said, her heart thudding painfully. "Just a friend."

Juliet watched her father to see his reaction. He scooped another photo from the box. "Oh, hey — here's one of you in your graduation cap and gown."

Unexpectedly, her eyes burned with tears. She quickly blinked away the show of emotion.

Unaware, her father burst into laughter. "You probably don't remember back when you were six." He held a different photo in his hand. "This is when you took my razor and shaved off an eyebrow. Your mom was horrified, of course. Even more so when you used a black marker and drew it back on." He extended the photo so she could take a look. "You sure kept us on our toes."

Like a robot, Juliet glanced at the photo and contrived an artificial smile.

No matter how you cook an onion — one burp and the true flavor appears.

She looked at her father, his attention already directed back to the box. Clearly, he didn't recognize the girl in the photo. But then, how could he? He'd remember her much differently.

"JuJu, is something wrong?"

Juliet stared at the photo in her trembling hand. "Why did you do that to Mom?"

He looked confused. "Do what?"

She looked up at him, challenging him with an angry silence. He noticed then — her eyes.

He sighed in desperate exasperation. "Juliet, those women. They meant nothing."

She handed him the photo. "Even her?"

Despite the shame that suddenly shadowed his face, her father stared at her in quiet protest. But then, how could he possibly explain?

Her parents' wedding portrait sat perched on the nearby sofa table. Beside it, a blue hydrangea from the casket spray lay drying.

Juliet lifted her chin and glared back at her father with renewed disdain. "Did you think I didn't know?"

His jaw tightened. "It was none of your business."

She looked at him with open-mouthed astonishment. "It was very much my business. She was my best friend."

She watched him look down at the photo.

"I could hear Mom cry at night." She shook her head. "She was never the same after — something inside her withered."

Her father leapt from the sofa. He paced the floor like a caged animal, fighting for control. "I made a mistake. I — I never meant to hurt either of you." He ran his shaking hand through his hair. It was clear her comments had hit the intended mark. "I spent years trying to make it up to her. To you," he said. "I swear, I stopped drinking and never looked back."

She looked at him, eyes blazing. "And she bought it."

"She forgave me," he corrected. "And I thought maybe you —"

Juliet tossed the afghan aside and pounced, her voice shaking with anger.

"Yeah?" She moved to within inches of his face. "Nancy was barely nineteen years old. When you climbed in bed with my best friend, who were you thinking of then?" Not able to stop, she added, "You killed Mom. And I'm not talking about last Sunday."

Her father's face grew dark. He raised his hand as if to hit her.

She glared. "Do it."

Suddenly, her father grabbed her shoulder with one hand. With the other, he scooped her purse and pressed it against her chest. "Get out." He pushed her toward the door. "Get out of your mother's house."

Breathless, she stumbled forward. Before she could catch her bearings, he took hold of her arm and pulled her to the arched door.

She tore from his grip. "What's the matter? You can't take the truth?"

"Get out," he repeated. He opened the door and shoved her onto the landing.

Blinded with tears, she quickly made her way down the front steps and scrambled to her car. Inside, she stabbed the key in the ignition and started the engine. Sobbing, she put her Jeep in gear and tore down the street, sending a screeching sound into the hot autumn night.

At the light, her fist pounded the steering wheel.

She hated him.

12

Juliet didn't drive home.

Instead, she headed downtown, to Greer's place. She stood in the brightly lit hallway and rang his doorbell and waited.

Showing up unannounced might be a bad idea, but she'd take that risk. She didn't want to spend the night alone in her condo. Not tonight. Even if it meant ignoring the small voice telling her Greer Latham could only be trusted so far.

She heard a click and the door opened.

Greer stood dressed in a robe over drawstring pants and leather slippers. He raised his eyebrows. "Juliet? What are you doing here?" He waved her in and gave her a kiss on the cheek. "You okay?"

"Not really," she responded, her voice breaking.

Greer visibly stiffened. "Well, I suppose that's to be expected, given everything you've been through." He tightened the tie on his robe.

Suddenly, she regretted her decision. Greer wasn't one drawn to emotion. She'd made a mistake thinking she could find solace with a man known for his calculated approach to life. "Look, I'm sorry. It's late and it was silly of me to —"

Greer pulled her close. "Nonsense," he whispered against her hair. "I'm here for you."

Juliet pushed the reservations from her mind and leaned against him, drawn to the warmth of another human being like a moth drawn to flame.

She resisted telling him what had happened with her father. She kept news of the fiery exchange to herself, and the fact it left her broken inside — how much she'd wanted to move beyond the past, but couldn't.

She wouldn't reveal how fragile she felt, and alone.

Greer pulled back and gave her a worried frown. She could sense his mind at work and knew her face had betrayed her. He'd never seen this side of her. Matching his approach, she'd always been careful to guard against appearing anything but accomplished and skillful at handling her emotions.

"I'm okay, really," she assured him, reining in her feelings. "I just missed you. That's all." She followed him into the kitchen. "I need to get back to work. The walls are closing in, know what I mean?"

He grabbed a liter of coconut water from the refrigerator. "Want some?"

She shook her head and watched him extract a glass from the cupboard. "Speaking of, what have I been missing? At work, I mean."

He filled his glass. "We've been focusing on the Water Circus fulfillment, and we're in talks to expand the original structure of that deal, which has us all crazy busy. But like I told you on the phone, there's no urgent need for you to return. The lab staff seems to have everything covered." He screwed the lid back on the bottle. "But I get what you're saying. For some, work can often be a solace."

Juliet stared at his leather slippers while he returned the bottle to the nearly empty refrigerator.

He was right. For people like them, work was as essential as air, the rest of life a distraction. She understood where she fit in the corporate world. Despite the politics, ambition and hard work would ultimately pay off. Simple rules. Juliet appreciated that.

Suddenly, Greer stood in front of her. He placed his hand on her chin and made her face him. "Look, it's okay to let your guard down. I care about you, you know."

But not enough to come to my mother's funeral.

Juliet pushed the intrusive thought from her mind. She and Greer weren't soul mates. Their attraction was based on mutual respect, an understanding that neither would burden the other with emotional baggage. Their affinity for one another didn't extend past complementary affection. That was all.

She'd be smarter than to reveal the depth of her need. The emptiness she felt inside. The fear that hole would never be filled.

Given that, she was as surprised as he when she looked into his eyes and pressed her lips against his, letting him taste the depth of her hunger.

"Stay the night," he whispered, his voice husky. He took Juliet's hand and led her out of the kitchen. And she let him. Anything not to be alone tonight.

She squeezed his hand. "Uh . . . I'll only be a minute."

He nodded and she headed down the hallway to his bathroom, with its wood-trimmed curved wall that served as a partition splitting the large space in two. On one side stood a walk-in shower lined with mosaic tiles in colors of the ocean and a full-height steam room. Juliet moved to the sink and vanity left of the curved wall. She leaned forward and examined her reflection in the mirror.

No wonder Greer expressed concern. Her face looked like a train had wrecked just south of her hairline — her eyelids red and swollen, blotchy skin. By all indications, she appeared not to have slept in days.

Juliet reached for a clean washcloth from the chrome rack mounted on the wall and ran the plush fabric under the water, then pressed the cloth to her eyes, letting the cold compress do its magic.

Greer Latham was a fierce competitor at work. He'd take every opportunity to position himself for success. Even if that meant not always being forthcoming with every detail she wanted to know. But there were ways he'd been there for her over these past months. He was the one who urged her to meet with Alexa Carmichael, saying Larimar Springs would benefit from someone with her level of expertise. On a personal level, he'd extended friendship and a level of romantic involvement that met both their needs.

And tonight, he'd be there for her at a time when she most needed to matter to someone.

Greer rapped on the door. "You okay?"

Juliet pulled the cloth down. "Yeah, I'll just be a minute." She quickly reexamined her face. Seeing little improvement, she shrugged and folded the washcloth, then laid it on the counter at the side of the sink.

That was when she noticed a pair of women's gold earrings.

Juliet swallowed. She stared at her reflection in the mirror, this time facing what she'd already known deep down. She bit at her lip, realizing no matter what she'd tried to tell herself, even her relationship with Greer Latham was nothing more than a lie.

She really was all alone.

13

Plenty of things had changed in her life in the past weeks, but the one constant Juliet could count on was her work.

She stepped into the lobby of Larimar Springs Water Corporation. As far as she could tell, everything remained just as when she'd last walked through those double glass doors and to the parking lot — before that tragic Sunday a little over a week ago.

The lobby was brightly lit with overhead lighting competing with sun shining through massive windows lining the face of the building. Juliet's heels clicked against polished floor tiles as she walked toward the familiar circular reception area, where two large pots with tall kentia palms flanked the corporate logo on the wall behind where the receptionist greeted everyone. LARIMAR SPRINGS — PURE QUALITY, GREAT TASTE.

"Morning, Dr. Ryan. Welcome back."

"Thank you, Lindsay. It's good to be

back." Juliet shifted the weight of her attaché to her other hand. "Is Alexa in yet?"

Their receptionist nodded. "She arrived about an hour ago." She lowered her voice. "She doesn't seem to be in a good mood."

Juliet took pause. "Any particular reason?"

Lindsay shook her head, sending her blonde ponytail swinging. "No idea. But she's not always a morning person."

Juliet nodded. "I've heard."

The front doors opened and in walked a group of women from the accounting department, followed by Dale Frissom, vice president of operations.

After accepting their condolences over her mother's passing, Juliet proceeded to the executive wing, down the wide hallway and past Greer Latham's door. She was glad it was closed. Especially now.

She'd stood in his bathroom last night with the earrings in her hand, contemplating how she should react. She grabbed the doorknob with every intention of confronting him. In the end, she simply hadn't been up to another nasty encounter. The screaming match with her father had left her depleted, and she didn't trust herself. Losing it would serve no good purpose and might place their professional relationship at risk.

Instead, Juliet carefully repositioned the jewelry back in the original spot on the bathroom counter exactly where she'd found it, took a deep breath, and joined Greer in his living room. He was reclining on the sofa, his robe casually open at the chest. He stood. "What took so long in there?" He looked at her and frowned. "Are you all right?"

Juliet imagined his arms around another woman. Suddenly, her mind involuntarily jumped to her father. To that photo.

Her jaw tightened. "Look, I've got to go."

"Now?" Frustration spread across his face. "You're going to drive home at this hour? Juliet, it's after midnight."

Juliet held up her hand. "I know. I — I'm just not good company. Not tonight."

"But you . . ." Greer let his sentence trail off. No doubt her expression left no question. She wasn't going to change her mind. Resigned to the fact, he rubbed at his barely shadowed chin. "Uh — do you need me to walk you out?"

She shook her head. "Of course not. I know the way."

Greer looked relieved.

She didn't even know when he'd started being with someone else. Neither of them planned on deepening their commitment, but somehow Juliet believed the relationship was monogamous. Given Greer's history, she might never learn the truth.

Decades back, she'd sat on the floor of her pink bedroom and marched her plastic-legged Barbie doll down a toilet paper aisle toward an imaginary Prince Charming. A silly game played by a little girl who had yet to learn the harsh realities of real life.

Going forward, Juliet promised herself she'd no longer assume any man honorable and good. Not until Prince Charming proved otherwise.

The trick now was to effectively redefine her relationship with Greer and extricate herself from the personal side with the business affiliation left intact.

Every magazine she'd ever picked up while in a medical waiting room warned not to get in this predicament. Blending professional and romantic aspects of a relationship often proved as toxic as mixing chlorine bleach with ammonia.

She neared her office. Why had she foolishly believed herself immune?

"Hey, Dr. Ryan. This is a surprise. I was told you wouldn't be in this week."

Juliet looked up. A young woman she didn't recognize sat at Tavina's desk.

The woman stood and extended her hand.

"I'm Angela Silva. American Staffing sent me over to cover for Tavina. Her little boy wasn't feeling well this morning."

Juliet hid her disappointment and shook Angela's hand. She was counting on Tavina filling her in on everything that had happened while she'd been away.

"I'm sure your assistant would have let you know. But no one expected you to be here this morning." She gave Juliet a sympathetic smile and sat back down. "I'm sorry for your loss."

Juliet nodded. "Thank you. Uh — my mail?"

"On the corner of your desk."

Juliet thanked her and retreated to her office, shutting the door behind her.

"Well, you made it."

She nearly startled out of her skin. She whipped around. "What?"

Greer rose from the sofa against the wall. "Sorry, didn't mean to scare you."

Juliet scowled, her heart pounding. Tavina would never let anyone in her office unattended. And she'd certainly announce if there was someone waiting.

As if reading her mind, Greer assured her the blame did not belong to the temp covering for Tavina. "I saw you pull into the parking lot and asked her not to say anything. I wanted to surprise you." He pulled at his perfectly starched cuffs, then moved across the room and placed a kiss on her cheek.

Juliet turned, but too late. Before she could stop him, his mouth shifted to hers and he pressed himself against her. She could taste the mint gum she knew he always chewed after his morning stop at Starbucks. "Glad you're back," he whispered. Boldly, his forefinger traced her jawline. "It was lonely here last week."

Repulsed, she pulled back. The backs of her legs knocked against the coffee table strewn with food safety magazines. "Greer, what's gotten into you? Not here," she snipped.

Suddenly, there was a quick knock and the door opened. Greer pulled back, but too late. Angela stood in the open doorway. Her eyes widened. Clearly, the temp had assessed the situation. "Uh — sorry for interrupting, but Alexa Carmichael is heading this direction."

Juliet threw the girl a scalding look. "Next time, please buzz me."

Greer brushed his sleeves. "Alexa moved the Monday morning meetings up an hour. She sent an email."

Juliet scrambled to her desk, looking for her meeting file. "And I'm learning of this just now? I didn't get any email."

Greer waited until Angela shut the door. "You left in such a hurry last night, I hardly had time to mention it."

Juliet's phone speaker buzzed. "Dr. Ryan, Alexa Carmichael is here to see you."

She glared at Greer. "Tell her to come on in."

The door opened and Alexa entered, dressed in an off-white pantsuit with gold jacket buttons and teal shorty boots. A patterned scarf in the same shade of teal was tied at her neck. "Welcome back, Juliet. I hope you got the flowers the company sent."

Juliet pulled her meeting file against her chest. "Yes, I did. Thank you so much."

"You certainly didn't have to rush back," Alexa assured her. "But now that you're here, we have a lot to talk about. Wasn't sure if you had a chance to learn of the meeting, so I thought I'd drop by to make sure you joined in." She turned to Greer. "I arrived this morning to a message from Cyril. He's on board with the extra capital we'll need to service Water Circus's California and Florida operations." She fingered her scarf. "But he believes the distribution costs are sorely miscalculated. We'll want to talk strategy. In the meantime, I've got the appropriate individuals reworking those estimates." She frowned and checked her Rolex. "Why don't you both follow me on down to the boardroom?"

Alexa turned and headed for the door. Greer glanced back at Juliet. He ventured a quick wink before following.

Juliet grabbed the projection spreadsheets off her mail pile, slipped them inside the file, and hurried out the door as well. She passed Angela on her way, careful to avert eye contact, not wanting to expose herself to any judgment.

She could stomp Greer for his indiscretion.

Juliet had been back at work less than an hour, and already a mental checklist of to-do items was forming. First, she needed to contact Tavina, see when she planned to return. Her trusted assistant would be back at her desk soon, Juliet hoped.

Second, and more important, she needed to cut things off with Greer. In particular before he pulled that kind of stunt again.

"Dr. Ryan?"

Juliet turned. "Yes?"

The temp pointed. "Your skirt. It's, uh — your skirt's twisted."

Juliet glanced down. The side hem was nearly in dead center front. She let out an angry huff, wedged her file under her arm, and readjusted her skirt so the seams were lined up properly.

She drew a deep breath. "Thanks," she told the watching woman reluctantly. In a miscalculated afterthought, she added, "And that in there . . . That wasn't what it looked like. With Greer, I mean."

The temp folded her arms on the desk and slowly nodded, looking eerily similar to a female version of Jiminy Cricket. Or maybe Juliet suddenly felt like Pinocchio.

"No problem," Angela murmured. She directed her attention to the computer monitor, but not before Juliet caught a slight grin forming.

Juliet cringed. Had Alexa also noticed the skirt?

She gathered what was left of her professional dignity and hurried down the hall toward the boardroom. She needed to take Greer to dinner. Make a clean break and end this thing.

The sooner the better.

14

From her position at the head of the conference table, Alexa Carmichael leaned forward and shot a look out over the polished granite. "Could someone please explain how these figures are still off by 20 percent?"

The executive team members glanced nervously at each other.

Juliet knew Greer, who was VP of marketing and sales, had worked closely with Alexa to determine volume, so his sales projections were likely accurate. Fred Macklin, the comptroller, simply took the numbers others provided and plugged them into his spreadsheet calculations. And certainly, Juliet's area had nothing to do with the error.

That left Dale Frissom, VP of operations. Distribution fell under his direction. Clearly in the hot seat, he adjusted his tie at his neck and dropped his attention to the spreadsheet in front of him.

Alexa jiggled her pen, snapping the expensive Waterman against the granite table. "I know you are all thinking this snafu falls solely in Dale's lap, but everyone in this room — including me — reviewed those numbers. None of us caught that the estimates were off." She drew her free hand into a fist and leaned forward. "We missed it, and Cyril Montavan raised the issue." She pounded the table in frustration. "Which is unacceptable."

Greer clasped his hands neatly in front of him. "We have a short window of time to commit to this opportunity with Water Circus without competitors issuing bids that could potentially undercut ours," he reported in a manner that irked Juliet. "The task was certainly not easy, considering we've never serviced a national account of this magnitude, but I have this valuable customer convinced we can perform. As a company, we have to do whatever it takes to save this deal."

And your fat sales commission, Juliet thought.

Fred Macklin fingered the back of his white hair. "If distribution costs are off by 20 percent, we'll have to adjust elsewhere."

Again, Greer intercepted the conversation in his favor. "Exactly. We have no choice but to make cuts in order to maintain necessary profit margins." He opened a folder in front of him and passed a stack of papers around the table. "I took the liberty to evaluate current budgets and believe I found a viable solution."

Alexa rewarded him with a smile. "Well, that's good news." She tapped her pen against her fingers while studying his proposal. She lifted her head. "Greer, you're onto something here."

Over the next hour, the executive team studied the figures in Greer's spreadsheets. There were minor reductions to extraction, bottling, warehousing, and trucking expenses. With the increase in production, everyone agreed very little could be done to squeeze those costs down.

Human resources under Dale was definitely vulnerable, but by far the largest cut was to quality control.

Clearly, the people in the room did not understand the critical need to ensure product safety. Juliet wasn't naïve enough to believe FDA regulations were as compelling as new accounts with huge profit potential, but one slip didn't just mean a monetary fine for regulatory noncompliance — outbreaks of foodborne illness could take whole companies down.

Her father's voice rang out in her mind. "See, what did I tell you? Profit-hungry corporations always cut corners when it comes to safety."

She pushed away the unwelcome mental intrusion. On the surface, it may appear that way, but he was wrong.

Of course Larimar Springs needed to watch the bottom line. But Alexa had granted assurances before hiring her that safety mattered.

The critical task fell to her to educate and influence decisions in matters relating to safety as zealously as Greer argued profit margins.

"Look, I'm not going to bore everyone with regulatory standards or give a verbal thesis on viable and necessary methods to maintain acceptable levels of contaminants —"

Greer smirked. "That's welcome news."

She didn't let his sarcasm derail her. "I'm not going to put everybody to sleep with scientific data, but I would be remiss in my duties if I didn't point out that the quality control cuts represented here could place this company at risk."

He raised his eyebrows and let out a chuckle. "Really? How so?"

Ignoring the uncomfortable expressions

on the other men's faces, she took up the challenge, countering with something she hoped would matter to Alexa and her executive team. "Have you been watching the news lately? It means we keep Larimar Springs free of negative media attention. Or worse."

Now out of the hot seat, Dale climbed on Greer's self-serving bandwagon. "I can see the concern if we manufactured hamburger, but we're a bottled water company. How many E. coli cases do you see on the news associated with good old H_2O?"

Juliet drew a deep breath to temper her response. "Exactly. Because of proper sanitation and testing conventions, water collected from sources vulnerable to contamination, via fecal matter from nearby livestock or otherwise, rarely makes it into the market." She turned to Alexa, trying to ignore the sour look on her face. "That is why I strongly recommend going forward with the upgrade to a PCR thermal cycler. As I stated in my report, most pathogens reproduce rapidly in high temperatures, of high concern here in San Antonio."

Her boss scowled and studied the figures on the spreadsheet. "The size of that expenditure is a hard one to swallow, given our current predicament."

Greer pulled at his cuffs, a habit Juliet was coming to hate. "Well, the only solution I can ascertain is to postpone the QA department's equipment acquisition until Larimar cements this deal with Water Circus. We adjust these numbers to satisfy Montavan accordingly, keeping our bottom line solid and moving our partner to release the capital we need to go forward."

Juliet tried to grab the conversation back. "But that doesn't take into account —"

Greer continued making his point despite her objection. "Certainly, when profits start rolling in from the realization of this significant marketing coup, I'm sure all things could be back on the table."

Alexa dropped the finger she'd lifted to her mouth while listening. "I agree with Greer. Larimar Springs satisfies the minimum standards that are currently in place. That will have to be sufficient until we are in a position to reconsider."

She stood, signaling the end of the meeting. Following suit, those around the table collected their files and prepared to head back to their offices.

Greer needled next to Alexa, chatting her up on the way out of the boardroom. Juliet hung back, following at the rear of the procession.

Months back, at the end of her job interview, Alexa had told her, "Consumer health and safety are at the very core of what we do today, and what Larimar Springs has always done." She leaned over the desk and smiled. "We need a person of the highest caliber coupled with state-of-the-art technologies to guide our product development and to ensure our water continues to be absolutely safe."

Juliet was thrilled to join a company that felt like she did about food safety. At no time since coming on board had she doubted Larimar's priorities. Until today.

She tucked away her disappointment and headed for her office.

Certainly, her father had never taken her seriously. Now it seemed she had little credibility with Alexa Carmichael. Greer had seen to that.

When her father warned that corporations too often focused on the bottom line, shortsighting what was in the best interest of food safety, Juliet had taken issue with his pompous and misguided attitude, demanding he recognize the contribution corporations like Larimar Springs made to the scientific advancement of food safety.

Today, it seemed, the moment of truth had arrived.

No matter what Juliet had been led to believe, or how zealously she argued to the contrary, managing the risk of exposing consumers to foodborne illness was indeed subject to profit.

She'd thrown a fit that ended with her mother crumpled on the ground — in the end, a fit that never even mattered.

15

Juliet returned from the lab to find Alexa Carmichael standing at her assistant's desk, her phone against her ear.

"Oh, good. There you are." Alexa slipped her iPhone into her pants pocket.

"I'm sorry. I was meeting with my staff to let them know about the upcoming budget cuts." Juliet gave the smug-faced temp a wary glance. Tavina would've texted and given her a heads-up. "Is there something you need?"

Alexa followed Juliet into her office. "I hoped you would join me for lunch."

Surprised, Juliet turned. "Today?" She saw something flash through the eyes of her boss then, a look of respect.

"Yes. I know you just returned after a week away and must be swamped, but will your schedule allow you to slip away for a couple of hours?"

Alexa could have called or sent an email.

Instead, she'd come to her office personally to extend the invitation. She warmed and gave her boss a slow smile. "Uh — sure. I'd like that."

Her boss looked pleased. "We haven't really had time to talk — just the two of us — well, since the interview." She checked the time on her Rolex. "Why don't you meet me in the lobby in, say, a half hour? I'll have Muriel book us at the University Club."

Without waiting for Juliet to answer, Alexa's perfectly tinted lips lifted into a smile, and she turned for the door. "I'll drive," she added, and then she was gone.

Juliet stared at the closed door, confused. *What just happened?*

In the morning meeting, Alexa had shown no confidence in her recommendation and had sliced the budget by eliminating a key piece of equipment she believed necessary. Now, the businesswoman she most admired had turned cheek and wanted to take her to the University Club.

A tiny thrill slid up her spine. She'd never been to the University Club. And just wait until Greer Latham got word that she'd lunched with Alexa — alone.

Juliet mentally chastised herself. She'd gotten upset far too quickly in that meeting, again allowing her raw emotions to get the best of her. In the future, she'd need to recognize how depleted she felt after losing her mother.

Budget decisions had to be made, and unfortunately her department's needs for additional equipment were viewed as nonessential. Stepping back, Juliet might see how meeting the minimum standards could be considered sufficient by someone outside the food science community.

Besides, Alexa might be open to repositioning the proposed thermal cycler back into the budget as soon as Larimar Springs had met their capital needs for the expansion. A compromise Juliet knew would restore her credibility with the executive team.

A hint of a smile played at the edges of her mouth as she slid into her desk chair and clicked her mouse, opening her email. She scrolled through a number of messages, deleting some, moving several into folders for later action. Suddenly, a directive from the CDC appeared on the monitor, catching her attention.

The Centers for Disease Control and Prevention reports thirty-six patients in the San Antonio metro area with hemolytic uremic syndrome (HUS) — a type of kidney failure that is associated with Shiga toxin–producing Escherichia coli (E. coli) infections — and three deaths associated with HUS.

The CDC is committed to isolating and eliminating the threat to the public as quickly as possible.

As of today, the CDC announces they have narrowed their investigation to less than a half dozen possible sources. Officials are monitoring the situation closely and are conducting tests to subtype the bacterial pathogen. The results of these tests are expected to identify a single origination point within the next forty-eight hours.

A further announcement will be made at that time.

Until then, anyone with severe stomach cramping, bloody diarrhea, or vomiting should seek medical attention immediately, especially children and the elderly.

Juliet swallowed as her priorities jerked back in line with her prior sensibilities. The numbers were growing. San Antonio was smack-dab in the middle of what was now considered a major foodborne illness outbreak.

She clicked over to a food safety chat

forum she often monitored. The buzz had picked up. Clearly, members were nervous. And for good reason.

Findings from this outbreak would steer the course of consumer health mandates in the years ahead. Monitoring processes would be challenged and adjusted, and everyone in her profession would suffer closer scrutiny. Not that advancement in food systems was a bad thing. Food scientists everywhere wanted a safe environment in place.

From a public relations standpoint, any company responsible for an outbreak of this magnitude might as well hang a DO NOT EAT HERE sign in their window. Even a hint of an outbreak would mean a close order and loss of profits.

Most of all, Juliet knew the public's confidence would significantly erode with every hour that passed without answers. Especially those in hospital waiting rooms.

Juliet clicked off the forum and closed down her laptop.

Thankfully, even without the thermal cycler, Larimar Springs had adequate monitoring in place, ensuring little risk for exposure to liability.

She grabbed her purse and headed for the

door, never realizing that thought was her first mistake.

16

The exclusive University Club was located atop the Energy Plaza Building in north San Antonio. At an early age, Juliet heard her dad tell her mother that memberships to the exclusive business club opened up rarely, becoming available only when the board of governors voted to increase or a member passed on, leaving a spot to fill. He'd also raved about the food, claiming the cuisine and service could not be matched.

When Juliet learned Alexa Carmichael had secured a membership, she'd secretly hoped to be invited at some point. Even though she was inundated with work after being gone for a week, she'd jumped at the chance to join her boss for lunch.

The minute they stepped from the elevator, Juliet took in the dark wood-paneled walls, the carpets with the club's logo woven into the design, the blue and gold draperies that adorned windows showcasing the San Antonio skyline.

Her boss stepped to the concierge desk. "Alexa Carmichael. I believe I have the Club Room reserved."

A suited gentleman pointed a white-gloved hand. "Welcome, Ms. Carmichael. This way, please."

Juliet followed Alexa past the main dining area where guests sat at linen-draped tables, sipping from water goblets garnished with mint leaves and lemon curls. The air smelled of cedar and smoky meat aromas.

Suddenly, she was starved.

"I hope you don't mind that I had Muriel book us a private room. That way we can talk freely without the risk of being over-heard." Alexa grinned. "Don't let all this pomp and circumstance fool you. That dining area has as many gossips as you might find in any senior citizen's bridge club."

Once they were seated, one waiter passed elegant board menus, another placed napkins on their laps. Alexa ordered grilled quail served with roasted red bell pepper sauce. Juliet studied the menu and selected jumbo shrimp served over fettuccine pasta with lemon beurre blanc.

Alexa fingered her silverware. "This morning, I sensed you were more than disappointed by my budget decision."

Juliet looked up, feeling a little like the proverbial deer caught in the headlights. "Oh?" Inside, she groaned. She normally didn't take a passive-aggressive route, preferring to own up to an honest expression of her feelings. But something about the way Alexa looked at her left her feeling like a fourteen-year-old. "I mean, yes — of course I was hoping for a different outcome. But I understand decisions have to be made. Sometimes those decisions aren't popular."

"Exactly." Alexa paused while a server placed a basket of hot bread on the table. "As you move up at Larimar Springs, you will face more of these situations yourself."

Did she just hear Alexa indicate she'd be moving up in the corporation?

"Frankly, between you and me, Frissom provided the miscalculation. He should've taken the entire hit this morning. Unfortunately, for the reasons I stated in the meeting, our rapid expansion will not tolerate cuts to the operations area." She reached for the basket and pulled a piece of sourdough bread from under the linen napkin. "Except for the staffing resources I indicated." She offered the basket across the table to Juliet.

She nodded and took the basket.

Alexa stopped buttering her bread and leaned close. "Look, I'm going to be entirely frank here. I hated to decide the matter counter to your counsel. I understand the food safety issue. Given recent news stories, believe me, I do."

Juliet listened intently and pulled a dark squaw roll from underneath the linen napkin.

"You see, this is the thing," Alexa said. "An opportunity for this kind of quick growth comes along once in a lifetime. In my wildest dreams, I never imagined the relationship with Water Circus would blow up like this, especially given how relatively new we are to their vendor roster."

Alexa placed her butter knife on a small plate. "Larimar Springs has a chance to go big, especially with Montavan capital backing us. We can't afford even a slight mistake." When she looked back at Juliet, her eyes almost glistened. "*But* — if we do this right — well, Larimar Springs pops into the realm of Nestle, PepsiCo, and Perrier. Our name would be internationally recognized. We'd have divisions across this country." She leaned back in her chair, flush with excitement. "Everyone on the executive team would be wealthy. And you, Dr. Ryan, would be vice president, directing an operation twenty times the size of what you currently oversee. You'd have your pick of speaking opportunities at conferences and science forums — worldwide."

Alexa took a bite of her bread, letting her words sink in.

As the waiters served their entrées, Juliet took the bait and let herself imagine the world Alexa had just painted. Her eyes darted from the expensive art on the walls of the exclusive members-only club and the small team of waiters scurrying to serve them, to the woman across the table who clearly believed in her and had just extended an invitation for Juliet to ride her business meteor as it launched into a wide world of possibility.

More importantly, Juliet imagined soaring past her own father's career trajectory. She let herself dream of the look on his face when he learned of her incredible success.

"Don't worry, Alexa," she promised, smiling with renewed confidence. "You have my full support."

17

By Thursday, Juliet finally felt caught up at work. She'd reviewed monitoring reports from the week she'd been out for her mother's funeral, randomly pulling individual test results to back up the findings. She'd sifted through nearly four hundred emails, listened to numerous voice messages left on her phone, and redid her budget proposal and submitted it to Alexa. Well, actually to Alexa's assistant, Muriel Parke, who huffed and barely said thank you.

Frankly, Juliet didn't see how Alexa put up with that old bat.

She unlocked her condo door and headed inside. After kicking off her heels, she moved to the kitchen, wishing she'd remembered to pick up some soda on the way home.

She was pondering how lucky she was to have Tavina, and lamenting the fact her trusted assistant still hadn't returned to work, when her cell phone rang.

Juliet stepped back from peering inside her nearly empty refrigerator, closed the door, and quickly moved to the counter. She picked up the phone and checked the face.

Well . . . speaking of Tavina.

She slid her thumb across the tiny screen and brought the phone to her ear, grateful for the chance to finally talk to her. Each morning that her assistant phoned in, Angela Silva had taken the call. Juliet had been reluctant to telephone her in case she was catching some sleep after caring for her sick son.

"Hey, Tavina. It's so good to talk to you. How's little MD?"

A muffled cry broke through from the other end.

"Tavina?" Juliet frowned. "Is everything okay?"

"Juliet — it's MD. He's getting worse."

"How worse?"

"He — he's been vomiting off and on for nearly twenty-four hours. He's lethargic and a little feverish." Fear laced Tavina's voice. "Juliet, I'm watching the news, and I'm scared."

"Tavina? Listen to me carefully. Has MD been experiencing any loose stools? Diarrhea . . . any blood?"

Tavina sniffled. "Yes — I seen it just now."

Juliet's throat tightened. "Get him ready. I'll pick you up in about twenty minutes and take you to the hospital."

"Is — is my baby gonna be okay?"

Juliet wished she could say yes, but she couldn't bring herself to assure Tavina with empty promises. "We'll take him to Children's. I promise MD will get the best possible care. I'll see you in a few."

Juliet scrambled to grab her keys and purse, not bothering to change.

Traffic was still heavy, but they arrived at Children's Hospital in record time, in part because when Juliet pulled up to Tavina's apartment complex, the scared mother ran out to the car with her son wrapped in a thick quilt.

Juliet pulled into the hospital entrance off Houston Street. She turned past the iconic eight-story mural of a guardian angel watching over a young boy and braked at the emergency room entrance, her tires screeching.

Together, Juliet and Tavina scrambled inside. "We have a really sick little guy," Juliet hollered at the woman behind the registration desk. Breathless, she quickly added, "Bloody stools, severe vomiting — very likely O157."

The hospital staff tore into action, bullet-ing questions at a frightened Tavina. A guy in scrubs scooped MD from her arms and told them to follow. Juliet handed off her car keys to the lady at the registration desk so someone could park her Jeep.

Seconds later, they were shuffled into a dedicated elevator. MD was rushed in one direction while they were led into a waiting room by a middle-aged woman in scrubs with a stethoscope around her neck. The woman gave Tavina a kind smile and guided her to a stiff green chair.

"Can I get you anything? Coffee?"

Tavina shook her head and sat. Neither she nor Juliet said a word. Instead, both of them stared at the news anchor on a wall-mounted television monitor near a rack filled with battered magazines.

Minutes later, a second woman appeared and handed Tavina a clipboard with insur-ance paperwork. "Here, honey. We'll need this information filled out."

"Give me your insurance card, Tavina. I'll help with that," Juliet offered, taking the clipboard.

Tavina's hands visibly trembled as she dug in her purse for her wallet.

Despite the brightly colored butterflies painted on the ceiling, this was no picnic in the park. Not for Tavina. And not for Juliet, who clearly understood what was at stake.

Juliet worked to fill out what seemed like a small mountain of forms. Finished, she took them to the woman volunteer sitting at a tiny desk near the door. "Can you alert registration these are ready?"

The white-haired woman smiled and nodded. "Of course, dear."

On her way back, Juliet directed a weak smile to a battle-weary couple sitting against the opposite wall. The man leaned over his knees, hands folded. His wife nervously picked at her nails and stared at Styrofoam cups littering the table to her right.

Juliet slipped into the chair next to Tavina. She looked up, her big doe-like brown eyes puddled with despair. "When do you think they'll let me see him?"

"I'm not sure." Juliet placed her hand on her assistant's back. "Tavina, I promise you these doctors are monitoring MD closely. Any hint that his situation is turning and the medical team will be right on top of it."

She watched, helpless, as tears pooled in Tavina's brown eyes. "I knew something was wrong. I should've brought him earlier. It's just — he got so bad so quickly."

"He's here now. That's what counts."

Her efforts to comfort the frantic mother

sitting beside her were interrupted by a breaking news banner threading across the television screen on the wall. Suddenly, images of her and Tavina running into the hospital with MD wrapped in the blanket were broadcast with a voice-over.

"Minutes ago, another severely ill child arrived at Children's Hospital. Sources tell the KENS-5 news team that this appears to be another case linked to the deadly outbreak of E. coli ravaging our city. That brings the current number of illnesses to thirty-seven. Three children under the age of seven have died."

Tavina buried her head in her hands. "Oh, Lord Jesus . . . please take care of my baby."

Juliet scowled and smoothed Tavina's hair back from her damp face. She hadn't noticed cameras when they arrived. But then, both she and Tavina were focused on getting MD the medical attention he needed.

Nearly an hour passed before a doctor in blue scrubs showed up in the waiting room, his exhausted expression confirming Juliet's worst fears. "We won't know until certain test results are back, which could take up to forty-eight hours to confirm, but all indications point to hemolytic uremic syndrome."

Tavina's big brown eyes filled with tears. "Is — is MD going to be all right?"

Juliet hated the terror she heard in her assistant's voice. She hated how her own gut twisted.

The doctor sighed. "I'm not going to sugarcoat this. He's a very sick little boy. Thankfully, you got him here fairly early and we can take necessary precautions. We have your son in the ICU and will monitor his condition round the clock." He paused, letting what he'd said sink in. He bent and placed his hand on Tavina's knee. "The next twenty-four hours are critical. But I promise you this hospital has the finest medical professionals, and we're going to provide the best care possible for your little guy. And right now, he's stable."

The physician went through the details of MD's condition, explaining carefully the little boy's illness, carefully maneuvering every word so as not to frighten Tavina with potential outcomes no one could really predict. He turned to Juliet. "We've notified authorities, and they are on their way to collect information. Officials will want a detailed account of where MD ate and drank in the relevant time period. Are you family?"

Juliet shook her head. "No, I'm a . . . friend."

Tavina swiped at her tearstained cheek.

"I'm going to stay here with Marquis." She dug in her purse and pulled out a pen and an old receipt. She scribbled on the back. "Here's my mama's number. Could you please call her and tell her what's going on?"

Juliet nodded. She tucked the receipt inside her purse. "Anything else I can do? I mean, I can stay with you if you —"

Tavina shook her head. "Thanks, but no. You go on home." She held up her phone. "I'll call you if he worsens."

Juliet hated leaving her. Her assistant looked beaten, like someone had emotionally walloped her and left her struggling for breath. Juliet gave her a tight hug. "I'll be here in minutes if you need me," she promised.

Before leaving, Juliet left her contact information at the nurses' station, with instructions to call her if MD took a turn for the worse. She headed for the bank of elevators, wishing against any hope that there would be a cigarette vending machine somewhere in this medical facility. Never had she longed for a drag of the calming acrid smoke to fill her lungs more than now.

Juliet retrieved her keys, then passed through the lobby on the way out, with its bright blue floor tiles and wall aquarium filled with tropical fish. A little boy held the hand of a toddler, her hair in ringlets and a bow. "See, Sissy? See the fishes?"

Juliet's heart ached. For those children lost in Seattle years back in the Jack in the Box outbreak, and for all the ones since. And especially for little MD Mosely, who lay upstairs in a seriously ill condition.

Her hand slammed against the big silver button, opening the sliding glass doors to the drop-off portico. *Why?* Why, after all food scientists had learned, did these outbreaks still occur, putting little ones and people with compromised systems at such risk?

The doctor was reluctant to paint a grim picture, but she knew if Tavina's little boy worsened, the situation would turn grave. Unless he was lucky, the deadly microorganisms in his digestive system would cause his kidneys to fail and his organs to shut down. He could even die.

As she'd recently learned, death was final, or at least for a very long time.

Juliet stepped outside into the heavy air, heated and carrying a hint of the garbage-filled alleys nearby. She looked up to a nearly starless sky.

If you're up there, Mom — please ask God to let MD Mosely be one of the lucky ones.

18

Before leaving the hospital parking lot, Juliet telephoned Tavina's mother, who was now living outside of New Orleans with Tavina's oldest brother. Juliet answered the frightened woman's questions as best she could, and then Tavina's mom passed the phone over to her son.

"Hey," he said in a low voice. "Straight up. How bad is it?"

"There are kids who make it," Juliet explained, trying not to make any promises. "The medical personnel are monitoring his hydration status closely and will use potassium-free fluids until his renal function has stabilized."

"Is he in renal failure? That can be fatal."

"MD is showing some indications of stress on his kidneys, but the doctors assured your sister his condition is not at an acute stage at this point."

When the call ended, Juliet clicked off her

phone and tossed it in her purse. She started the engine and backed out of the parking spot, then pulled onto Martin Street and merged onto the 35 going north, leaving the hospital and the past several hours in her rearview mirror.

In some ways, Children's Hospital was a shiny cup filled with sour milk. The bright exterior and colorful landscaping camouflaged an interior filled with anxious parents and children in pain.

Juliet couldn't imagine being in Tavina's place tonight, her torment too deep for words, only authentically expressed in her brown eyes, pooled with heart-wrenching agony.

She swallowed hard, wishing she could call and dump some of her own emotion into her mother's caring lap. Her mom would know what to say to make Juliet feel better. She'd tell her the outcome of MD's medical crisis was in a loving God's hands, and Juliet would want to believe her.

The randomness of life, with all its tragedy, had never settled well with Juliet. She'd like to be convinced that some master being was indeed pulling the strings and orchestrating everything. Because then she'd have someone to blame when nothing made sense and hurtful events hurled into your lap like a steaming potato too hot to pick up and toss back.

At least Tavina had a mother and brothers who loved her and would support her through all this.

Juliet stared at the rear lights of the car in front of her, considering the fact she had no one. In only a short time, she'd lost her mom, sliced her father out of her life, and discovered her relationship with Greer was nothing but pretense.

Her existence was filled with co-workers and professional connections, and girl-friends she'd occasionally meet for dinner or drinks — but Juliet had no one to share her heart with. No one who understood she was a capable woman struggling with inse-curity. Who would grasp that she was a bundle of contradictions, a person who was bold and fearful all at the same time? Who — except her dead mother — would truly know her and love her?

God would.

Unexpected tears burned at her eyes as her mother's voice formed in her head, as if she were sitting in the passenger seat talk-ing.

"Maybe so, Mom," she tentatively whis-pered. "But he's not here right now."

You know better than that.

Juliet chewed the inside of her mouth, rolling that thought in her head. Clearly, the night's events had taken their toll. Now she was hearing her dead mother preach.

Up ahead, she caught sight of a McDonald's sign. Juliet rarely indulged in fast food and shouldn't now, given how long it had been since her last run. But she was starving. With food in her stomach, she might think more clearly. Certainly, she wouldn't find anything to eat in that empty refrigerator at home.

Juliet sighed, put her blinker on, and exited. Minutes later, she sat alone in a hard, plastic-backed chair in a dining room filled with empty tables, a greasy odor, and stained tile.

Her hands lifted the Big Mac from the tray and pulled the wrapped paper back. She prepared to take a bite when a buzzing sound came from beside her.

She set the burger back down and grabbed her bag, pulling her iPhone from its pocket, remembering she'd set the ringtone to mute in the hospital.

Greer.

Juliet rolled her eyes. She didn't have the energy to pretend with him tonight. She placed the phone, still buzzing, on the table and picked her hamburger back up. She took a bite, watching the phone finally go dark. As expected, a ding soon alerted that he'd left a voicemail.

Juliet indulged in a handful of hot, salty fries, letting the caloric intake do its trick. There was a reason carbs fried in hot grease were often called comfort food.

The phone rang again.

What could Greer possibly want at this time of night?

She pulled the protective paper from her straw and plugged it into the lid opening, ignoring the call, then took a drink from her super-sized Diet Coke.

The phone rang yet again.

Frustrated, she slammed the disposable cup to the table, grabbed the phone, and picked up. "Greer, it's late."

"Where have you been?" he shouted. "I've been trying to reach you for over an hour. I drove by your house and left you phone messages. Why haven't you been picking up?"

It was then Juliet noticed multiple missed calls. "Sorry, calm down. I was at the hospital with Tavina. Her little boy —"

"Juliet, have you seen the news?"

"Yes, I certainly didn't look my best. Not when I was so tired."

Greer huffed. "You have to get to the office. Now!"

"What are you talking about? What's so important I'd have to get to the office this time of night?"

"The CDC just made a big announcement."

The alarm in his voice caused the patterned tile to undulate in her vision, like she was suddenly shooting the rapids on the Comal River in a flimsy raft. "An announcement? What about?"

"They've identified the source." On that, his voice broke.

Juliet nearly spilled her drink. "What? Where?"

"Officials are reporting the source . . . is Water Circus."

19

Juliet eased her Jeep through the nearly empty front lot at Larimar Springs and parked under a light pole near the entrance, next to Greer's Jaguar. Alexa's Aston Martin was parked in her reserved spot near the front door. She spotted Dale Frissom's car as well.

She'd barely used her security card and stepped inside the lobby when Greer charged across the floor. "It's about time." He reached for her elbow and guided her down the hall toward the conference room.

"Well, hello to you too," she said, noticing he'd rolled up his cuffs.

Without responding, he almost pushed her through the conference room door. "She's here. Now we can get started."

From her spot at the head of the table, Alexa looked up. "I'm relieved to have you with us, Dr. Ryan. Sit down. We have a lot to consider."

Even at this late hour, Alexa looked put together. She wore designer jeans, calf-length boots, and a cream-colored turtleneck with a leopard print vest over the top. Her hair was pulled back into a chignon at the back of her neck. She even wore lipstick. The only change to her normal appearance was the glasses she wore in place of contacts.

"What did I miss?" Juliet took a spot at the table, trying to ignore how she must look. It'd been hours since a comb had seen her hair, and she probably smelled like French fries.

Alexa wasn't a woman for small talk. She got right to the point. "I'm not going to sugarcoat what's happened tonight. This announcement has placed Larimar Springs in a perilous situation." She opened her leather portfolio. "I've been in very brief contact with the Water Circus people. I'm told it's a madhouse over there. This finding is very serious for everyone concerned."

"How serious?" Dale Frissom nervously rubbed his neck above an open-collared shirt. "Look, I'm not sure what all this means." His hand moved to the side of his face. "Practically speaking."

Juliet placed her folded hands on the table. "I made a call to my contact at the CDC on my way here, and Dr. Breslin confirmed every test sample resulted in the exact same subtype cultures — the O157:H7 antigen as well as the Shiga-like toxins which are associated with these pathogenic strains."

Dale ran his hand through his hair. "In English?"

"Those test results, integrated with the established epi curve, are conclusive — every victim visited Water Circus during the window of time they are looking at," Juliet explained. "The park is under a close order until a team comprised of the CDC, USDA, and Texas state officials can coordinate the effort to pinpoint the suspect food or drink and identify exactly where the pathogens originated."

Alexa's face turned grim. "Not only will our future expansion be placed on hold for an indefinite period, but while that close order is in place, we stand to lose a lot of profit. Nearly half of our current business is with Water Circus."

Her manicured fingers rubbed at her temple. "No question, this development will significantly impact our operation here at Larimar Springs. We'll be faced with a multitude of decisions very quickly." She swiveled her chair toward Juliet. "Dr. Ryan, we're looking to you to help us assimilate the information and guide us going forward. Why don't you start at the beginning and fully brief the team?"

The fact Alexa had formally addressed the situation by looking to her didn't pass by Juliet. Neither did the immense responsibility. She took a deep breath. "In these early stages of bacterial outbreak, an epidemiologist's task is a lot like assembling a big jigsaw puzzle. Disparate clues have to be identified and connected."

While Juliet spoke, Greer quietly paced in front of the windows, his hand rubbing at his jaw.

"Step one is to inventory what those with symptoms have consumed during the relevant incubation period. And where." Juliet poured herself a glass of water from the ice-filled pitcher on the table. "A few days ago, officials narrowed the focus to three potential sources, based on early interviews and their case control study. From there, further tests were necessary to rule out consumed food products that were common to all."

Greer stopped. "What products?"

"Because those products have now been ruled out, officials will keep that information confidential. For obvious reasons."

Dale scowled. "How do they rule something like that out?"

"Well," Juliet answered, "they test the product. If the results fail to match the findings in the stool samples, the lab issues a negative finding and that possibility is crossed off the list."

Alexa steepled her fingers. "So, at this point there is no reason to question the tests?"

Juliet nodded. "No, the tests are conclusive. No scientific challenge can be made."

"But do they know what these people ate at Water Circus?" Greer asked.

"No. That's the next phase of the investigation," Juliet explained. "And to complicate matters, the puzzle pieces are a bit scattered. Beyond consumptive items, the investigators will test other things, like the water in the fountains and waterslides. I'm afraid toddlers wear diapers, and fecal matter can contaminate areas where other children can come in contact with the E. coli bacteria."

Greer scowled. "But the news said many of the people who have become ill are older. I haven't seen any senior citizens zipping down a waterslide lately."

Juliet conceded that was true. "Like I said, this is a very complicated process. Until this whole thing concludes, the governing agencies won't take chances, which is why they issued a close order to the Water Circus here in San Antonio. Thankfully, all the reported cases are local." She leaned back. "Things could be much worse."

Greer almost sneered. "What could be worse than losing our biggest account and knocking out a planned expansion that could have quadrupled this company's profits?"

Juliet ignored his comment and turned to Alexa. "As you might guess, Larimar Springs is on the vendor list they've compiled. I've been asked to meet with the authorities first thing tomorrow morning for a special meeting to provide records they've requested."

Alarm crossed everyone's faces.

"What kind of records?" Greer snapped.

"Our internal test results from our sampling program, log books, and procedure manuals. They will already have the audit reports from the health inspections, which we always passed with flying colors." Juliet worked to appear confident. "I assure you, everything is in order. We run a clean ship. Besides, bottled water products boast the rarest number of pathogenic outbreak incidents among consumer products."

Juliet could see Alexa and the others carefully considering the information she'd provided, making mental calculations of the cost to the company and to each of them personally. Especially Greer. The biggest accomplishment of his career was now swirling down the toilet. Clearly, he was not happy about his future being flushed away.

If Juliet were a mean person, she might find some joy in that. But she knew how devastated he must feel right now. Which is why she'd left the really bad news until last. "I'm afraid I have more."

Alexa furrowed her brow. "More?"

Juliet nodded. "My assistant, Tavina Mosely, called me earlier this evening. Her little boy has developed symptoms consistent with the O157 hemolytic uremic syndrome reported on the news. I was with her at Children's Hospital this evening when you all were looking for me." Juliet noticed Greer gazing out the windows into the dark, his back to the rest of them. "Doctors have yet to confirm, but all indications are that Tavina's son has HUS and is in the early stages of renal shutdown."

Alexa's face visibly paled. "Is he — will he be all right?"

Juliet shrugged. "The medical professionals will closely monitor him, try to keep him hydrated. But this is a virulent disease. Statistics show that nearly 85 percent of children under the age of six who contract the O157 strain and develop these symptoms fail to come through the ordeal."

"He could die?" Alexa teared up, clearly upset. The normally self-assured woman seemed to come undone in front of everyone. She glanced at Greer, then turned and stared at the table in front of her. "I'm so sorry to hear that," she said, her voice nearly a whisper.

From where she sat, Juliet could see the tendons in Greer's neck muscles flex.

Several seconds passed in silence. Finally, Alexa raised her head. "Is there anything she needs? What can we do?"

"I'm not really sure at this point," Juliet responded. "The next twenty-four hours will be critical."

Alexa stood. "I'll make some calls. My husband knows several of the hospital board members. We can arrange special attention for Tavina and her little boy."

Greer rubbed at the side of his face. He stepped to the table, looking oddly flustered, and cleared his throat. "We still need to evaluate what this will do to us financially. And make a plan," he said in a low voice, as if wanting to move on to a less emotional topic.

Alexa turned her exhausted face in his direction. "Not tonight. Besides, we'll need

Fred to run numbers before we can truly assess the hit we'll take, and make any appropriate decisions." She gathered her purse from the floor. "I'll call Cyril first thing in the morning. I don't want him hearing about this from anyone else." She looked across the table. "Go home, everyone. Get some sleep. Then let's plan to gather back here first thing in the morning." She turned to Juliet. "Please keep me posted. On everything."

Juliet nodded. "When I return from meeting with the authorities, I'll bring an update."

Before leaving, Juliet grabbed her white coat from her office and headed for the lab to collect some records stored there. The production lines ran shifts around the clock and were located at the rear of the complex. But the admin offices were eerily quiet at this time of the night.

Juliet made her way past darkened cubicles. As she rounded the break room, ahead she noticed light coming through the door leading to the lab. *That's strange. Who left the lights on?*

She swiped her security card and followed the sanitation protocol. With her shoulder, she hit the large red button and waited for the buzz that would release the door. Inside, something moved at the back counter. She startled. "Malcolm? Malcolm, what are you doing here?"

He startled as well. "Uh — Dr. Ryan." His eyes darted around the room. "I didn't expect you'd be here this late."

Juliet's eyes narrowed. "I wouldn't suppose so. It's nearly eleven." She moved closer to his petite frame. "Why are *you* here this late?"

"I heard the news, figured we'd be the target of further investigation, and thought I'd make sure the girls had gotten all our test results in the notebooks." He stared at her. "They'll want to see them, right?"

Juliet slowly nodded. "That's why I'm here." She walked to the filing cabinets against the wall opposite where they were standing. Her fingers ran across the spine labels until she located the records she'd need. "And everything is in order?" she asked with her back to the QA supervisor.

"Everything's there," he assured her.

She turned, her arms loaded with two large three-ring binders. "I didn't see your car out front."

"I parked out in the back lot."

Juliet eyed him warily. "But that's quite a walk."

"Security patrols that lot at night," he

answered, challenging her suspicion. "Safer when you're walking to your car alone."

Juliet mentally chastised her cynical distrust, unsure why she continued to believe she had to watch her back with him. She nodded. "Makes sense." Then she added, "Thank you, Malcolm, for taking the initiative to make sure we have everything."

Malcolm nodded. His black eyes stared at the floor. "Sure. Let me know if you need anything else."

Juliet thanked him again and moved for the door. Suddenly, she turned. "Malcolm? Would you like to go with me in the morning? To the meeting, I mean."

His face brightened. But surprisingly, he turned her down. "Nah, I'd best stay. Lucy's out tomorrow. A dentist appointment."

Juliet looked at him thoughtfully. "You sure?"

He nodded and straightened some beakers on the counter.

"Okay. Good night then." Juliet gave him a weak smile. "See you tomorrow."

Before she drove home, she called the hospital to check on MD. "No change. He's holding his own," the charge nurse reported.

Juliet let out a sigh of relief and thanked the nurse. She started the engine. *Let's hope God will keep it that way.*

20

The following morning, a meeting was held at the Texas Center for Infectious Disease. Health officials from multiple agencies were in attendance, as well as members of the media and, unfortunately, a few lawyers. No doubt victims were already gearing up to seek compensation from whoever was determined to be responsible.

First, there would be a general informational session. Right after, each of the Water Circus vendors would have a private interview with the health authorities in charge. Records would be turned over, and a number of questions would be answered. Ultimately, product confiscated on-site would be tested, and one by one, vendors would be ruled out until only one remained.

The man leading the effort stepped to the podium. "Could I have everyone's attention?" He waited for the room to quiet. "Thank you. I'm Dr. Henry Breslin from the Centers for Disease Control in Atlanta. I am the team leader and am charged with coordinating this multidisciplinary effort to identify the source of the E. coli O157:H7 outbreak here in the San Antonio area. I am also working with individuals from the City of San Antonio Metropolitan Health, the Texas Department of Health Services, the Texas Center for Infectious Disease, the US Department of Agriculture Food Safety Inspection Service, and officials from several local universities, hospitals, and public food safety organizations."

Juliet glanced around the room filled with all the food science heavy hitters. Like physicians, these men and women hoped to never have occasion to use their training. Sadly, the situation in San Antonio warranted every bit of their attention.

"What I'd like to do is brief you all on the new developments since last evening when we announced we'd narrowed the focus to Water Circus. We are fully aware of the economic impact a close order has on an enterprise of this size, and we're committed to doing everything in our power to isolate the product source and get the park back open."

He spent the next minutes delineating the process they'd gone through to assemble a list of vendors and revealed their plans in detail. He ended by telling everyone that they hoped to produce a definitive answer within forty-eight hours.

Hands shot up around the room.

"I'm sorry, any time I devote to answering questions takes away from more important tasks. I will keep everyone appropriately updated with any new developments. Thank you."

Dr. Breslin stepped down.

Juliet felt a hand on her shoulder. She turned to see Dr. Keller Thatcher, director of the North American Food Safety Symposium.

"Dr. Thatcher, this is a surprise." She stood and they shook hands.

"Good to see you, Dr. Ryan. We enjoyed having you on the panel in Chicago."

Juliet nodded. "Thank you. It was a treat for me as well. As you know, food safety is a subject I care very much about." She smiled at the small-framed man. Unfortunately, he'd joined the ranks of men wearing bad toupees. His had slipped, forcing Juliet to look away quickly before she chuckled.

A familiar figure stood across the room. Her father had his back to them and was talking with a small group. He was taking notes in a little pad he held while they spoke.

Juliet's heart quickened. She refocused on Dr. Thatcher. "I'm sorry. What were you saying?"

"I'm hearing through sources that your name is on the vendor list."

She reluctantly disclosed that Larimar Springs was indeed a product provider. "But as you know, Dr. Thatcher, water products have the lowest incidence of pathogen-related contamination. That, coupled with the fact our protocols are impeccable and are followed to a tee, and every audit has been clean in the past five years — well, I'm not terribly worried," she assured him. In the back of her mind, she still didn't care for the fact someone was leaking names. When this was over, she'd place a call and make her concerns known.

Juliet risked another glance in her father's direction. He was heading their way.

A voice called out from behind. "Dr. Ryan? You're up next."

Juliet let out a sigh of relief. Thank goodness.

She quickly bid Dr. Thatcher goodbye and turned and scurried down the hall, following the woman who had called her name into a room that eerily reminded Juliet of an interrogation room you'd see on some cop show on television.

A small table occupied the center of the windowless room, surrounded by five chairs. A whiteboard was mounted on one wall. Large printed posters with flu warnings and information about vaccinations covered the opposite wall.

The woman didn't introduce herself when she motioned Juliet to take a seat. "Dr. Breslin and his team will be right in."

She closed the door, leaving Juliet wishing they'd at least left some water in the room to drink. She glanced at the clock on the wall. Hopefully, this wouldn't take long.

The door opened. "Hello, Dr. Ryan. Thank you for coming in."

Juliet squared her shoulders and smiled as the white-coated man, followed by two other similarly clad men, filled the room and made their way to the seats around the table. The inflection of his greeting almost sounded as if she'd been invited to a social event instead of a mandated interview. But then again, perhaps his light tone reflected the reputation she'd tried to build in the food science community — one of working to place food safety as the highest priority. Certainly, her protocols and testing proved that true.

No doubt the team was exhausted and glad this interview would be brief.

"Gentlemen, it's good to see all of you. On behalf of everyone at Larimar Springs, I'd like to express how grateful we are for your efforts to get to the bottom of this quickly." She leaned over and unsnapped the closure on her large wheeled document case. "I think you'll find we have everything you requested and will find our testing in order."

Dr. Breslin nodded. "We have one other —"

The door opened then, drawing everyone's attention. Juliet looked up from her open briefcase. Her posture immediately stiffened.

"Sorry I'm late." Her father marched into the room and pulled out the single empty chair. He nodded in her direction and sat.

Dr. Breslin leaned over the table, his hands folded. "Let me make some introductions." He prefaced the effort with a weak smile. "I believe you know Dr. Bennett Ryan."

Juliet pasted on a stiff, close-lipped smile before responding. "Yes."

Her father gave a more relaxed smile. "We're — uh, well acquainted. Juliet is my daughter."

The others looked at each other nervously and nodded. Juliet felt esteem for her position at the table circle the drain. By showing up to this inquest, her father had just scrubbed her confidence and ability to shine.

Dr. Breslin finished the introductions, and over the next thirty minutes the men around the table posed questions and Juliet responded, taking care to highlight the fact that no internal testing revealed a hint of contamination. Further, the lab protocols at Larimar Springs surpassed minimum standards and those employed by most companies.

Her father remained strangely quiet. He focused on scribbling notes and studying the contents of her binders. She hoped he was happy. He'd finally gotten his audit, so to speak.

Dr. Breslin leaned back in his chair. "Well, the information you've provided has been very thorough, Dr. Ryan. Again, we appreciate your time."

Her father pulled his reading glasses from his face. "I have one more question."

All eyes moved in his direction. A heavy feeling settled in Juliet's stomach as she masked her apprehension with a broad smile. "Yes?" Her single-word response was as glossy as the porcelain on a toilet bowl. She averted her eyes and reached for one of the binders on the table.

"First, we'll need copies of some of those test results," he said in a thinly veiled attempt to put her on the spot.

"Of course." Juliet smiled again and nodded. "The team is welcome to have anything they need."

"Second, I didn't see any source water or transport documentation."

Juliet's eyebrows lifted. "Well, I don't believe the scope of the document requests extended that far. But certainly, if you want them, we'll provide copies."

Her father perched his glasses onto his graying hair. "Could we examine originals?"

Tension blanketed the tiny room. Juliet's jaw stiffened. "Of course." She glared at him. "Like I've said, Larimar Springs fully supports this team's objectives and welcomes any level of examination."

Dr. Breslin cleared his throat. He slid his chair from the table and stood. "We appreciate that, Dr. Ryan. People like you make our job much easier."

Juliet stood. She extended her hand across the small table and shook his hand. "My pleasure."

The meeting adjourned and Juliet gathered her things. With careful intention, she swiftly positioned herself directly behind Dr. Breslin and followed him out, never bothering to look back at her father. The slight may have raised some eyebrows, given their familial relationship, but her emotions took over. Frankly, he was lucky she didn't go toe-to-toe with him and take him down a notch or two.

She was crossing the parking lot to her car when she heard his voice calling out. "Juliet, wait."

She turned as he hurried toward her. "What do you want?" she nearly hissed.

"JuJu, wait a minute. I need to talk to you."

"What? Wrecking my life wasn't enough? Now you're bent on toppling my career?" She turned and opened her car door. "It's all I have." The minute the words left her mouth, she regretted saying them. The admission made her sound weak and vulnerable.

He touched her shoulder. "Please listen. I — I'm on your side here."

She jerked away, hating that tears formed. She blinked quickly so he couldn't see her anemic attempt to appear strong. "Look, Dad. Take your pom-poms and go home. Shake them for some other team."

Juliet slid into the seat and shut the door. Holding her ragged breath, she started the engine and pulled away, leaving him standing.

21

Juliet headed directly back to the office and reported the meeting with the health officials had gone well. As expected, no specific issues had been raised. She skipped telling them her father had shown up and showboated at her expense. She also advised no new information had been released, and warned not to expect any developments for forty-eight hours — when the test results on the vendors' products would be concluded.

"Cyril Montavan arrives from Italy later this afternoon," Alexa said. "I'd like you available to answer questions he might have about the investigation and alleviate any concerns that pop up. It's critical we maintain his full support — especially now."

Juliet agreed. "Certainly. I'll lend whatever help I can."

Since the company was now in a waiting game, and the focus of the efforts at Larimar Springs would be on accounting measures and profit recalculations, Juliet excused herself from the conference room and returned to her office so she could check back on Tavina's son.

Greer followed her into the hallway. "Hey, can you slip away for lunch?"

With everything happening, Juliet's mind had ventured far past the situation with Greer and the earrings in his bathroom. She did need to close things down with him so Mr. GQ didn't feel entitled to reenact the inappropriate scene in her office from a few days ago. The temp already suspected something was up between them, and the last thing Juliet needed in the middle of following an E. coli–related outbreak was to have to repair her credibility if he chose to pull that baloney again and they were caught.

Lunch away from the office might provide the best and fastest opportunity for a clean break and to clarify their relationship going forward as strictly professional. "Yeah, sure," she said, looking at her watch. It was eleven thirty now. "Where? I'll meet you after I check on Tavina's situation."

Greer rubbed the space above his left eyebrow. "Yeah, tell her we're all pulling for her little boy." He lowered his voice. "Want to meet at my place? I've been a little stressed and . . ."

Juliet cringed inside. What? She was now his antianxiety medication? A few minutes in the bedroom and he'd return to the office feeling less tense?

"No. That's not a good idea. I'll meet you at the Buckhorn." Juliet wanted to meet at an out-of-the-way place. The popular eating establishment and museum was a short drive, and they weren't likely to run into anyone they knew.

"At twelve thirty," she added before quickly moving on.

As Juliet neared Tavina's desk, the temp handed her a stack of mail. "I took the liberty of calling the hospital for an update. HIPAA privacy rules limit what they would disclose, but they did confirm your assistant's little boy is no worse this morning."

"Thanks, Angela." Juliet scowled. "Where's the framed photo of Tavina and MD? She keeps it right here on the corner of her desk."

The temp nodded. "Yes, I know. That little boy smiling in my direction all day creeped me out a bit, given the awful situation. So I slipped the photo inside her desk drawer for now."

The action irked Juliet. As every day passed, the overbearing girl, with her eighties hair and bad complexion, inched in and assumed more ground. Selfishly, she wanted her trusted assistant back.

She looked away from Angela's smile, which seemed far too close to a sneer, and buried her attention in the pile of mail.

The sooner, the better.

No more had Juliet stepped up to the bar and ordered a club soda and lime than she felt a hand at her back.

"Juliet, you're right on time, as usual." Greer's familiar cologne scented the air. "I have a table waiting." He instructed the bartender to put the charge for her drink on his lunch tab. "Ready?" he asked.

Juliet nodded and followed him to a table at the back of the café. Around them, the walls were filled with mounted taxidermy. On the wall across from her, a hairy-faced wild boar with fierce tusks protruding from either side of his mouth stared with glassy eyes.

She quickly diverted her eyes back to the table and the situation at hand.

Before this lunch was over, she planned to take charge and poke through the pretense of this relationship, finally letting the unhealthy liaison with her ambitious co-worker die.

Greer ordered a brisket sandwich. He brought the napkin to his lap. "With extra jalapeños." He waited until Juliet ordered her chicken Caesar salad before he made his move.

He reached across the table and caressed her fingers. "I've missed you." Before she could gracefully pull back, he boldly rubbed the side of his foot against her thigh under the table like some common redneck, despite the fact that no tablecloth hid his action.

"Not here," she scolded, pulling her hand back. Suddenly, nerves hit and she lifted her club soda to her lips to wet her throat.

Across the table, Greer's eyes narrowed. Sales prospects rarely turned down Greer Latham's proposals. That same intensity carried over into his personal life. "Juliet, if I didn't know better, I'd read your actions as being a bit hostile. In fact, you've been acting strangely for days."

Juliet tried to recover. This was going too fast. She needed time to explain and make this transition as painless as possible. Nothing good would come of escalating the dismantling of their romantic attachment to a contentious level. She certainly didn't want to be goaded into revealing what she'd discovered the other evening. She and Greer Latham still had to work together.

Juliet scrunched her face into puzzled amusement. "I think the stress of everything at the company is getting to you, Greer." She managed not to look him in the eyes while she took her passive-aggressive approach.

She felt him studying her as the waiter stepped to the table carrying their order. "That was quick," she said brightly as he placed their food on the table. She picked up her fork and thanked the young guy dressed in a green polo with the Buckhorn logo on the pocket. As he walked away, Juliet stabbed a forkful of romaine covered in creamy dressing and Parmesan. "I'm starving."

Greer went into a silent pout. He ate his sandwich while Juliet chattered on about the timing of health authorities' efforts to stop the progression of the outbreak, how anxious she was for Larimar Springs to be cleared, and tried to encourage him with the notion the company would be on the path to recovery once Water Circus reopened. "I have to say, I'm impressed with the way the park has managed their public relations effort through all of this."

She put her fork down, noticing Greer's silence. She also knew the clock on the wall was a reminder that she needed to focus on why they were here. She looked across the table. "What's the matter?"

"You don't get it, do you?"

Juliet drew her chin back. "Get what?"

"We're likely to lose our jobs before this is all over. If Montavan pulls out, this company is dead in the water. We'll never recover from the reversal of profits."

She waved off his comment. "I think you're exaggerating a bit."

He let his fork fall to the table. "Do you? Well, clue in. I know you're a scientist and numbers aren't your game, but trust me — things are likely to get ugly." He leaned forward. "Look, between you and me? Before she partnered with Montavan International, Alexa had the company assets leveraged to the hilt. I had a hard time convincing her to hire someone of your caliber, instead of that milquetoast supervisor who was in line to get the quality assurance position when the former director got pregnant and wanted to go home to play mommy." He sat back and picked up his sandwich again. He took a big bite and chewed, watching for her reaction.

His remarks hit their target. Juliet tried to

207

swallow the salad that seemed to double in size inside her mouth. Greer had needed to talk Alexa into hiring her? And Malcolm Stanford had wanted her job. No wonder the friction.

Juliet forced herself to recover and reminded herself again what needed to be done.

"Look, Greer. I'm grateful for your recommendation and anything you did to advocate for my hire. I love heading up the quality control function at Larimar Springs — even now in the middle of this outbreak. I'm hoping the company weathers this storm and we end up better than ever." She looked him in the eye, feeling a bit empowered knowing what lay just ahead. "You've done a marvelous job marketing our products, and if we all band together, we'll see this through. No doubt the company may struggle, but Alexa is no dummy. And she's assembled bright people to help her lead and grow the company. She'll not be quick to let her own investment tumble. You'll see." Juliet risked reaching over and patting his arm.

"But I guess I haven't been totally honest," she continued. "I think what you've been noticing is the fact that we've been growing apart, especially now that our responsibilities and commitments at work are racing forward at breakneck speed."

Greer dropped his sandwich to his plate. "You've got to be kidding me! You're breaking it off? Now?"

An image of those gold earrings on his bathroom counter formed in Juliet's mind. She'd accepted his professional dishonesty on occasion. But duplicity in the intimacy department was nothing she would ever accept from him. She bit the inside of her cheek and forced herself not to break his gaze.

"Yes," she confirmed. "I think that's better for both of us at this juncture. Besides, we both knew we weren't in this for the long haul."

His chiseled jaw set, and she could see the vein in his neck pulse. He wiped his hands clean, then pulled on his cuffs. "Speak for yourself," he said as he pushed the chair back and stood. He waved over the waiter.

Greer nodded in her direction. "Give the check to her." He slammed the chair back to the table. "My lady friend with the brass nerves is buying."

He threw the napkin to the table, turned, and walked away.

Juliet apologized to the wide-eyed waiter for Greer's outburst and handed him her

credit card. She sat stunned at Greer's reaction as the waiter took the card from her
and went to ring up the check.

While waiting for the waiter to return, Juliet picked at her salad. Unfortunately, she'd
lost her appetite. She placed the fork down
and looked up at the wall. The wild boar
stared straight ahead.

She sighed. "Well, that went really well.
Don't you think?"

22

Juliet returned from lunch to find Cyril Montavan exiting a cab. He saw her about the same time and waved as she neared. Despite the news he'd recently learned, he continued to wear a warm smile.

"Good to see you again," Juliet greeted him, extending her hand.

He draped his folded overcoat over one arm and shook. "Likewise, Dr. Ryan." He gave her a sideways look, and she couldn't help but admire his tanned skin and the way the sun created hints of midnight blue in the black color of his hair.

She smiled. "Please, call me Juliet." She led him inside, glad for the air conditioning. "Where are you staying?"

"The Mokira," he answered. "It's a lovely establishment, and the service is impeccable. The feel of the lobby reminds me of my favorite hotel in Turin."

"I've never been to Italy," Juliet admitted,

stopping at the receptionist desk for messages. "But I'd like to go someday. If things at work ever settle down, that is."

Greer sauntered across the lobby. "You'd like to go where?" he asked with a hand extended in Cyril's direction, not bothering to look at her.

Cyril shook Greer's hand. "Perhaps the entire Larimar team could make a visit to our headquarters in Italy at some point." He turned back to Juliet, a slight smile nipping at the corners of his mouth. "I'd love to show you around."

Greer's eyes narrowed. No doubt he'd caught not only Cyril's charming way of emphasizing the wrong syllable but the way the company's benefactor had directed his attention at her.

"Alexa and the team are assembled in the conference room." Greer thrust a piece of paper in her direction. "Juliet, could you find someone to place this dinner order and have our food delivered by six o'clock?" He placed his hand on Cyril's back as if to lead him away. "I'm afraid we're looking at a long night ahead."

Juliet didn't take the offered piece of paper. "I'm sorry. On the way back to the office, I got a couple of critical email alerts regarding the outbreak. I'd hate to delay passing this important information on to the team." Her eyes narrowed. "Perhaps the receptionist would be willing to help you with your dinner order."

If Cyril Montavan caught the shots she and Greer volleyed in the lobby, and their verbal tête-à-tête, he didn't let on. Regardless, Juliet knew these early exchanges with Greer were critical. She'd have to hold her own with him now or forever acquiesce to his demeaning actions, which were really a poorly hidden attempt to assuage his wounded pride and settle the score.

He frowned and dropped his hand. "I thought you reported there wouldn't be any new developments for forty-eight hours or so?"

"That's what the CDC announced at the meeting, but several of us in the food science industry are part of a special group. We get far more access to inside information than is typically released to the public."

Cyril nodded his approval. "An inner circle?"

"Yes," she confirmed, hoping their investment partner was impressed.

Greer's neatly manicured nails flicked at the sleeve of his custom suit jacket, as if he were more interested in some imaginary lint than her connections with the CDC.

Clearly, she'd encountered the downside of ending her personal relationship with a vice president of this company. Juliet would have to maneuver carefully to minimize future risk. But she most certainly wasn't going to allow Greer to subordinate her in front of Cyril Montavan. Greer's influence with Alexa Carmichael did not alter the fact that Juliet also reported directly to the CEO of this company, even if she didn't yet have the VP title he enjoyed.

Alexa immediately stood when Juliet and Cyril entered the conference room, leaving Greer back in the lobby explaining the food order to Lindsay. "There you are! Much earlier than I expected. I hope your flight was comfortable." She moved and shook his hand. "Please, have a seat. I'm sure you have questions, and we're anxious to bring you up to date."

After reacquainting him with the executive team sitting around the table, Alexa looked to Juliet. "Anything new?"

Juliet nodded as Greer reappeared and took his seat across from her. "About two hours ago, another case was confirmed. This time outside the San Antonio area. Officials are on their way to Corpus Christi to conduct interviews with the patient's family and the medical professionals in charge."

Fred Macklin looked up from his stacks of spreadsheets. "Does that mean a delayed reopening of the park?"

Juliet took a deep breath. "Possibly. On the other hand, depending on what officials discover, a slight potential could formulate for an alternative source."

Alexa raised her eyebrows. "You mean, Water Circus would be off the hook?"

Juliet nodded. "I'm answering with caution here. But yes. There could be a scenario where the health officials determine the common factor is not connected to Water Circus. But again, I would not predict that as a strong possibility."

Alexa's face brightened. "Well, that's certainly welcome news, even if only a slight possibility. Especially if the close order gets lifted sooner than later."

Cyril Montavan was watching Juliet. She liked the idea that he and Alexa were focusing on her to collect and disseminate information critical to the operation of the company. "I've also confirmed that Tavina's little boy has not worsened since early this morning," she added, aware their attention could never be comparable to more serious matters at hand.

Dale Frissom leaned back in his chair. "That's even better news."

Alexa agreed. "It's hard to believe such a common bacteria can wreak such havoc." Her boss's gaze quickly darted to Greer before returning to Juliet. "Dr. Ryan, the team appreciates the update. Now that Cyril is here, we'll focus our efforts on what all this means to the company P&Ls and develop a financial strategy going forward."

Greer nodded. "I told everyone how busy you are with the outbreak issue. There's no reason you have to stay for the remainder of the meeting."

His proposed exclusion stung. Moments ago, the people in this room had hung on her every word. Now, he was trying to have her dismissed as if she wasn't an essential member of the executive team. Worse, from the look on Alexa's face, she was buying in.

"Actually," Juliet ventured before she could lose her nerve, "with the slowed production, my department is ahead of the game at this point. I'd prefer to stay." She glared at Greer, who now seemed to believe she was a lesser planet in his orbit.

Cyril lifted his briefcase to the table and clicked it open. "I'd like Dr. Ryan included in our discussions. Given what's developed here lately, and the vulnerability this outbreak has imposed on this company's bottom line, I strongly urge even more emphasis be placed on the quality control functions led by Dr. Ryan. She's obviously done a superb job orchestrating the information flow between the health officials and our team, and because of her careful attention to needed testing, this company's interests have been well protected." He pulled a set of documents from his briefcase. "I looked over the revised financials. The budget reflects elimination of a line item I believe was recommended by Dr. Ryan."

Alexa stiffened. "The equipment requested was simply put on hold, not eliminated. Profit margins are often maintained by juggling priorities . . . temporarily."

Greer moved into a seat near the head of the table and inserted himself back into the discussion. "Alexa guided our effort to revise the budget to bare bones when revenues did not support sizeable expenditures. A necessary maneuver given that so much was out of her control. I'm sure even Dr. Ryan wouldn't argue that point."

Juliet held her breath, knowing the budget cut predated the outbreak. Clearly, Alexa Carmichael was not used to anyone questioning her judgment, not even someone of Cyril Montavan's stature, and Greer was using this opportunity to show his support for her and bring Juliet down a notch.

Regardless, Juliet appreciated Cyril Montavan's advocacy and knew exactly how she needed to respond.

"Mr. Montavan, thank you for your recognition of my department's contributions. One of my most important considerations before I came on board here at Larimar Springs was whether or not food safety would be a number one priority." Juliet took a calculated pause to emphasize what she was about to say. "I have found this company, and particularly Alexa Carmichael, completely genuine in their commitment to these very important issues. When she was forced to revise the company budget, Alexa personally assured me the thermal cycler would be purchased at the earliest possible occasion."

The woman sitting at the head of the table, in a gray sheath dress and pearls, noticeably relaxed upon hearing Juliet's remarks. No doubt Juliet had scored points.

Greer's face, on the other hand, paled like sour cream. She'd stolen his thunder.

Hopefully, by not throwing Alexa under the bus, Juliet had established credibility as a professional in all their eyes. The choleric vice president of marketing and sales sitting across the table would have to reassess his scraped ego and his need to vent at her expense, or risk diminishing his own stature in the group.

Sometimes, the best way to keep a bad pimple from festering was just to pop it.

Over the next four hours, she joined the team huddled together over the table, working and reworking the income projections for the coming months. During a quick break, Cyril Montavan joined her at the coffee service. He leaned close and confided with a low voice, "Your response to my budget observation was impressive."

Juliet popped a K-Cup into the Keurig machine and pressed the button. "I'm sorry?"

He smiled. "A true leader always supports her team." He turned the storage carousel and selected a tiny container of dark French roast. "I'm serious about you coming to Italy. In addition to your duties here at Larimar Springs, perhaps you'd consider consulting for several of our other enterprises. Food safety is as important in Europe as it is in the United States."

She blushed at the compliment. "Thank you, Mr. Montavan. I appreciate that."

"Cyril," he corrected.

Juliet nodded. "Cyril." She smiled. "I'd very much like to consider your offer at some point. Perhaps when all this has settled down." In her pocket, her iPhone buzzed. "Uh, sorry — would you excuse me, please?"

"Of course." He stepped back to allow her freedom to move toward the door while she picked up.

"Hello?"

"Dr. Juliet Ryan?"

She frowned, trying to place the voice. "Yes, this is Dr. Ryan."

"Dr. Henry Breslin with the Centers for Disease Control. I'm afraid I have bad news."

23

Juliet hung up and tried to breathe. She stood in the lobby with the phone in her hand, frozen, while the memory of Dr. Breslin's words churned in her mind, a riptide of cold, dark water threatening to suck her under.

"Our trace-back investigation has concluded. Granted, earlier than anticipated. But team epidemiologists reported less than an hour ago that cultures from Larimar Springs bottled water have confirmed presence of Shiga toxin–producing Escherichia coli. The clinical specimens were subtyped and are consistent with O157:H7."

Juliet's arm flesh turned cold. Her neck flushed hot.

How could that possibly be?

For the first time in her life, she thought she might pass out.

Juliet looked across the lobby to see the receptionist barreling toward her.

"Dr. Ryan? Are you all right?" The receptionist rushed to her side and wrapped her arm around Juliet's shoulder and pressed her into an armchair. "Would you like something to drink?"

Juliet focused on the company logo mounted on the wall. "No, I'm fine. I — I just felt a little lightheaded, that's all. I — I'm okay now." She stood despite her shaking legs and the look of worry on her co-worker's face.

Her entire professional life had been devoted to food safety. How could Dr. Breslin's report possibly be true?

Years of higher education and the recommendations of every respected food safety source available had been incorporated into Juliet's protocols. She'd monitored regularly — personally.

Yet multitudes had fallen ill. Three little ones had even died.

Under *her* watch.

An image of Tavina's anguished face formed in Juliet's mind. Her treasured assistant was going through hell on earth — because Juliet had failed.

She'd failed.

She glanced at her watch through tear-filled eyes. In less than an hour, the health investigation team would march through the front doors with briefcases and comminute the company brand and the reputation of every person in that conference room. All because Juliet had missed something so critical.

Thankfully, Dr. Breslin promised to keep the findings quiet until after he'd met with Juliet in person. Right now, before his team stormed the lobby, Juliet needed to tell Alexa and the others.

With trembling fingers, she pressed her phone into her jacket pocket and headed back down the hall. With each step, the notion she had to drop a bomb of this magnitude left her pulverized. The rumble of devastation would reverberate through this company for years to come, if Larimar Springs even survived the blast.

When Juliet entered the conference room again, the team members were already seated and talking.

Alexa Carmichael was in her place at the head of the table. Less than ten years ago, she'd left a lucrative marketing career in Houston to purchase a feeble bottled water company about ready to close its doors. Under her tutelage, Larimar Springs turned a profit three years later and had been expanding each subsequent year, making her one of the most respected businesswomen in the state of Texas.

Fred Macklin had spent nearly his entire career here. First for the family that started Larimar Springs, and then as chief financial officer for Alexa. He was scheduled to retire soon, with plans to tour Europe with his wife of forty years.

To Alexa's right sat the vice president of operations, Dale Frissom. On several occasions, he'd proudly shared he was financially supporting his only daughter through medical school. She wanted to specialize in oncology, to fight the terrible disease that had taken her mother two years ago.

Cyril had his head buried in a stack of pro formas. He'd been extraordinarily gracious about recent developments, given his investment in Larimar Springs. He trusted her.

And finally — Greer. She'd never known a man so entirely wrapped up in his career, which had made him the perfect match for Juliet for so long. She'd never felt the need to justify her priorities with him.

Could she even muster the necessary courage?

With her stomach cinched and bile bitter on the back of her tongue, Juliet cleared her throat. "Excuse me, could I have everyone's attention?"

She wished her soul was stronger, but with

every word, a little piece of her insides died. She alerted everyone in the room to the call she'd just received from Dr. Breslin and carefully explained the team's discovery. By the time she finished, her face felt hot, despite the chill that had descended over the room.

"I'm — sorry," she said quietly.

She could tell from the looks on their faces, frosted with panic, what her gut had already revealed. With this mistake, her heels had slipped off the corporate ladder. For good.

In years to come, Juliet would remember this day.

The day her career ended.

24

Juliet stepped into the nearly empty parking lot at Larimar Springs so bone-tired, she believed her cells might never stop quivering. The last time she'd pulled an all-nighter, she'd prepared her dissertation while holding down a full-time job at a small laboratory in upstate New York — more than a few years back.

The sky wouldn't lighten for at least another hour, even though she could hear the buzz of traffic in the distance, signaling many had already started their day. People who lifted from their beds and showered, ate breakfast, and opened up the *San Antonio Express-News* to learn the bottled water they'd trusted was tainted with E. coli. Mothers who scurried to their refrigerators to check. Just to make sure their families were in no danger.

Juliet rubbed at her eyes, sighed, and trudged toward her car. She needed to get home, catch some shut-eye for an hour or two, then shower and get back. The last twelve hours had been hard, but in contrast, the coming hours would only get worse. If that was even possible.

She unlatched the door to her Jeep and slid into the leather seat, willing her gritty eyelids to remain open for the drive home.

As expected, in the past hours, Dr. Breslin and his team of health officials had swarmed the offices. She was provided copies of verified lab reports in a brief meeting, fulfilling the mandate to communicate the methodology that formally tagged Larimar Springs as the source. State-of-the-art polymerase chain reaction (PCR) methods had been used. PCR is a molecular technique that targets sequences of nucleic acids, leaving no doubt in anyone's mind the testing had been entirely accurate.

Teams of epidemiologists and microbiologists scanned copies of sample test reports, distribution documentation, and evidence that the quality assurance process had met all Hazard Analysis and Critical Control Points (HACCP) regulations.

Pallets of bottled water in the warehouse were impounded.

And finally, a close order was formally issued.

The CDC issued an extensive press release. In a feeble attempt to diminish the hit to the company, Alexa immediately hired a public relations firm to develop a crisis management strategy and prepare a counter press release on behalf of Larimar Springs.

Media trucks swarmed the streets surrounding the Larimar Springs facilities.

In a few short hours, everything would start again.

Juliet dug for her keys and started the engine, realizing it didn't take a finance expert to understand that this equation added up to doom for Larimar Springs and its employees. Personally, she could kiss goodbye not only the promised promotion but the hope of rising to the top of any company as a food science expert. Her credibility was shot.

About two-thirds of the way home, she spotted an H-E-B sign off to the right. Suddenly, Juliet realized she hadn't eaten all day and pulled off.

Inside the grocery store, she squinted against the bright lights and grabbed a cart, pushing it in the direction of the bakery in hopes of snagging a muffin fresh out of the oven.

On the way, she passed a rack filled with copies of the *San Antonio Express-News*.

Her mind lingered on lifting a newspaper from the stack to see just how bad the media had painted the story.

In the end, she passed on the idea. She didn't have to scan the headlines to know she'd appear incompetent. The reporters would quote statistics, give updated information on the victims, and inevitably mention the E. coli outbreak of the nineties that had educated them all.

Like Ken Dunkley, the QA director who was painted the villain in the Jack in the Box case, her name would be noted in the annals of food science lore for years to come. Her calamity might inspire some young person in school to focus their career on keeping the public safe. Some young woman like herself, who mistakenly believed that if she did everything right, her career would turn out and her work would make a difference.

Juliet snatched a box of cold pastries from the shelf and tossed it into her cart.

Worse, her father would end up being proved right. Corporations could not be trusted to put ethics above profits, safety above dividends. She'd personally handed him that win on a platter.

She jerked her cart in the direction of the coolers. She'd need milk and juice.

Two guys in the produce area unboxed apples and stacked them in a bin. One heaved a box off the cart. "Hey, did you hear?" he said to the other. "They found out where all that E. coli stuff came from."

"Oh, really? Where?"

"Some bottled water company. You know, most of those places just use tap water and then turn around and charge a buck fifty to drink the same thing us taxpayers already paid for once."

"That right?"

"Yup. I don't know why we get up at this awful hour every morning, when we could just get us some pretty bottles with bright-colored labels and fill 'em up at the sink. Make a mint."

Both men shook their heads and laughed.

She supposed the situation was farcical to them. Many people didn't understand the extraction process and the care a company like Larimar Springs took to ensure that the source water pulled from the springs was never exposed to the light of day, let alone any contaminants. Few understood that the water was transported in stainless steel piping that cost millions, and then a costly oxidation process was used to purify the water before it was added to triple-sterilized PET bottles labeled with USDA-compliant disclosures.

Only two of Larimar's water sources were above ground. Those carried slightly more risk for contamination, but testing was performed every hour, both at the extraction site before the water was pumped into sterile stainless steel containers mounted on semitrucks for transport, and again when the water arrived at the plant.

Those bozos she'd just overheard in produce had no idea the microbial counts recorded, the inorganic components measured, the analysis on residual by-products carefully noted. Did anyone understand that her department conducted nearly two thousand tests each and every week? Did they know that she personally reviewed the results through a carefully planned sampling protocol?

Juliet shoved her cart past the meat department until she reached aisle C. Across from shelves lined with cereal boxes, a grinder emitted the rich aroma of coffee. She was reaching for a package of French roast beans when a loud noise caught her attention, causing her to nearly jump out of her exhausted skin.

She quickly opted for a package of pre-ground and threw it in her cart, then wheeled back down the aisle toward the sound.

At the wall of glass doors lining the rear of the store, a team of men in protective coveralls labeled TEXAS HEALTH DEPARTMENT worked to remove cases of Larimar Springs bottles from the cooler. Even their hands were covered with disposable blue gloves.

The sight struck a tender nerve.

Juliet diverted her eyes and quickly pushed her cart toward the front of the store to the courtesy counter. "Uh, ma'am. Excuse me?"

An older woman with a unibrow strangely resembling a big black caterpillar stopped placing a rubber band around a stack of papers. "Yes? What do you need?"

Juliet pointed. "A carton, please."

"Brand?"

"Uh, doesn't really matter. Marlboro Lights, I guess."

"A whole carton?"

Juliet nodded. "Yes. Oh, and a lighter. I'll need a lighter."

She quickly got in the checkout lane and paid for the few items in her cart, crossed the parking lot, and loaded the purchases into the back of her Jeep except for one small sack.

The truth was, her dad was right. Somehow she'd become a food safety scientist in theory and not in practice.

She couldn't even figure out where her safety protocols had gone wrong.

After getting in her car, she turned and dumped the contents of the sack in the passenger seat, then inserted her key into the ignition and started the engine.

Without giving the matter a second thought, Dr. Juliet Ryan chain-smoked the entire way home.

25

Juliet forgot how nicotine could act as a stimulant and interrupt sleep patterns. As badly as her body needed rest, she couldn't seem to quiet her mind and drowse off after giving in to her former habit. She tried drinking warm milk. She tried taking a hot bath. She closed the blinds to keep out the light. Eventually, she resorted to turning on the television, hoping the background noise would lull her mind into sleep.

Even so, as she drifted into slumber, Juliet's mind seemed caught on high-whirr mode and she slept fitfully.

She dreamed she was a little girl wearing a tiny white lab coat with her name embroidered across the upper front pocket. The room was — yes, it was her classroom, with her standing by Mrs. Myers's desk and the rest of the students sitting at their desks. Susie Beckler and Janice Kirkland were parked in the front row with their hands neatly folded on their desktops. The curly-headed girls were smiling at her. Stinky Sam sat in the back, clearly not happy that sour-faced Mrs. Myers stood near.

They all kept staring, not saying a word.

Suddenly, Juliet's father appeared next to her. "Okay, JuJu. Go ahead and add the food coloring," he urged.

She was afraid.

At the back of the room, Mrs. Myers scowled and looked at the wall clock mounted above the classroom door.

Juliet felt her father's hand on her back. "Go ahead."

She looked up at his face, gathering needed confidence before she tentatively removed the lid on the tiny bottle of coloring. She let her hand hover over the beaker. Her heart pounded as she carefully squeezed.

The red coloring dropped into the beaker. Immediately, the substance inside exploded into a foaming mass. But instead of turning red, the ingredients morphed into a nasty brown and emitted a horribly foul odor. A smell she'd encountered before.

All the kids covered their noses. "Oh, yuck. That stinks," they said in unison.

At the back of the room, Stinky Sam laughed . . . louder and louder until she couldn't see anything but brown foam and hear anything but his laughter. She couldn't breathe — the smell overwhelming.

Frantic, Juliet's arms moved through the air, trying to locate her dad. She needed to climb into his arms, feel the security of his embrace.

In a full panic, her arms flailed at empty space next to her.

Nothing.

She heard his voice and called, "Dad? Dad, where are you?"

Suddenly, Juliet heard a loud ringing.

She startled awake. The brown foam receded. The laughter faded.

Her eyes snapped open.

Juliet sat up in bed, sweat beading her brow. She reached across the side table and slammed the top of her alarm clock, shutting down the loud noise, her head pounding as she peeked at the digital numbers displayed on the face.

Eleven o'clock.

Juliet rubbed her temples and tried to focus, fighting remnants of the weird dream, even her father's voice.

Suddenly, reality materialized out of the fog. The voice was her father's.

She reached for the remote and turned up the volume on the television, where the esteemed Dr. Bennett Ryan stood before a bank of microphones.

"E. coli O157:H7 was first confirmed in the United States in 1982. People of all ages can be infected, but young children and the elderly are more likely to develop severe symptoms related to hemolytic uremic syndrome, commonly known as HUS."

A reporter threw up his hand and interrupted. "Could you pronounce that syndrome name again, please? And give us a spelling?"

Her father nodded. "HEE-mo-li-tic you-REE-mic syndrome." He spelled the name and then cleared his throat before continuing.

"The types of E. coli that can cause illness can be transmitted through contaminated water or food, or through contact with animals or people. As demonstrated in the Jack in the Box outbreak in January of 1993, failure to incorporate proper measures to identify and eliminate this deadly pathogen in food products can have a catastrophic result.

"To counter this, in 1998, the Hazard Analysis and Critical Control Points program was established to identify critical checkpoints in the food production plants to prevent pathogens from contaminating meat and other food products. Sadly, since then, we've seen over a dozen major outbreaks. This incident at Larimar Springs is yet another example that more needs to be done to protect public safety."

Juliet had had enough. She clicked off the television.

For several seconds, she sat on the edge of the bed with her hands clutched and head bowed, her heart an empty chasm. She had no right to get angry. Not really. Everything he'd said was justified.

Despite her best efforts, his daughter had let down her company, her industry, and especially the public. Three children had died on her watch. Even now, her own assistant's little guy remained in a hospital bed, severely ill.

The only upside was that her mother had never witnessed her public humiliation. If she were here, all her mom would've had to do was look in her daughter's eyes, and she'd have seen the depth of her shame.

"Oh, Mom — what have I done?"

She slipped from the edge of the bed onto the carpeted floor, gripped her stomach with both arms, and rocked back and forth, letting the full force of the past twenty-four hours pound her spirit.

Then Juliet did something that was long

overdue.

She broke down and wept.

26

By that afternoon, the frontage road leading to Larimar Springs swarmed with reporters, television camera crews, and satellite trucks, forcing Juliet to take a calculated shortcut through the neighboring facility belonging to a restaurant supply distributorship.

After maneuvering carefully past a loading dock, she drove alongside several large blue dumpsters and cut into the back parking area where the warehouse workers normally left their pickup trucks, some with jacked-up wheel bases and others showing off mud flaps featuring chrome-silhouetted women.

Tavina's warning played in her head, the one where she cautioned never to wander the plant alone at night. The thought triggered a fresh ache in Juliet's heart. Who warned her assistant that drinking bottled water could make her baby sick?

Juliet wound her car to the front parking area, only to find her spot was taken. A cerulean blue Lexus sedan. Local plates.

She pulled into one of the many empty spots and exited the car with a file folder held up to block any shot some ambitious cameraman with an amped-up lens could capture.

The lobby was empty, as expected on a weekend. Music pumped from the speakers in the ceiling, and voices drifted from the hall leading to the executive suite. Juliet braced herself and headed in the direction of the open conference room door.

As she neared, she could hear Greer's voice. "Look, Alexa, I'm telling you. We need to hire legal counsel ASAP." He sounded frustrated.

Alexa cleared her throat. "What do you recommend, Ellen?"

A woman's voice responded. "I strongly urge you to wait," she said. "At least until after the press conference this afternoon. If the first thing this company does is protect themselves legally, it'll look bad."

Juliet paused at the open door, trying to renew her will to move inside.

Greer paced at the windows shrouded with closed blinds. "Ha — guarantee it'll be a lot worse if we start saying things that will come back to bite us legally."

Alexa looked up. "Come on in. You're late."

Juliet nodded. "I know. I'm sorry." She glanced at the empty seats around the table littered with empty Styrofoam cups and sugar packets. "Where is everybody?"

Greer smirked. "Probably hiding out from the media."

"Sit." Alexa motioned to a chair. "We have a lot to go over before the press conference." She pointed to the woman. "This is Ellen."

Alexa returned her attention to her laptop, banging on the keyboard with hard, eager strokes.

The woman — Ellen — wore cream-colored slacks with a cashmere sweater of the same shade, accented with thick gold jewelry that appeared to be the real stuff. She wore bright red lipstick and an air of confidence Juliet wished she felt.

Juliet fought a jolt of irrational nerves. She held out her hand. "Hello, Ellen."

The woman smiled. "You don't recognize me?"

Juliet stared at the dark-haired lady. "No," she said slowly. "I'm sorry, I —"

"I'm Ellen Shaffer." She paused, waiting for the information to register, then added, "We went to school together. You and your father did a science experiment on Career

Day. Elephant toothpaste, if I recall correctly."

Juliet's eyes widened. "Oh — of course. I'm sorry."

Ellen shook her head. "No, don't be. That was a long time ago."

Juliet pulled the file folder tightly against her chest. "And — your father brought the teleprompter." Ellen must work for her father's public relations firm, which should have brought Juliet some level of comfort. Instead, she felt humiliated.

The woman standing before her was a force, driven and focused. Juliet used to be one of those women. She couldn't explain how it had happened, but now, of course, she'd turned back into that girl sitting at the back desk — punished for something that wasn't her fault.

But this time everything was her fault.

Although no one in the room said so.

Ellen clapped her hands together. "Well, let's get started. We have a lot to cover." Her phone buzzed. She picked up, her face drawing into a scowl while she listened. When she clicked off, she turned to Alexa. "Two more toddlers have been admitted."

Alexa buried her forehead into the palms of her hands. "They pulled all the product. When does all this stop?"

Juliet swallowed. "Incubation is usually one to four days. Often a diagnosis isn't made until several days after that."

Ellen made a tsking sound. "Look, I don't want to burst anyone's bubble . . ."

Greer glared in her direction. "Believe me, there is no bubble."

Looking frustrated, Alexa held up her hands. "Let's focus."

Like a woman who knew her way around trouble, Ellen Shaffer moved to her place at the table and lifted a newspaper. She opened it and spread the pages on the conference table. "We have to get in front of this, and quick. I know the news director at KENS-5, and he's agreed to hold any major story until after the press conference, provided I give him first access to any developments. But I'm afraid this *San Antonio Express-News* article isn't very flattering. And no doubt the entire story will go national."

Juliet leaned over the table and read where Ellen pointed.

She was identified. By name. And the account quoted her remarks made at the North American Food Safety Symposium in Chicago.

Consumer health and safety are at the very core of what we do every day, and because of the collective efforts of dedicated food scientists and quality assurance directors in companies across America, outbreaks are now rare, with fewer reported each year than ever before.

Kids across the metroplex were falling ill. Some were dying. The article made it clear — everyone in San Antonio blamed Juliet.

This came as a shock, that she was in the center of a scandal. While she'd once been known as brilliant and talented, her rising star's light had dimmed and was plummeting, soon to hit the ground and implode.

At least that was what her smoldering gut told her.

27

Greer remained more than testy throughout Ellen's prep sessions. Especially when she dropped a bombshell and recommended that Juliet stand with Alexa to field technical questions during the press conference.

"Well . . . isn't that opening the company up to a lot of negative press?" he questioned, his forehead wrinkled. He looked to Alexa, clearly hoping she'd agree and change her mind.

When Alexa backed up Ellen's decision, Greer rolled his neck, making a popping sound. "Suit yourselves," he huffed, and turned to the window. He pulled on his cuffs, then carefully lifted one of the slats on the blinds and looked out. "Just as a reminder, the wolves will be looking to bite a chunk off somebody's backside. Do you really think she's up for the meal they're going to want to make of her? This ain't no picnic, you know."

Juliet gritted her teeth, put out that Greer spoke of her in the third person like she wasn't even in the room. "I'll try not to wear my red riding hood when I step in front of the microphones," she snapped back, not meaning to sound so shrill.

Unaffected by her sharp words, Greer dropped the slat and backed away from the window. "Cyril just pulled into the parking lot."

Alexa closed her eyes while squeezing the bridge of her nose between her middle finger and thumb. "We're going to have to tell him."

Ellen clicked off her tablet and looked up. "Tell him what?"

Greer and Alexa exchanged nervous glances. Alexa pushed back from the table and stood, then cleared her throat. "Our primary lender called me this morning, threatening to pull the loan. Apparently, these events trigger a default under one of the clauses. Technically, we're in breach."

Ellen looked like someone had just placed a gun to her head. She took a deep breath. "Anything else you haven't disclosed? I can't help you if I don't know what's coming."

Juliet felt the heat of Alexa's and Greer's stares, in the way they looked at her, disappointed they'd placed their trust in someone so untrustworthy. No doubt they believed, like everyone else in the room, that she'd driven Larimar Springs into a rock and was solely responsible for the company now sinking.

Frankly, how could she blame them? Their tense animosity was completely understandable. She felt like the villain in all this, and with every development, each new revelation, it was becoming harder to live in her own skin.

This made stepping into the public arena even more difficult. Even so, she was determined to show Greer, and everyone else, that she was a professional and up for the challenge.

The press conference took place in the Larimar Springs lobby, with reporters representing the local market, as well as Dallas, Houston, and Austin news outlets. Juliet noted one camera even held the CNN logo. The overcrowded room added to the pressure, but Ellen Shaffer knew the best way to stay in control was to host the event on their own turf. In keeping with her promise, she arranged for a private interview with the KENS-5 station people after.

By the time everything was finished, Juliet almost wished Greer had won his earlier argument. She definitely ended the media sessions with a large measure of her reputation chewed up.

Despite Ellen's best efforts and Cyril Montavan's encouraging support, when the questions turned accusatory in nature, Juliet had a hard time focusing on the talking points. "You stray from this outline," Ellen had warned both Alexa and Juliet, "and anyone with a financial stake in this company will wish they were wearing Depends."

Alexa, on the other hand, stood in front of the reporters with confidence. Near the end, when faced with a particularly rude remark, she formed a resolute smile.

"We have implemented an aggressive response plan, which places the highest priority on the health and safety of our customers and the public. Larimar Springs is fully cooperating with health officials. We've completely opened our company records for review and are assisting as needed with the recall. Lastly, our hearts and minds are with those affected, and we pray for quick recovery."

Juliet prepared to step away from the microphones, feeling relief that the press conference was finally over, when a local talk show host stepped forward with a particular barb that harpooned her heart.

"What do you want to tell the families of these children?"

Alexa squared her shoulders and leaned into the microphones. "Larimar Springs will do what is right." She looked over the crowd of reporters. "The right thing to do is to own up to our responsibility and pay for these poor people who had to put their children in the hospital."

Out of the corner of her eye, Juliet caught a glimpse of Greer's paled face. Their attorneys were going to have a fit over that comment.

By the time the press conference ended, the clock on the lobby wall read nearly four o'clock. Alexa's warning that they'd face another full day tomorrow followed Juliet out the door, but right now she didn't care. She was free to head to the hospital to see Tavina and check on her little boy.

In the parking lot she opened the door to her Jeep and climbed in, fighting off exhaustion. The last eight hours had seemed to stretch forever, the tension suffocating at times.

She'd like nothing more than to go straight home and fold into a weary puddle, but she forced herself to keep going, knowing Tavina's world was far worse.

Juliet entered the hospital lobby, took the

elevator to the pediatric critical care unit, and walked into the waiting room just as the news broadcast changed over to the weather on the television mounted against the wall. She felt the few people in the room staring at her with recognition as she passed through.

At the help desk, she leaned close to the volunteer and lowered her voice, not wanting to draw any additional attention. "I'm here to see Tavina Mosely."

The white-haired woman wore a broad smile and a corsage made of crepe paper flowers. She picked up the phone receiver, held it midair. "And you are?"

"Dr. Ryan — uh, Juliet."

When the woman at the desk provided the go-ahead, Juliet made her way down the long corridor, a pallor of unease resting over her heart. She neared the bustling nurses' station, smelled the tang of antiseptic and fear hovering in the air.

The pediatric critical care unit was serious business. Especially when those hard metal gurneys held little ones fighting to survive.

Little MD Mosely was in one of those beds.

Tavina's face wore signs of a mother who had spent the last forty-eight hours clinging to the bedside of a little boy with tubes everywhere — a catheter down below his groin to catch fluids, a chest tube to drain the fluid from around his lungs, and a breathing tube delivering oxygen to his truffle-colored torso. An IV transported crucial drugs into his system, lowering his dangerously high blood pressure, and flashing lights on machines surrounding his bed recorded every breath and heartbeat.

"The blood became so profuse, it soaked through his diapers," Tavina lamented, her voice low and ragged. "Over the past four hours, my baby turned lethargic and his belly swelled up like a cantaloupe."

Juliet covered her assistant's hands with her own, feeling helpless. She wasn't a medical doctor, but she knew these signs. Tavina's son was worsening.

The frightened mother's lip quivered. "I just don't understand. How . . . why did my baby get so sick?" She pulled one hand from Juliet's and wiped her forearm across her damp, despondent face. "Do you?" she asked Juliet.

Standing at the sliding glass panels leading to the hallway, Tavina's mother shook her head and patted her chest, her face painted with worried sorrow. "We haven't told her," she admitted out loud.

A sudden involuntary intake of air filled Juliet's lungs. A chill crawled down her back. "She . . . ?"

"No." Tavina's mother looked at the floor. "Larimar Springs has been so good to my girl. I didn't know what to say." The older woman ran her hand through her graying hair. Her eyes held no disapprobation. "Maybe you could explain."

Tavina scowled. "What are you talking about, Mom?"

Juliet took a deep breath. She squeezed Tavina's hand, unsure which of them extracted more comfort from the gesture.

In the end, there was little Juliet could do but disclose the facts as gently as possible, trying to sound calm and hopeful. She reiterated what the doctor had said about MD's diagnosis and told her about the health investigatory team's findings, taking care to avoid Tavina's eyes as she spoke.

When she finished, Tavina's head tilted wildly as she tried to assimilate what she'd been told. "No — none of what you're saying makes sense." Her expression turned limp, and she looked Juliet in the eyes. "We're careful. I don't have a fancy science degree, but I see the testing and all our department does." She buried her face in her hands and rubbed her tired eyes. "Something's not right."

Sympathy surged through Juliet. She hugged her assistant, holding on to her shoulders for several seconds. Tavina had a right to choke with emotion. No matter what, Juliet would extend unwavering support.

Back in the parking lot, Juliet's ragged emotions surfaced. She cupped her hand over her mouth, letting the impact of what was going on upstairs in that hospital carry her into a dark place.

Tavina's resounding endorsement warmed Juliet's heart but did little to lift her self-reproach.

How could she deny the stark reality that children were dying because of product passed through her laboratory? The microbial counts were sufficient to classify the liquid inside those bottles as poison.

She'd poisoned babies.

Tavina's baby.

Through eyes flooding with tears, Juliet stumbled to her car. Her hand blindly felt for the car door handle.

That was when she discovered the envelope taped to her window. In carefully blocked black letters, the front read, *Dr. Ryan — Read This.*

Juliet wiped her eyes with the back of her

hand and pulled the envelope from the window. With shaking fingers, she slipped her forefinger under the seal.

She quickly unfolded the piece of paper — a copy of an analysis report dated almost five months prior to when Juliet started employment with Larimar Springs. A Mylar sticker with a black arrow had been positioned on the line reading *Total Coliform Units — MCL.*

Instinctively, Juliet's hand went inside her purse. She fingered her cell phone, thinking she should call somebody.

But who? She unlocked the car door. *And what would I say?*

Suddenly, her phone rang, making Juliet jump. Her eyes darted around the parking lot. Whoever had placed that envelope for her to find might be watching.

Wary, she quickly climbed in her Jeep and locked the door, then answered her phone. "Yes, hello?"

"Dr. Ryan, this is Dr. Breslin. The investigation has produced a new development that has us scratching our heads."

Juliet's bedraggled nerves went on high alert. The last thing she needed was more bad news. "Yes? What is it?"

He cleared his throat. "The team is a bit puzzled by a pallet of product confiscated from your warehouse. The pallet label is dated back in November of last year. That alone wouldn't concern us, but there's a huge gap in time between this pallet and the others in the warehouse."

Juliet's fingers tightened on the test report dated in that same time frame. "I — I'm not sure I understand," she said, her mouth suddenly cotton-dry.

"Given what we've been able to piece together and what Larimar executives have reported, your company has been turning over product quickly for weeks in order to meet the demands of the Water Circus account." He paused as if piecing together his thoughts. "So — why the old product?"

Using care not to reveal her own alarm, Juliet admitted she didn't have the answer. Warehouse and distribution fell under operations, and that was Dale Frissom's area.

When she said as much, Dr. Breslin's voice turned even more concerned. "I know tomorrow is Sunday, but we'd better talk with both of you in the morning," he said. "Let's plan on nine o'clock."

She thanked Dr. Breslin for the call and promised they'd be there. Hopefully, with answers.

From inside her car, Juliet quickly dialed

Dale Frissom. When he didn't answer, she left a message. "Call me, Dale. It's important."

Despite her exhaustion, Juliet made the drive back to the office in record time. Since the outbreak, night production had been placed on hold, lending the entire facility an empty atmosphere that was almost eerie as she pulled into the parking lot.

Since the outbreak had been connected to Larimar Springs, Juliet had taken to living, eating, and sleeping the situation. To everyone, she acted cool and in command — she was the point person, after all — but when alone, she questioned every decision she'd made since coming on board. Binders of test reports were strewn across her carpet at the condo. Her office looked much the same. She'd searched for some hint, some understanding of how all this could have happened.

In all those hours, she couldn't remember seeing anything unusual. Especially from last November.

At the double glass doors leading to the lobby, she glanced over her shoulder, hoping Alexa had maintained their security force, given their financial strain. Shaking, she pulled her entry card from the pocket in her purse and swiped.

Nothing.

She tried again.

Still nothing.

Exasperated, Juliet stood in the chilly air and phoned Greer. She nearly barked at him when he didn't pick up until the fifth ring. "Greer, I can't get into the building."

"Yes, I know. Under the circumstances, Alexa felt no one should have access when others are not in the building."

"You mean *me*."

He gave her a patronizing sigh. "You're getting paranoid."

"Are you telling me my security card has been suspended?" Juliet rubbed her forehead in frustration. "Am I the only one?"

"Perhaps you should take this up with Alexa," he responded, his condescending tone grating on her nerves. "I'm sure she'd be willing to explain her decision in the morning."

Juliet groaned. "Oh, never mind." She hung up without saying goodbye. And without telling him why she was trying to get into the building this time of night. Strangely, he hadn't asked.

Tavina might be right. Something didn't feel square here. The events surrounding this horrible outbreak might not be what they seemed on the surface.

Juliet tightened her fists.

Before she knew what was happening, she'd changed course and made a critical decision. Perhaps none of this was her fault after all. A pallet of bottled water unaccounted for in the records. An analysis report mysteriously left on her car. Who had left that envelope?

Everything pointed to something sinister going on.

Starting immediately, she'd get to the bottom of this mess. Somehow she'd find a way into that building. She'd collect and analyze every piece of information available, put her budding suspicions through every test. Every lab report, bill of lading, and invoice would be placed under a microscope and examined — yet again.

Highly respected food scientists weren't born, they were made. At least that was what her father had drummed in her head back when she'd dared to mention how difficult her doctorate program had become, how little sleep her worn-out body got for all the studying required.

To lay all this to rest, she'd have to use everything she'd learned to nail down the answers to this mystery — or Dr. Juliet Ryan might as well hand over her lab coat.

28

Juliet searched for any sign of security personnel that might let her in if she showed her ID. As suspected, the financial situation at Larimar Springs meant there were none. Frustrated, she headed for her car.

Then she got an idea.

The company server could be accessed via her iPhone, allowing her to open the employee roster. Surely an employee might live close. Not a sure thing, but certainly worth trying.

Bingo!

One of her lab assistants, Lucy Patrick, lived less than two miles away.

Juliet checked her watch. Convincing herself ten thirty was not too late to call, she went ahead and dialed. She didn't have much choice.

A female picked up. "Hello?"

A plane cut through the dark sky overhead, the undercarriage lights flashing in the chilly night sky. "Is this Lucy?"

"Yes."

"This is Dr. Ryan. I'm afraid I've misplaced my access card and need to retrieve a file from my office. I know it's late, but could I possibly impose and come borrow yours?"

"Tonight?"

She scrunched her face, hating that she had to ask. "Uh, yes. I'm so sorry." There would be a record of her accessing the building, should anyone choose to check. She'd die on that sword later.

"Well, sure," Lucy said. "That'd be fine."

A little over an hour later, she stood at the front door of Larimar Springs, took a deep breath, and swiped Lucy's card, prompting the clicking sound that unlocked the doors. "Just as I thought. Only *my* card wouldn't work," she fumed, not liking how things were adding up.

The lobby looked much different empty and in the dark. She didn't dare turn on the lights and illuminate the fact she was here alone. She fumbled in her bag and retrieved her car keys. On the ring was a tiny flashlight with a bright LED bulb with enough illumination to get to her office.

Thankfully, her office window faced the rear of the building. She flipped on the light and opened up her Mac.

Juliet spent all night scouring lab records and found that everything lined up for the suspect report. Not sure whether that was a good thing or not, she continued her audit for all the tests conducted well before the date on the pallet Dr. Breslin was concerned about.

The work was tedious and took hours. Every cell in her body quivered in protest, and her eyes burned like someone had poured anhydrous ethanol across her pupils. She doubted any amount of caffeine could make her feel alert.

Still, she kept on.

Despite eating up a large percent of her budget, Juliet had tightened the company's processes to effectively safeguard bottled water from contamination. Nothing here indicated her established practices had been violated.

By the time light peeked through the windows, she'd found no discrepancies. Nothing that left her concerned, not even with the test left on her car window.

Armed with this information, she followed Dale Frissom into the meeting with Dr. Breslin, unsure how to play her findings in a way that would satisfy the investigators.

After initial greetings, she handed over

copies of her audit records. "I reviewed everything personally and found everything in order." Her voice had an edge, counter to her intent. She could only hope the man guiding her to the table clued in to the fact she'd been up all night performing the audit. With the slightest provocation, she might get sharp with even Mother Teresa at this point.

Dr. Breslin stared at her for several seconds, or perhaps he was looking at the dark circles under her eyes. "Thank you for that effort, Dr. Ryan," he said, taking the large folder from her hands.

He invited them to sit, then pulled some documents from his briefcase and spread them out on the small round table. "This is what caught our attention," he said, pointing to a line item on his product inventory. A paper clip attached a photo of the suspect label.

Juliet studied Dale's eyes as he leaned close and scanned the records. Looking puzzled, he lifted his head. "I'm afraid I don't have any answers." He opened his own attaché case and pulled a folder. "Our bottles come in twenty-four-count cases. For twelve ounce, we package ninety-one cases per pallet." He pulled a set of stapled documents from his folder. "When Dr. Ryan alerted me of your concern, I pulled all our shipping and receiving documentation. Strangely, nothing matches back to that particular pallet."

Dr. Breslin took the offered records and scowled. "Your records have to be in error. The production date is clearly indicated on the pallet." He pointed to the label. "We won't know for twenty-four hours or so, but if that pallet tests positive for the coliforms we found in the product at Water Circus, we've got a major problem."

Dale's face paled as he realized Juliet was no longer the only one in the hot seat.

Dr. Breslin went on. "The worry here, of course, is that there might be contaminated water still out in the marketplace. The recent development erodes my confidence that we've accounted for all the suspect product." His face grew solemn. "I'm afraid we may have to go public with this new development."

"But won't that only serve to increase public anxiety?" Juliet didn't want to over-step her bounds, but nothing would be achieved by making mothers in the San Antonio area worry even more until they could prove consumers were in actual danger. "Seems to me there's been a mas-sive recall of Larimar Springs bottled water, and you've confiscated any product Larimar Springs had on site. Without records to prove for certain, the possibility of additional bad product remaining out in the marketplace is conjecture at this point. We don't even know if that pallet will test positive. Nothing in the FDA regulations requires you to report suspicion — only fact."

Dr. Breslin's expression told her she'd connected with his scientific sensibilities.

"Of course, Larimar Springs will support whatever decision you make," she quickly assured him. "The entire investigation team has our full support."

Juliet made that promise no longer entirely certain it was true. In her mind, the foundation of truth at Larimar Springs was quickly crumbling. Measures had been taken to keep her out of the building, a suspicious envelope was left taped to her car, and now warehouse records couldn't be matched with product. How could Juliet be certain of anything, given all this?

She wasn't normally a person given to suspicion and distrust, but only a fool would turn her head and not stare this dog in the eye.

Dr. Breslin stood, signaling the meeting was over. "Your argument is well taken, Dr. Ryan. I expect it'll take some time to review all the information you've provided, but I can only assure you the CDC and our investigation team will weigh your point of view against our mandate to keep the public safe. I can't make any guarantees," he explained before escorting them out.

Visibly shaken, Dale voiced his appreciation on the way back to the office. "Thank you for that," he said, running his hand through his hair. "I mean it. The only thing I can figure is somehow paperwork errors occurred when Alexa forced a RIF and we were training temp workers in the middle of that big push. That decision opened us up to a margin of error in our day-to-day operations," he said, going on the defensive.

Juliet didn't point out that the suspicious pallet label suggested a date far before Alexa's demand for expenditure reductions. She didn't need to.

"I know the buck stops with me. But honestly? In my twenty-two years with Larimar Springs, nothing like this has ever happened on my watch. I mean, one time we had an issue with rats in the warehouse, but an exterminator solved that mighty quick. I can't understand how we have no transport documentation for that pallet." Then, as if she might have the power to protect his career, he confided, "I'm putting two kids through college right now, one is in med school. I can't afford to lose my job."

Juliet wished she could reassure him, persuade her co-worker he was a valuable member of the executive team and his employment was secure. She couldn't do that.

Surprised by her own instinct, she instead offered what she'd heard her mother claim so many times. "It's out of our hands, Dale. We'll just have to trust God to work all this out."

She dropped Dale off in front of the office door.

He grabbed his attaché from the floor of her car. "See you tomorrow."

She nodded. "I'll call you if I hear anything from Dr. Breslin before then."

Dale thanked her again and started to close the door. Suddenly, Greer burst through the office doors. "Juliet!" he hollered, heading for her car.

Apparently, she and Dale were not the only ones working over the weekend.

Dale glanced over his shoulder, then returned a weak smile. "Good luck." He nodded and backed away, nearly getting knocked aside as Greer approached and grabbed the car door, opening it wide.

"Where'd you and Dale take off to?" he

demanded, his face dark and agitated.

Juliet gripped the steering wheel with enough force to maintain composure. She desperately wanted to put him in his place. Instead, she measured her words carefully. "Dale and I had a meeting."

"A meeting? Where? With who?" His questions came at her like artillery fire.

She aimed back and shot off a response meant to shut him down. "Dr. Breslin had questions regarding our distribution and warehouse practices. That's why I took Dale with me." She forced an artificial smile. "I'll update everyone tomorrow, but right now I'm heading home."

There would be nothing lost in waiting to tell the team. Dr. Breslin would need at least twenty-four hours to review her findings against whatever test results came in. Then he'd decide how to move forward. If she told Greer now, he'd only panic and promulgate a lot of unnecessary and premature reaction.

Besides, at this point he'd lost her trust. If she told anyone, she'd make sure and tell Alexa directly. And with others present as a safety measure so there would be an adequate record of everything she conveyed.

Greer straightened and stepped back, a look of slight suspicion still evident on his face. But there was something else in his eyes. Something calculated. "It's just with everything that's going on, communication is critical."

She nodded, unsure how to reconcile the man she'd spent so much time with over these past months with the potential traducer standing at her car. "Of course, Greer."

"And about last night — the security card thing." He lifted his chin slightly. "I mentioned the issue to Alexa. Her decision had something to do with liability, given we no longer maintain on-site security at night."

She inclined her head, appalled at the liberties he took with the truth. She waited for him to ask why she'd needed access at such a late hour. When he didn't, she hurried to end the exchange. "Look, Greer. I really need to get going."

She drove home with her briefcase resting on the floor in front of the passenger seat. Safely tucked inside, a duplicate set of her research provided a level of safeguard against the developing unease in her gut. After hours of work, she'd not been able to unravel the mystery of the outdated pallet in the warehouse, or why there were insufficient records to resolve the unanswered questions.

One thing had become very clear in the process. Something was up with Greer. He'd lied on several occasions. No longer could she chock up his agitation to losing his key account, to his company faltering. His skills as a talented sales executive were indisputable. Greer could land another job any day of the week.

His hostility definitely stretched beyond a breakup pout. The typically calculated man she knew, who rarely showed emotion unless it was in his favor, seemed to be coming undone.

The notion stretched beyond rational, but something told Juliet he had something to hide.

But what?

For now, she'd keep the envelope a secret, especially from Greer. Eventually, she might have to go to Alexa with her suspicions. But she'd need more than misgivings and a gut feeling to garner the CEO's reinforcement. If she was believed, Greer's career at Larimar Springs would be tanked, of course. Without proper proof, the approach would backfire and simply underscore the idea that she was the incompetent one.

Her exit loomed ahead. After putting on her blinker, she turned onto a side road leading to her neighborhood. On second thought, perhaps she'd better keep her budding misgivings to herself. At least for now.

In the midst of these snarled thoughts, a sad realization moved to center stage. Over only a couple weeks, she'd managed to sour her love life. Her personal life was a mess, and now her professional reputation was fast crumbling at her feet. At times like these, her mother would provide much-needed support.

But she was gone.

In the short time since her mother's funeral, Juliet had barely allowed herself to grieve. Instead, she'd been immersed in an outbreak of foodborne illness that in some ways offered up an opportunity to hide from the real fear she couldn't yet face.

She'd never entirely bought in to the fact there was some guy upstairs orchestrating all the events on earth. If there were, why would he allow her mother to die when she was most needed? Or let innocent people fall victim to food pathogens?

Why would he let her career falter, sending all her hard work down the drain?

In so many ways, it would be easier to erase the notion of a supreme being from her reality, to completely give in to the notion there was no God.

Unfortunately, that truth was impossible.

She needed to believe. Because she needed little MD and the others to get well. And without a heaven — forever was a very long time to be without her mom.

At home, she folded onto the sofa with a cup of chamomile tea, hoping the warmth would quell her racing mind and allow her to doze off. She could afford only a few hours before she had to get back to her research, needing to retrace her steps just in case she'd missed something.

Juliet rested her head against the stack of pillows, remembering she and her mother used to sit like this, hands wrapped around steaming teacups, talking about everything, and at times nothing at all.

What would her mom say if she were here? If she knew her bright and focused daughter had skidded off her carefully planned career path?

Juliet had disdained so many of her mother's choices. Her simple faith, her steadfast commitment to a man who didn't deserve her loyalty, her willingness to empty her own dreams to fill the needs of others. In return, people had packed a church to pay their final respects and say goodbye.

Her mother was loved.

Carol Ryan hadn't strived for success, yet

her life mattered.

With her mother gone, Juliet meant to need no one, but now the emptiness of that decision haunted her. She'd scoffed at her mother's morals and literally slept with the enemy. Her reputation as a food scientist was in severe jeopardy. Her career potentially over.

Juliet's self-awarded trophies for studying the hardest, working the longest, and garnering respect in a field dominated by self-important men were quickly sliding off the shelf.

The façade was crumbling.

Worse, she was alone at a time when she needed someone the most.

Tears, warm and salty, slid down Juliet's cheeks. She fumbled and slid her cup onto the coffee table, then quietly moved into the bedroom, where she opened a drawer and retrieved her mother's Bible from beneath a silky folded nightgown.

In her mind, she could see her mother in her robe and slippers at their old kitchen table, underlining text with unexplainable confidence, despite the late hour and her husband still not home.

Juliet pulled the worn leather volume close to her chest, sheltering her heart from waves of disappointment and longing crashing against the walls of her soul.

The events of these past weeks had thrown some rip currents, left her a bit shipwrecked. Frankly, she didn't know if she could swim against the current and land safely on shore.

Perhaps she was simply overtired, worn out, and not thinking with a clear mind. But Juliet couldn't help but ponder an idea she'd never dared to consider.

She was definitely sailing without a rudder. What would it be like to face what was ahead with her mother's quiet strength?

Juliet opened the volume to a well-worn page in Isaiah and noticed that her mother had highlighted verses.

Do not be afraid, for I have ransomed you. I have called you by name; you are mine. When you go through deep waters, I will be with you . . . For I am the Lord, your God, the Holy One of Israel, your Savior.

In the margin, her mother noted the date and a single word.
Nancy.
Juliet's heart thumped painfully.

For a long time, she'd thought if her mother ever found out about that one, she would fall to pieces. But she'd not only known about Nancy, she'd forgiven him even that.

Juliet sank to the floor and cast her head back against the thick carpet. Covering her eyes with her forearm, she conjured the smoothness of the skin on her mother's face, her eyes that expressed love without restraint. Somehow her mother had been released from the need to paddle, even in the worst times. Nothing, it seemed, could sink her boat.

She'd never known a woman with more strength, more dignity.

Closing her eyes, she let her mind form another memory — her mother's hand closing over her own, her practical short fingernails lightly spattered with paint from her latest project. Juliet's nostrils drew in air, easily recalling her mom's fragrance hinting of lilac and clean laundry.

God, if you are there — tell her I miss her.

29

Lindsay looked up from the receptionist desk. "There you are. The meeting's been changed." She pointed to the executive wing. "Her office."

Juliet nodded and headed that direction.

Lindsay seemed on edge, like everybody else around here in the past days. No employee escaped feeling the heat of working for a company in the glare of the public spotlight. Worse, they knew even if the company survived with their brand intact, the financial strain from this outbreak would likely mean future layoffs.

Her staff was particularly unnerved. Since the outbreak had been pinned on Larimar Springs, her lab techs' chins had dipped to their chests as if they couldn't quite bring themselves to hold their heads up, their disorientation nearly palpable. Especially Malcolm Stanford, who answered her questions in monosyllables and kept his eyes drilled to the floor. She wondered if, like all the others, her QA supervisor blamed her for this fiasco.

As she neared her own office door, she handed off her purse and attaché bag to Angela, keeping a single file tucked beneath her arm. "Any updates from Tavina?"

The temp shook her head. "No, not this morning."

Juliet took the stack of mail Angela offered. "Thanks. And could you pen me out this afternoon for a couple of hours? I want to go to the hospital and check on little MD, and see if Tavina needs anything." She turned to head to the meeting, moving several yards before Angela dropped her proverbial bomb.

"Uh — I won't be here when you get out of the meeting. And I won't be back."

Surprised, Juliet whirled around. "What? Why?"

Angela shrugged. "Got word this morning that I won't be needed anymore." She pointed down the hallway to Fred Macklin's assistant. "I was told to hand off my work to Alva Jacobs. So I guess I'll catch you later."

Juliet couldn't help but turn and stare in the direction of the woman who was nearing retirement age. Not only was Alva known for snooping through people's desks, but she refused to use a computer, clinging to her IBM Selectric typewriter from the seventies. The polyester-suited woman still wore support hose and refused to use a cell phone. "Why should I when I have a perfectly good telephone on my desk?" she was often heard explaining.

Rumor had it the guys in the mailroom were directed to print out all emails and place them on Alva's desk no later than ten a.m., and then again at two in the afternoon. Even more puzzling was that she wore an elastic coiled bracelet with a tangle of keys dangling from her wrist. Funny she kept her own files locked up when she felt so free to open other people's desk drawers uninvited.

Yes, Angela was pushy and difficult to warm up to, but Juliet would choose the temp over Alva Jacobs any day. Based on the way Alva stared back, she wasn't terribly keen on the idea either.

Though pressed for time, Juliet quickly returned to Angela's desk and shook her hand. "Thank you for filling in, especially during . . . well, all this."

"Yeah, y'all got your hands full at this place, I'll give you that."

Minutes later, Juliet headed for Alexa's door, first passing by her assistant. Muriel

Parke stood and shuffled a stack of papers into a neat pile, a scowl painted across her colorless face. "Don't you carry your cell phone anymore? Alexa's been calling you." Her features reminded Juliet of a pit bull with Ringo Starr's haircut from the sixties.

"Sorry." Juliet moved past, not bothering to offer any further explanation. A fact Muriel didn't care for, based on the way she huffed.

Under normal circumstances, she'd maintain the politically correct stance with the old battle-ax. Despite the overblown sense of power of some in this group, Juliet knew the expediency of keeping on the assistants' good sides. Lately, however, no amount of deference seemed to matter. Their chatter silenced every time she entered the break room to fill her coffee mug. Overheard whispers in the cubicles included words like *blame, incompetent, bungled.* The staff's cold stares said everything — she'd been iced out.

She didn't have many fans on the executive team either.

Around the small granite conference table in the corner of Alexa's office sat Dale Frissom and Fred Macklin. Greer was perched on a small sofa over near the windows with his arm thrown over the back, chatting about reactions to their press conference with Ellen Shaffer, who seemed to be embracing his smooth and polished charm.

Everyone stopped talking and stared when she entered the room.

She checked her watch despite knowing what time it was. "Sorry I'm a bit late." She moved to the table and took her place by their chief financial officer. "I understand we'll be sharing an assistant going forward."

Typical of his gruff, outspoken approach, he simply blew out a puff of angry air. "Don't look at me. Wasn't my idea."

She turned to Dale, wondering if he'd take the opportunity to defend his decision since the human resources area reported to him. He said nothing. Instead, he kept his focus on the loose papers in front of him.

Alexa walked into the room then. Instantly, she took control. "Listen up. We have a lot to consider this morning."

Dale sat expressionless as Alexa dropped her bomb. "Since QA was unable to provide adequate documentation for an outdated pallet found in the warehouse, the CDC believes there may be additional tainted product in the marketplace. They are threatening to go public."

Juliet's fists locked in anger. *That weasel.*

Using every bit of self-control she could

muster, she repressed any reaction, instead forcing herself to remain stone-faced despite the fact she was seething mad.

She'd been sold down the river so Dale could reach shore in this deal. No doubt he'd painted the scenario in his highest favor.

While clinging to her threadbare composure, she struggled to form a strategy to restore her own credibility.

Alexa opened her leather portfolio. "We need to give Dale credit for convincing them to push the pause button. Because of his efforts, Dr. Breslin felt confident that if he gave us another twenty-four hours or so, Dale could connect the dots and shed light on why his warehouse was holding an outdated pallet without shipping manifests."

Everyone turned their attention to Dale, who still wouldn't look her in the eye.

"Uh, yes — we committed to investigate further," he said, his voice unnaturally high.

Alexa sat with her fingers steepled, deep in thought. "We need to get to the bottom of this," she said. "This company will never win if we're forced to keep playing defense."

Fred threw up his hands. "I don't understand how you people could miss such critical facts." He grabbed a wad of financials in his fist and shook them. "We're losing hundreds of thousands daily. Do you understand what is at risk?" Clearly, he referred to his retirement as well as the company's P&L position. And *you people* meant Juliet.

Ellen Shaffer stood, her face composed and silky hair loose on her shoulders. "I probably don't need to remind you that Larimar Springs has already used up all its markers with the public. If you ever want a chance of regaining customer confidence, you'd best find the answers before the CDC."

From the sofa, Greer leaned forward and tugged on his shirt cuffs. "I don't mean to stir the pot here, but perhaps it would be advisable to appoint a company liaison with the CDC." His gaze drifted in her direction. "Someone who has less personal stake in the information flow."

Juliet's jaw clenched. "What you are implying, Greer?"

"Let's not let emotions supersede our judgment." Alexa rubbed across her lips with her forefinger. With the other hand she tapped her Montblanc pen on the tabletop several times. Finally, she lifted her chin. "Under the circumstances, perhaps that's a good idea."

The decision kicked Juliet's gut. Her boss's directive cemented the notion she'd lost all confidence within the company at every level. Juliet's career here was over. The best she could hope for was to salvage her image as a professional who wouldn't melt under the heat.

"Again, I don't believe that move is necessary. But I'll concede and work to dispense my duties in the way you see fit." The words stuck in her throat as she said them. She could play the puppet, if that was what they wanted, in the short time she had remaining in this position. In any other situation, she wouldn't accept this blatant shift in confidence from her superiors. She'd resign and move on. But there would be time to focus on getting some semblance of a career back on track later. The main thing was to make certain the company complied with the CDC investigation to facilitate efforts to end this outbreak as quickly as possible. For everyone's sake.

Alexa turned to Greer. "Who do you suggest?"

"Well, clearly Dale and Juliet are out of the question, and Ellen isn't an officer for the corporation. That leaves Fred or me."

Fred immediately appeared uneasy. He held up his open palms and shook his head. "No thanks. Leave me out of this. I'm the numbers guy, that's all."

Alexa lifted her chin. "Then it's settled. We only have one option, really." She stood and moved to her desk. "Besides, Greer can hardly direct a sales or marketing effort while the company is struggling through these issues. So, looks like you're the point person, Greer."

"Happy to," he said, giving Juliet a look that radiated superiority.

"Another thing. No — and I mean *no* — information is to be disseminated to the public or to Cyril Montavan or our bankers without first going through me. Is that understood?" She waited for everyone to nod. "Okay, meeting over."

Fred and Dale stood and collected their papers, then headed for the door.

Ellen, recognizing the shift in power, coyly smiled at Greer. Following her lead, he awarded her with a smile of his own and followed her out the door, listening intently as she gave pointers on how to remain noncommittal when providing information.

"Juliet, could you stay? I'd like a word — privately."

She raised her eyebrows and glanced at her boss with caution. "Uh . . . sure." Maybe she wasn't going to be given the opportunity to stay after all.

Alexa moved for the door.

Despite preparing herself for this eventuality, she felt her heart race. She had hoped this company needed her, would use her expertise to maneuver the outbreak. Given that Alexa had just seen the need to appoint a babysitter of sorts, now she wasn't so certain.

After closing the door, Alexa moved to the sofa. She patted the place next to her, inviting Juliet to join her there. "I want you to understand my position."

Juliet took a deep breath and sat next to the polished and confident woman she'd so admired. From the outset of accepting employment with Larimar Springs, she'd viewed Alexa Carmichael as the epitome of everything she longed to be. Which made her boss's decision to appoint Greer to play liaison stab deeper. Juliet vacillated between anger and dismay that the target of her admiration no longer trusted her to do what was best for the company.

"You may have misunderstood what just took place." Alexa's face grew sympathetic. "That decision was made to protect you."

"Protect me?" she murmured, a bit confused.

"Don't think people haven't tried to step on my back the times my career hit a low," Alexa confided. "Weak managers always dispel blame by pointing at others. Recently, I've come to realize it may be time to realign my . . . support system within the company."

Juliet felt baffled by these new pronouncements, and said so.

Alexa patted Juliet's knee, her eyes steady. "You handled yourself well today. Let Greer shadow you. It'll do no harm and will protect you from rumor and innuendo. Besides, sometimes the greatest show of power is to let others think they've won."

Her vote of confidence caused Juliet's spirits to lift considerably. Somehow in all this mess, the smart and savvy businesswoman had seen through her detractors after all. "Thank you, Alexa. I appreciate your support."

Her boss kicked off her gray alligator stilettos, stood, and moved across the plush carpet in her bare feet to her desk. She pressed a button on her phone set. "Muriel, hold my calls, please. I don't want to be interrupted."

Alexa returned to the sofa carrying a tray of fresh croissants from her desk. After placing the tray on the table, she sat next to Juliet and folded her feet up under her aqua pencil skirt. "Eat," she urged.

The last thing on Juliet's mind was eating, and she was hardly hungry after the waves of nerves she'd been riding over these past hours. Still, she reached for and buttered a croissant.

Alexa dabbed the corners of her lips with a napkin and looked Juliet in the eyes. "I realize you might be a bit confused here." She brushed crumbs from her skirt. "Look, I like you, Juliet. I admire your knowledge and talent. Now, I need to know if I can trust you."

"Of course." She took a bite, unsure where Alexa was heading with these comments.

"Good. Because I need to confide something. Something that must remain between the two of us."

The tenuousness in Alexa's voice took her by surprise. She nodded her agreement.

Alexa placed the unfinished portion of her croissant back on the tray and focused on a few wayward crumbs. Finally, she looked up.

"I think I know where the E. coli came from — and why there was an outdated pallet in the warehouse."

30

Unable to sleep, Juliet got up before dawn, pulled on her Patagonia Ultrarunners and an extra sweatshirt to ward off the chill, and headed for the trail near Levi Strauss Park. The parking lot held only one other car at that early morning hour — a couple she recognized from a marathon she'd been in last year. She waved and they waved back.

She sat in her Jeep, drinking coffee and listening to Trey Ware's morning talk show on the radio, waiting for the sky to lighten enough to make out the running path.

As soon as the faintest pink hinted at daybreak, she hopped out and did her stretching routine, with a safety whistle in her mouth for good measure. Whenever she needed to think, she went running. And after yesterday's meeting with Alexa Carmichael, she had a lot to consider.

She'd not been able to get everything Alexa revealed off her mind. Especially the astounding revelation dropped in her lap and how she'd barely been able to respond.

"What — what do you mean you know where the E. coli came from?"

For the first time that day, Alexa fidgeted. Barely able to maintain eye contact, the typically self-assured owner of her company picked at her skirt as she explained. "Initially, when the CDC pointed the finger at Larimar Springs, I had no reason to put two and two together. Not really. I mean, I had a niggling suspicion, but when an outdated pallet was discovered — well, then I knew."

"You knew what?" The sharpness of Juliet's tone surprised even herself.

"Let me explain — from the beginning."

The phone set on Alexa's desk buzzed. She rolled her eyes and stood. "Excuse me." She marched to her desk and punched a button. "I said to hold my calls, Muriel."

"I'm sorry, Alexa. It's Harris. He . . . uh, he says it's urgent."

"Fine." Alexa turned to Juliet and apologized. "I'm sorry. I have to take this."

"Do you want me to . . . ?" Juliet let her words trail as she pointed to the door.

Alexa shook her head. "No, sit tight. I'll only be a moment."

She grabbed the receiver and pulled it to her ear, then punched a button. "Harris.

I'm in a meeting." As she listened, her eyebrows pulled together. "Well, I appreciate that, but I can't do anything about it now." She turned her back to Juliet and lowered her voice. "So reschedule. It's not like your surgical procedures are a matter of life or death."

Juliet cringed. Nothing felt so uncomfortable as overhearing a marital spat. Alexa rarely spoke of her family, but framed photos of her plastic surgeon husband and teen son lined the credenza on the wall opposite her desk. Several of the images included the tony couple posed with actress Lara Flynn Boyle and her real estate mogul husband Don Thomas. It was rumored Thomas and Alexa's husband were in several business ventures together.

"Well, did you ever consider the academy might be right? Perhaps Adam needs to miss soccer if he's failing Latin." She rubbed the bridge of her nose. "Regardless, Harris, you just need to take care of the situation. I'm too busy right now." She hung up.

"I'm sorry about that," she said, appearing even more uneasy. She poured herself a tumbler of water from the glass pitcher on her desk, looking like she wished it held something much stronger. She returned to the sofa and cleared her throat. "Okay, let me start at the beginning."

Alexa commenced by telling about Juliet's predecessor, a woman named Robin Ford. "I'm afraid the young woman was a bit over her head to begin with. When she wasn't able to return to her position after a disability leave, we knew we needed to fill that critical spot with someone with your background and caliber."

"She wasn't able to return?"

"She had scheduled a maternity leave, but unfortunately encountered a high-risk situation that prompted an early departure — and then she resigned."

Juliet remembered Tavina telling her a bit about the situation, and Greer had said something about a maternity leave, but she'd never discussed the woman with either of them much past a casual mention. There was no need, really.

"Anyway, I'm afraid Robin's head wasn't entirely in the game during all that." Alexa took a quick sip of water and placed her glass on a nearby table, next to a Fiesta San Antonio commemorative paperweight. She shifted, trying to get comfortable. "About that same time Malcolm Stanford brought something directly to my attention."

Without thought, Juliet chewed at her lip, wary about what she was about to hear.

She'd never entirely understood her QA supervisor's story — and why he never seemed entirely on board with her work to improve the laboratory systems. At first, she'd thought he just resented the proposed changes, taking each of her assessments as criticism. But lately, she'd suspected his reserved nature might have a deeper cause.

"Admittedly, my knowledge of pathogens and coliforms was limited at the time. But Malcolm voiced concern that microbiological levels were showing up in the high ranges in our source water samples."

"You mean, from the aquifer?" Juliet asked, the skin on her neck tensing. The Edwards Aquifer provided water to nearly two million people in south central Texas. "I'm afraid I don't understand. If samples raised concerns, why was the water allowed into production?"

Alexa fingered her neckline. "That's my point. At that same time, Robin Ford's attention was directed at her serious health issues. Understandably, of course. She assured me necessary precautions had been taken. I trusted her."

Understanding dawned. Juliet slowly nodded. "Oh . . . I see." So Malcolm had raised serious issues and his concerns went nowhere. No wonder he was a bit reluctant to play team ball. His prior coach had left the field in the middle of the game and the ball had been fumbled.

Alexa rushed to add, "We had no reason to suspect —" She faltered. "I mean, there was no way for us to know until all this." She lifted the glass and took another drink. Her voice choked with emotion. "I — I should've paid more attention, given her health issues. It's just — well, I was campaigning for this merger, and —"

Juliet placed her fingers on Alexa's forearm. "I understand you never meant for this outbreak to occur, but the issues Malcolm raised were serious. None of that product should have made its way into a consumer's hands. Ever."

"Robin assured me the levels were low and that our filtration and disinfection systems assured the water was safe. Even so, we held back the pallets. Which is why they remained stored in the warehouse but were never logged into distribution." Alexa faltered. "When demand increased with the Water Circus expansion, something must have happened and the pallets were delivered."

Alexa stood and paced, clearly distressed. "If I could turn the clock back, I would. I can't." Her arms swept the room. "Now, I have this company's future to consider. Not only for myself, of course." She stood and wandered to the windows, gazed out at the gardens. "Did you know Fred Macklin is less than a year from retirement? And Dale Frissom has kids in college." She turned abruptly. "Do you have any idea the pressure of keeping this company viable, for everyone's sake?" Her chin quivered and she stared at the floor.

"Or —" she said, her voice nearly a whisper — "what it feels like to know you are responsible for children dying? For Tavina's little boy?" She nearly crumpled then.

Juliet rushed to her side. "Oh, Alexa. Don't — you didn't mean for this to happen." In a strange warp of worlds, she found herself comforting her boss, rubbing little circles on her back the way her mother used to when Juliet's heart was hurting.

She took a deep breath, trying to let all the information sink in.

Alexa Carmichael had made a fatal error in judgment and would indeed need her if this company was going to survive this mistake. "We'll figure this out together," Juliet promised.

Relief flooded Alexa's face. She quickly wiped at her eyes with her perfectly manicured nails and thanked Juliet for her understanding.

Alexa claimed the former QA director had failed to properly perform her duties. More than as a career, the woman had obviously viewed her role at the company as a mere job. "She probably would like to have resigned earlier, but she'd lose her insurance," she suggested. "Not an option for a woman with a high-risk pregnancy."

Still, how could someone with any knowledge of the potential risk choose to look the other way and take a chance others might be harmed?

And Juliet had other questions. Like, who had deposited the envelope on her car? And why couldn't she find any discrepancies in the testing, the lab statistics, and the tracking systems?

She posed the most obvious question.

"Why are we not talking to this woman?" she asked Alexa, making a quick decision to keep the envelope to herself. At least for now. "Surely this would not only provide closure on this investigation, but culpability could be transferred. At least to some extent."

"Larimar Springs would still be liable for any employee's actions that caused damages. As an ex-employee, she could be a loose cannon and we wouldn't be able to control what she said or what she might do to deflect her own liability. This way, I stay in control and save the company. In terms of the victims, I can make certain anyone damaged by this mess is made financially whole."

The fact that money could never recompense the lost life of a toddler remained unspoken.

Alexa placed her hand on Juliet's forearm in an insistent gesture. "I've taken charge of the situation out there in the warehouse, and I'm absolutely confident there is no additional tainted product available to the public. The CDC will conclude that very soon." She released her grip on Juliet's arm and leaned back. "I've mulled this over and over. Crisis managers everywhere would advise to let the story run its course and die quickly. And they're right." She lifted her chin, seeming to have no illusions about the gravity of what was ahead for the company she loved. "I'm not prone to starting another flurry of media right now. Larimar Springs has taken a huge hit, but we'll weather this. In the end, our company will become a beacon for food safety. I've instructed Ellen to research and make a recommendation as to how we could form an auxiliary nonprofit to raise funds and champion these issues.

Every move I make in the days ahead will ensure the Larimar Springs brand will be synonymous with compassion for these victims and with food safety."

Juliet now rounded the bend in the path, feeling a certain comfort from the rhythm of her shoes hitting the pavement. She breathed deeply, taking in air quietly scented with notes of cherry sage and dormant cottonwood stands on the limestone bluffs just ahead.

What her boss had said next, no one could have seen coming.

"Going forward, this company can't afford any risks. That's why I've made a critical decision." The woman's eyes lit with feverish commitment.

Alexa Carmichael stood with her hand on the back of a side chair, a woman of no illusions, not of her personal goals or of what she wanted for her company. "I'm impressed with how you've handled this entire situation, of the integrity and commitment you've shown."

Juliet let a humble smile form. "Thank you. I appreciate that."

"Your level of expertise is critical to our future progress. That is why as soon as this is safely behind us, I plan to name you president."

Her heart stopped beating, then drummed several beats to catch up. She tried to catch her breath. "I'm sorry. What?"

Alexa gave her a confident smile. "You heard me, Dr. Ryan. But we have to keep this between us at this point. The timing for the announcement will be delicate. Still, I'm confident this move will serve to further our company focus on safety going forward, and will provide a greater level of confidence with our bankers and with Montavan International. Cyril really likes you, I can tell."

Her boss clapped her hands. "As I see it, my decision is a win-win." She moved to her desk and wrote in her day planner while explaining that Dale, Fred, and even Greer would report to Juliet in her new role. "Your compensation package will reflect your advanced position with the company, of course."

Juliet tried to act cool, hoped her wide-eyed surprise was not clearly evident on her face. This sudden turn of events was more than she ever dreamed could happen. Especially on the tail of this foodborne outbreak.

She'd spent the last weeks feeling like she'd dropped the ball somehow, that everything she'd been trained to do had fallen short. A consumer product she'd been charged with keeping safe contained deadly

O157:H7. People had fallen ill. Little children had died.

Now, she could embrace the knowledge that the situation had not been created by a lack of diligence on her part. Someone else's actions had instigated the outbreak. Her role had been to minimize the effect. She was the hero after all.

Better, even, her father would learn the truth at some point. He'd find her career had been accelerated.

President of the company.

She let that thought linger, savoring that all her hard work had finally paid off.

"So, are you in?"

"I'm flattered, Alexa." Taking a deep breath, she extended her hand. "You can count on me."

31

The Riverwalk in downtown San Antonio used to be one of Juliet's favorite spots, especially in the weeks leading up to the holidays, when teams of decorators fastened lights and greenery to the light poles and walking bridges. Merchants all along the tourist attraction started before Thanksgiving, transforming their establishments into festive venues.

In years past, she'd strolled the lush banks of the San Antonio River with her mother, guided by more than six thousand luminarias — warmly glowing candles in sand-filled bags lining the walkways to symbolically mark the "lighting of the way."

That was before.

Now, painful visions of the fateful day she'd lost her mother marred the memories and the way she felt standing along the Riverwalk.

"Can I get y'all something to drink while

you wait?"

Startled, Juliet looked up from her riverside table. "Uh, sure. Iced tea would be fine. Thank you."

Despite a slight chill in the air, the waitress wore a short-sleeved blue T-shirt with printing on the front that read "The County Line — Legendary BBQ." She had big hair, a bigger smile, and smelled slightly like the smoky meat she served all day. The woman pointed at the activity up and down the sidewalks lining the river. "Can you believe it's almost Thanksgiving? Seems I was just fixin' to carve pumpkins."

"Yes, the weeks certainly fly by," she agreed with a sigh.

The waitress leaned her head to one side. "You know, you sure look familiar." She shrugged. "Ah, but then I see a lot of people every day. Hold right here, I'll go get y'all's tea."

Glad to have escaped the connection to recent media stories, she glanced at her watch. It wasn't like her mother's best friend to be late. Since the funeral, Sandy had been leaving messages that she was praying for her, offering to take her to lunch. Until today, there'd been no time to squeeze in anything social, even that. She'd barely had time to eat and sleep.

For example, after meeting with Alexa on Tuesday, she'd had another conference with Dr. Breslin, with Greer tagging along, of course. Thankfully, once Juliet fully answered his questions and Dr. Breslin reviewed her early findings, he'd gone along with her recommendations and concluded there was no need to further alert the public. In fact, recent admissions reports from the local hospitals indicated the outbreak had peaked. Given this, the team had reached the conclusion that they needed nothing further from Larimar Springs.

Everyone involved breathed a sigh of relief at the news.

Except Tavina.

Her little boy continued to worsen. MD's prognosis was growing dimmer by the day. Medical professionals said only a miracle had got him this far, but they warned a real possibility for further deterioration remained — he could easily lose the battle and succumb to the virulent pathogens compromising his critical internal systems.

The report left Juliet heartbroken and feeling helpless.

Many at Larimar Springs felt the same. Ladies in the office filled Tavina's freezer with meals and sent cards filled with Starbucks gift cards and well wishes. Not to be outdone, men passed an envelope and made sure her utilities were paid for several months. Malcolm Stanford led this effort, a fact Juliet found endearing, if not a bit surprising given his aloof personality.

Alexa had directed HR to pay Tavina's salary in full and asked that all medical bills be sent to Larimar Springs, despite warnings from legal counsel that the act could be characterized as an admittance of liability. Alexa also rented a small condominium for the family and had a town car made available for transporting them to and from the hospital as necessary.

Ellen Shaffer dubbed the action a brilliant move from a public perception standpoint. "Everyone will connect these efforts to a company of compassion — minimizing the image of an entity that tried to maintain their bottom line at the expense of public safety. Larimar Springs will be seen as a group of benevolent people who care about not only one of their own but every person who fell victim to this common yet virulent pathogen." Her eyes had nearly gleamed as she pounded out a press release on her MacBook Air, hoping the information would grant her client clemency in the public's mind.

One person who often vilified Larimar

Springs in the media was Juliet's own father, a subject that rarely came up when she was in the room. But she'd seen the same news reports, read the same interviews. For everything Ellen and her team were doing to raise the perception of Larimar Springs in the public's mind, her father was working diligently at just the opposite.

"Here ya go, honey." The waitress placed her tea on the table before scurrying on to the next table. The movement startled two ducks from their quiet respite by the edge of the water, where they'd been tucked against the shoreline, nearly out of view for the lush and low-lying philodendrons. They quacked and dove into the river.

Juliet smiled, remembering how her mother would sneak food to them, despite posted signs and her father's warnings that feeding ducks bread was unhealthy and could lead to malnutrition, diseases, and behavior changes.

Amused, she watched the ducks paddle away when her phone alerted she had a text.

So sorry. Hate to do this at the last minute, but I must pick up my sick grandson from daycare. Rain check?

After replying not to worry, they'd get together another time, she clicked off Sandy's message, suddenly feeling immensely lonely. Only now did she realize how much she'd needed time with the woman who served as her only connection to her mother. Perhaps it was being on the Riverwalk, but sadness permeated her soul this afternoon.

Grief's full impact had been held back while her attention was directed at maneuvering pathogens, coliforms, and microorganisms. Coordinating a response to an outbreak and focusing on Tavina, with frequent treks to the hospital to check on little MD, had in some ways prevented her from dealing with the loss.

But today, being so near where her mother had left this world, well . . . she'd simply underestimated the impact it would have on her emotions.

She took a drink of her tea and watched a man in a portable hoist attach large ornaments to the greenery on a wrought-iron balcony across the river. The holidays were just ahead. The first without her mom, a notion Juliet could barely consider.

"Dr. Ryan?"

She turned. Cyril Montavan stood at her table, almost unrecognizable in jeans and a sports coat in place of the tailored suits he normally wore.

She stood and extended her hand. "Cyril,

what a surprise."

He urged her to sit back down. "It's nice to run into you, Dr. Ryan. As you know, I'm staying nearby. Some issues with the European financial market required me to be on the phone with headquarters through most of the night, because of the time difference. Afraid I found it necessary to sleep in a bit." He gave her a broad smile, revealing deep dimples and crinkles at his eyes.

Her hand motioned for him to sit. "Please, join me?"

"You had such a solemn look on your face," he said, taking a seat across from her. "This outbreak mess has been difficult on you."

She sighed. "Yes, I won't argue that. The whole thing has been a struggle on multiple levels."

His finger brushed across the grain of the wooden table. "You've handled a difficult situation with grace. I told Alexa she was lucky to have you in this key position during such a trying time. Frankly, knowing you were at the helm of this incident gave me the confidence to follow this investment through instead of pulling back. Especially when it became necessary to put up additional funding so I was no longer subordinate to the primary lender."

She looked across the table, feeling extraordinary gratitude and a bit surprised he'd chosen to share so openly regarding his financial relationship with Larimar Springs. "I appreciate your support, Cyril. Truly, I do." She jingled the ice in her glass. "Frankly, there was more than one occasion over the past week where I was ready to hang it up. I thought my career was over. So much easier to look at the bigger picture on this end of the outbreak."

The corners of his mouth turned up slightly. "Oh, someone with your talent should never cease bringing your knowledge and expertise to bear. Obviously you are passionate about these issues, and in the end we all win because of that."

His compliments were like soft blue ocean water to her still crusty and barnacled self-esteem. No one really understood what it was like to attain respect in her field, then have that regard ripped away, even temporarily, leaving her career adrift. Added to what Alexa had promised earlier in the week, his remarks helped her believe a day would come when she'd be able to fully lift her sails and catch wind again.

When she told him so, he awarded her with another of his generous smiles. "I've found things of this nature have a way of working out in the end."

The big-haired waitress showed back up at the table then and handed them both menus. The woman leaned in and cupped her mouth. "Take some advice, don't even bother trying to decide." She lowered her voice as if someone at a nearby table might steal her secret. "The brisket is to *die for* today. Slow roasted over eighteen hours — can't find any better."

Cyril grinned and handed back the menu. "Sold."

Juliet followed suit. "You better tell my friend here to save room for your homemade bread pudding."

Their waitress winked. "Well, that's a given, y'all."

She waited for the waitress to move on from their table. "Bet you don't find a lot of smoked brisket in Italy."

He shook his head. "No, at least none that smells quite like this." He lifted his nose and sampled the smoky aroma wafting from inside the restaurant. "Italians often claim food is like a great perfume — best when it's an accord of bold notes and subtle bouquet."

She grinned. "There's nothing subtle about the County Line's barbecue, aroma or otherwise."

He discovered that for himself when the platter of sliced meat was placed before him. No matter how carefully Cyril wielded chunks of the brisket onto the tines of his fork and into his mouth, traces of the dry rub and tangy sauce clung to the corners of his lips with every bite.

Amused, Juliet handed him a clean napkin. "You left some," she teased.

"What?"

When he frowned like he didn't understand, she reached over and wiped the sides of his mouth. As she did, he lifted his fingertips and lightly brushed the inside of her wrist, leaving her a bit unnerved.

Not for the first time, she admired his coffee-brown eyes, as inviting as her early morning cup of joe. With his classic looks and elegance, and the way the late afternoon sun highlighted the touch of silver at his temples, Cyril Montavan appeared to have stepped off a movie screen.

Unlike Greer Latham, who greedily consumed every room he entered, she found the man gazing across the table at her soft-spoken and incredibly intelligent. Even though he was quiet, Cyril Montavan saw everything. He understood things others couldn't, simply because he took the time to observe. She admired him for it. Yet in ways, she also feared the notion, worried he could see through her with a glance.

Which is why she quickly averted her eyes when he looked at her a bit too long.

"I hope you can find reason to return to San Antonio in April," she said, trying to move past the intensity of the moment.

He neatly crossed his fork and knife across the empty platter. "In April?"

She nodded and pushed her plate back. "Every spring, downtown San Antonio becomes the site of a citywide celebration with over a hundred events, including a series of parades and a huge carnival. We call it Fiesta."

A note of excitement crept into his voice. "Yeah? Tell me more."

She warmed at the interest shown on his face. "My parents took me every year. I loved the river parade with all the pretty lights at night, but admittedly my favorite is the Battle of the Flowers parade. The Daughters of the Republic of Texas stage a procession to the Alamo as a memorial tribute to the Battle of the Alamo and Battle of San Jacinto heroes. As a little girl, I was fascinated with the multicultural and brightly festooned floats. I still am," she admitted.

Cyril rubbed at his chin as if conjuring

memories of his own. "In Italy, we celebrate something similar. Carnevale is our huge winter festival. We celebrate with parades, masquerade balls, and parties. Children throw confetti, and older patrons pull pranks, hence the saying *A Carnevale Ogni Scherzo Vale,* which means 'anything goes at carnival.' For the feast of Carnevale, we Italians celebrate with bugies, which translated means 'little liars' — a sweet fried dough dusted in powdered sugar, meant to tattle on those who sneak off with them by leaving a wispy trail of sugar."

She laughed then, an easy laugh. He was a great storyteller.

They chatted for several more hours, even after dinner walking the riverbank and enjoying one another's company, comparing cultures and childhood memories. A strange thing happened during their time together. She forgot to be self-conscious and nervous, and found herself laughing breezily and sharing in an open manner she had no idea she was capable of. Even when his comments grew personal.

"I see a hint of sadness when you speak of your family."

She let her eyes meet his own, knowing yet again he saw much deeper than the surface. "My mother recently passed away."

311

She couldn't help it. Her eyes suddenly teared. "I'm afraid I miss her terribly."

He touched her forearm. "I'm so sorry. I didn't know."

"Yes, only a couple weeks ago. Here on the Riverwalk, just several blocks away from where we were sitting." Her shoulders trembled, from the chill in the air or her emotions, she wasn't sure. Regardless, Cyril removed his jacket and draped it over her arms, his warmth and the light terpenic scent of his cologne evident.

"I find it remarkable you made yourself available to intercede with the authorities on behalf of Larimar Springs during such a personally trying time. I'm also aware you are close with Tavina Mosely. Yet you didn't buckle under the pressure."

He knew her assistant's name, again pointing to the fact no detail missed this man. He cared enough to assimilate the things that mattered. Maybe she was being overly sentimental, especially given the raw emotion connected to talking about losing her mom, but Cyril Montavan was someone worth knowing. Instinctively, she knew this man was light-years different from the overly ambitious and self-centered Greer Latham. She needed a friend — at least she tried to tell her head that she only saw him as a friend — and hoped they'd stay in touch.

When he walked her to the parking garage and they stood at her car, he voiced the same. "Dr. Ryan —"

"Juliet," she reminded him.

He smiled and nodded. "Juliet. I had a lovely afternoon. Frankly, I never planned to spend that much time away from the work waiting for me in my hotel suite. Regardless, I enjoyed spending this time together. I hope we'll have an opportunity to do this again."

In a brave move, she placed her hand on his arm. "I was just thinking the same."

She learned he was flying back to Italy over the weekend. "I've done all I can do here," he said. "From all indications, Larimar Springs is past the most critical danger. Now all we have to do is buoy public confidence and weather the litigation we all know will come." In an even bolder move, he tucked a stray piece of her hair behind her ear. "But I have faith things will work out."

And for the first time since that awful day when her mother died, Juliet dared to believe the same.

32

The first lawsuit was filed on the day before Thanksgiving, at precisely three o'clock in the afternoon and in plenty of time to hit the nightly news broadcasts. Named defendants included Larimar Springs Corporation, with Harris and Alexa Carmichael and Montavan International as shareholders.

Larimar's counsel, John Davison Lucier (and yes, he liked to go by all three names), called an immediate meeting in his downtown office. Everyone on the executive board was required to attend, despite many having travel plans for the holiday.

Mr. Lucier was an intense person who seemed to take great pleasure in making people jump when he instructed them to do so. Juliet found him one of the most arrogant men she'd ever encountered.

The first time he'd shown up at Larimar, she was struck by his plastic appearance. Texas had its share of overstretched women, but rarely did you see a man so acutely preserved.

Regardless, he had some impressive courtroom wins, including defending a highly publicized cruise line when hundreds of passengers fell ill as a result of a norovirus outbreak. Victory came when Mr. Lucier convinced a Texas jury that only the ordinary head cold was more common and his client could hardly be held culpable for an illness they had no chance of eradicating.

The other thing Juliet found strangely odd was that he always sported a red tie.

Today was no different.

Wearing a slate-gray suit and a bright red tie, he stood when his receptionist showed them in, and invited them to sit. Alexa slipped into one of the guest chairs in front of the desk, with Greer quickly taking the spot next to her. Juliet held back and positioned herself with Fred and Dale on the leather sofa against the wall to the right. Ellen Shaffer moved to a chair in the corner and prepared to take notes.

He made introductions from behind a massive desk with a black marble top, with absolutely nothing on it except for a leather portfolio engraved with his name and a black enameled Waterford fountain pen. The guy also kept his credenza and bookshelves cleared of paper of any kind. In fact, the whole room looked like a showroom for executive furniture, without any files in view.

"Thank you for coming," he said, and explained the lawsuit that had been filed was on behalf of a single plaintiff, an elderly woman who had lost kidney function and remained on dialysis. "There will be more," he promised, explaining he'd just gotten off the phone with plaintiffs' counsel and learned several more filings were in the wings. "His plan is to file individual cases in federal court and then petition to have a class certified."

"A what?" Fred asked.

Mr. Lucier sat straight-backed in his chair. "In layman's terms, a class action is where one representative action proceeds through the court system on behalf of a number of plaintiffs."

"Isn't that to our disadvantage?" Greer asked.

"Not necessarily. I'll argue that administrative consolidation would be just as effective. However, I intend to move that damages be determined on an individual basis."

He directed his attention to Alexa. "This is where we'll have an opportunity to negotiate low settlements that favor you."

She nodded. "I only hope this litigation

won't drag out for years. Our plan to go global is stymied until we get our legal matters resolved."

"Well, if you're willing to write big enough checks, this and all future cases will go away. But I caution, that will be costly. And if I've understood correctly, you've hired someone of my skill to make sure you only have to use the company change purse." He grinned.

Juliet's ears perked at the conversation in light of Alexa's earlier plan to pay for all the victims' medical expenses. Most of them in this room knew the financial outlay could grow to be a substantial amount, but that's why businesses carry multiple layers of liability insurance.

She scowled, hoping this guy hadn't talked Alexa into something else so he could grandstand. Ellen was right. If Larimar Springs had any opportunity to regain public sentiment, the effort would require an extraordinary show of compassion to the ones hurt in the outbreak. Plus it was the right thing to do.

Greer pulled on his cuffs and asked, "Tell us about plaintiffs' counsel. Is he any good?"

Mr. Lucier straightened even more, if that was possible. "I'm afraid he is. Leonard Paternoster is one of the premier food poisoning attorneys in the country. Don't get me wrong," he said. "I'm going to give him a run for his money, but Leo will be an extremely tough opponent."

Her palms went moist.

Why hadn't she seen this coming?

Of course the guy on the podium with her at the food safety symposium would rush to be involved in an outbreak of this magnitude. If the past was any indicator, Leo would paint the entire situation as a fast-moving disaster that had been entirely preventable — especially given her level of knowledge and expertise. She could even hear him using her speech that day against her.

He'd made a name for himself in this kind of litigation, and he wouldn't stop until everyone associated with Larimar Springs' role in the outbreak had been pushed to the creek bottom, with no air to breathe.

Her fears were immediately affirmed.

"The biggest obstacle we'll face is in discovery. If any suitable fact is uncovered, Leo Paternoster will push for punitives. That's when we'll be talking serious money. I've even seen occasions where he's amended to name individual executives and board members to his list of defendants, and in some cases he's been successful."

Greer paled. "How could he name the executives individually? We don't share ownership. And except for Dr. Ryan, none of us were charged with the responsibility for detecting pathogens in our product and keeping these organisms from harming the public."

Juliet's blood surged. The creep was acting like a jilted junior high football jock in need of more acne medicine. Because of his bruised pride, he'd throw her under the bus at any opportunity.

Inside she dared to smile, knowing a day was coming when he'd be sorry he took that approach, given she'd soon be president and he'd report directly to her. Of course, as soon as Alexa made the announcement, Juliet fully expected that Greer would elect to resign. She took great satisfaction in anticipating that moment.

Even so, the pleasure she'd get from Greer's reaction wouldn't erase the risk she, and apparently the others in this room, faced.

Their wrinkle-free attorney had made his assessment clear.

Leo Paternoster would be out for blood.

33

Juliet woke on Thanksgiving morning feeling alone and restless. Rather than sitting home feeling sad, she headed for Children's Hospital to offer Tavina a break. If she'd even go for it.

Knowing Tavina had rarely left her little son's bedside since his admittance, Juliet had arranged for dinner for her and her mom and brothers at Morton's Steakhouse. The downtown location would be close to the hospital, and the town car Alexa had made available could transport them. She'd even thought to stop at Nordstrom's and pick up fresh outfits for Tavina and her mother, and jackets for the guys.

It would do all of them good to spend some time together away from nurses, heart monitors, and plastic dining trays of hospital food. Especially on a holiday.

Tavina put up a fight, of course. Thankfully, her mother gently guided her into changing her mind, reassuring her with the promise Juliet would take her place by MD's bed and would call them immediately back to the hospital if needed. They could get back in minutes should anything come up. Besides, her mama reminded her, little Marquis DeAndre had been holding his own now for days.

"C'mon, honey," she urged her daughter. "It'll do you good."

Tavina rolled her tired eyes. "All right," she said, finally giving in. After changing in the bathroom down the hall, she leaned down and kissed her son's forehead. "Be good, little man. Mommy will only be gone for a little while." She teared up while brushing the back of her hand across his cheek. "Bye, baby."

The Mosely family had only been gone a short time when Juliet moved from the larger chair by the wall to a small, hard plastic one next to the gurney holding the little guy hooked up to IVs, monitors, and catheters.

His black curly hair was sweaty and matted, his skin the color of dried-out mud. Deep blue circles rimmed puffy eyelids, shiny from ointment applied to lubricate and keep his tear ducts moist while he was on the ventilator.

The sight made her throat ache and left her chest cavity weighted like rocks. She struggled to swallow the emotion.

How did Tavina do it? Sit here all day watching her baby waste away?

Recent tests indicated a possibility his bowel was bleeding internally — at least intermittently. Very soon a decision would have to be made about whether he was strong enough to survive surgery to remove a portion of his colon, which doctors hoped would eliminate a great deal of the toxins from his system but would leave him dependent on a colostomy bag. Maybe for his entire life.

Out in the hallway, Tavina's brother had told Juliet the risks were very high. By doing the procedure, complications could arise, including severe hypotension and compromised cardiac functioning.

Until the surgical team gave the go-ahead, MD mainly slept, and his anxious family waited.

She gently rubbed his little arm. "I'm so sorry, little buddy," she said, remembering the Jack in the Box case that had pressed her into this profession in the first place.

She kept fingering his wrist, letting her mind drift to his mother. In normal times, she'd likely have ignored professional propriety and confided in her assistant that she'd seen Cyril Montavan yesterday when she got home.

She'd try to portray her interest as merely casual as she shared he'd been married, but lost his wife to cancer nearly four years ago. One internet article said he'd taken a leave of absence and never left her side.

He was even on the board of several nonprofit foundations. One was based here in Texas and raised money for a feeding program and to build water wells in some of the hardest-hit areas of Angola and South Sudan. Another focused on ending sexual exploitation of children in Thailand. Both had Christian affiliations. A fact that would've thrilled her mother.

She could hear Tavina say it was about time for her to hook up with someone like that. "Girl," she'd say, "life's too short to go living it alone."

Of course, then she'd have to remind her assistant she was a pot calling the kettle black.

Together, they'd have a good laugh. Especially at her choice of words.

Tavina was like that — easy to be with, a girl who had learned to travel life holding tight to a ticket with JOY printed across the front in large, bold letters. Despite much hardship, the beautiful girl knew what mattered and didn't bother messing around with anything that didn't.

She sure didn't deserve this.

Juliet had given a lot of thought as to how she could make up for the medical horror her spunky assistant had to endure.

When made president of Larimar Springs, she'd promote Tavina and provide a compensation package that would make these ventilators and heart monitors a far distant memory. She'd help her find a house in Stone Oak, a gated community filled with families. Despite any lingering medical frailties, little MD could swim and go to camp with other kids in the affluent neighborhood, even if a nursing companion was required. Private schools and the best colleges would be made available. Given the chance, Juliet would make things right.

She had to, because no matter what anyone said, her company was responsible for MD being here.

Suddenly, a machine to the right of the bed started buzzing loudly.

Juliet jumped from her chair, looking frantically at the foreign equipment. Another beeped — then another. And they kept beeping.

Something was terribly wrong. "Help!"

she screamed.

A nurse dashed to the door. One look and she yelled in the direction of the nurses' station, "Get the crash cart! STAT!"

Immediately, medical professionals swarmed the room. Someone grabbed Juliet's arm and pulled her to the door. "Out," she was told.

Frantic, she pulled her phone from her pocket and punched Tavina's number. When she answered, Juliet could barely choke out the words.

"Tavina — you've got to come quick."

34

Marquis DeAndre Mosely died at 8:32 p.m. on Thanksgiving Day.

Within only minutes of the machines alerting there was a problem, his little body reacted to a recent increase in platelet dysfunction, and MD started seizing.

By the time Tavina rushed back into his room, pushing through the crowd of white coats with her elbows to get at his bedside, he'd slipped into a coma, a result of acute and sudden cardiovascular collapse. After that, there was very little anyone could do to reverse the situation.

Within days, Mrs. Mosely packed up her broken daughter and moved her to New Orleans to be near family. There would be no funeral. "I can't," Tavina muttered between sobs. "I — I just can't do it."

Juliet helped her brothers hire a moving company and put her landlord on notice that Tavina would be terminating her apartment lease.

With the outbreak winding down, and Alexa's decision to place production on hold until after the first of the year, the quality control activities at Larimar Springs were on pause, allowing Juliet to take some much-needed vacation time.

The first week, she ended up wandering her house in pajamas, unable to clear her mind of the look in Tavina's eyes or stop hearing her animal-like moan when she learned her baby was gone.

She didn't eat. Didn't sleep.

Milk soured in the refrigerator.

The bed didn't get made.

Emails and phone calls went unanswered — even those from Cyril Montavan.

She'd spend her mornings watching hosts tout purses and kitchen mixers on QVC while thumbing through old *People* magazines her mother had given her last spring, thinking she might enjoy them. Her afternoons were filled with old movies on cable or network talk shows — the ones where real people openly revealed all their problems in front of a studio audience, something she'd never in a million years do.

She didn't need Dr. Oz or Oprah to know why she was an emotional wreck.

The combined loss of her mother, the

stress of the outbreak, and now the over-whelming sadness and guilt over MD's early demise had pulled her legs out from under her. She'd lost her ability to cope.

Over and over, she tried to tell herself that there hadn't been anything she could've done to prevent this outbreak, that the ship had set sail before she ever got on board. Without the understanding of what Robin Ford knew back in those critical months, what could she have done, really?

She could have followed up on that envelope. That's what.

Maybe the answers wouldn't have saved little MD, but she'd easily shifted the unanswered questions aside, relishing the promises of promotion Alexa made.

She'd even let herself consider a new friendship with Cyril Montavan, thinking of her own personal happiness, never realizing that in days Tavina's precious little son would take his last worn-out breath.

All these thoughts were threatening to take her under, so to speak. She was floating the Comal River in a leaky tub and would sink if she didn't start paddling — *but how?*

By the beginning of the second week, the walls of her place started to close in and she decided to take a drive, just to get out for a while. Maybe stop at the store, since the hall closet had only one roll of toilet paper left on the shelf.

Without bothering with makeup, she pulled on a pair of jeans and a sweater and headed for her car in the dim light of late afternoon.

Leaving her neighborhood, she became aware that brightly colored holiday lights lined the eaves of nearby houses and blanketed shrubs and trees.

Christmas was only a few weeks away, and she'd almost forgotten. Subconsciously, she must've realized she couldn't deal with the painful thought of a Christmas morning without her mom. Not added to everything else.

While driving toward downtown, she tried to conjure her mother's voice saying how pretty everything was this time of year — especially the blue lights. Her favorites.

For the first time, Juliet struggled to catch the cadence of her mother's sound in her head, how she drawled her vowels like a true Texan, as if she'd grown up here and not in the Pacific Northwest.

She couldn't hear her mother's voice.

Juliet's fingers tightened on the steering wheel. She needed to get a grip. Clear her head.

With that thought in mind, she exited the

freeway onto Commerce and turned north at the light in the direction of the Alamo, drawn to the Menger Hotel, where her father used to take her when she was little for her own personal history lesson.

She remembered standing at the entrance of the bar as a child, peeking inside while holding her father's hand. He'd let go and knelt beside her, pointing through the door. "That is the very room, JuJu, where Theodore Roosevelt organized the first US volunteer cavalry known as the Rough Riders, which valiantly fought the San Juan Hill battle in Cuba during the Spanish-American War."

Later at home, he'd helped her look up more information in their Encyclopedia Britannica set so she could write a report for extra credit at school. He'd even grabbed one of her Crayolas and joined her in coloring a crudely drawn picture of Teddy Roosevelt in his blue uniform.

Even in recent years, the bar was one of her father's favorite places to meet his professor chums. Which made the strange fact she'd ended up here now even more odd.

She walked through the nearly empty establishment, past dark wood-paneled walls to a stool perched at the bar counter.

A massive tavern mirror mounted behind the bar reflected her image, and a taxidermy moose head hung on a nearby wall.

For the first time in over a week, her mouth turned up at the corners. She couldn't help but smile, considering the fascination her father had for this place.

"Evening." A gentleman with wide sideburns compensating for a balding head greeted her while wiping the counter. "What can I get you?"

Not a frequent drinker, she wasn't sure. Her eyes roamed the collection of liquor bottles. A small voice inside her head warned she might want to order a safe glass of chardonnay, but after this past week she decided to throw caution to the wind.

No matter what Alexa and Cyril had tried to tell her, she struggled with the feeling that she should have been able to do something — that Tavina's little boy was gone because of an outbreak under her watch. Even given the former QA director's issues, what good had all those increased safety protocols been if little boys like Marquis DeAndre Mosely would never grow up because of what had happened at her company?

"I'll, uh . . . let's see, let's try a bourbon on the rocks." She wedged her purse on the floor at the base of the stool.

"Any particular label?"

She looked up. "No . . . uh, on second thought, I'll have a beer. That one." She pointed to a bottle with a long neck.

The bartender nodded and folded his bar rag. "We have that on tap as well. Which would you prefer?"

She scowled. "Do people drink beer in frosted mugs?"

He grinned. "Some do."

Juliet smiled back. "Yeah, then. I'll have that. A bottle and the mug. Thank you."

The beer tasted harsh and slightly acrid. Despite how the amber liquid tasted every time she took a swallow, she grimaced and took another. In between long, carefully measured breaths to catch her air.

Unsure exactly how long she'd been sitting there, only that her mug had been refilled a lot of times, she summoned the bartender by wiggling her fingers. "Excuse me? Do you sell cigarettes? I'm dying for a smoke." She smirked and lightly jiggled her mug, sending the tiny bit of beer in the bottom sloshing over the top. "I quit. Awhile ago, actually. Oh, except for that one night." Lifting an unsteady arm, she waved off her comment. "But that shouldn't really count."

He pulled his attention from the television

mounted on the wall. "Sorry, we don't. I think there's a vending machine out by the gift shop."

She let out a heavy sigh. "Yeah, okay."

He leaned back against the counter holding the cash register and folded his arms. "You look like you're having a bad night."

Her finger slid around the rim of the glass. "Do you know that nursery rhyme 'Itsy Bitsy Spider'?"

"You mean the one about the spider that climbs up the waterspout but keeps getting washed out every time?"

She nodded, her head suddenly feeling heavy. "Yeah, that one. I'm that spider."

An older guy in a button-down with the collar open who'd been sitting at the opposite end of the bar stood and picked up his beer bottle. He sauntered over. "Whatcha drinking there, sister?"

Before she could answer, he leaned over the bar. "Hey there, Hank, fix the lady up and put it on my tab." He slid onto the barstool next to her and extended his hand. "I'm Stanley."

She shook his hand, noting a heavy gold-link bracelet at his wrist. "Hi . . . I'm Juliet."

"Yeah? What do you do?"

She took a deep breath and looked him

straight in the eyes. "I'm a professional killer."

She could tell from his expression her comment took him back a bit. He gave her an odd smirk. "Like your work?"

She squinted. "Yes and no. Long hours and a lot of stress — but when your head hits the pillow at night, you're blessed with a warm feeling knowing you tore someone's heart out." Her eyes pooled with tears and she gave a loud sniff.

The bartender stood, wiping his hands on a bar towel. "Maybe you've had enough."

She looked at him in misery. "Ha, that's where you're wrong. There's never enough."

"Juliet?"

Startled, she turned to face the familiar voice. "Oh great!" Juliet waved her arm in that direction. "See what I mean? That waterspout thing again."

Her father bent and grabbed her purse. "C'mon, let's get you home."

She pulled away. "No."

His face grew sympathetic. He turned to the bartender. "Could you call us a cab?" He gently placed his hand on her back. "Look, I know you're going through a rough time."

"Oh, don't give me that smug look. I've survived worse, you know." Juliet nodded sloppily. "Yes, you do know."

He leaned close and whispered, "Yeah, I made mistakes, including too much of that." He pointed to her mug. "I'm different now."

"Ha, says who?"

Her father winced. "In so many ways, you're still that same little girl in class wearing her white lab coat, trying to hide her feelings."

"I am not," she argued. "How would you know anyway? You were never around enough to know." She narrowed her eyes. "You were too busy with *Naaancy.* And all the others."

She hated seeing the hurt in his eyes, hearing the miserably mean sound of her own voice. Her mother would be ashamed.

He stepped back and sighed. "JuJu, you have many admirable qualities. But remember this very important thing." He brushed a damp strand of hair off her forehead. "Without a heart and soul, you have nothing."

Her father retrieved her keys and handed them to the bartender. "Make sure she gets in that cab." To the guy hitting on her, he said, "No offense, but this one's off-limits tonight."

She frowned. The guy nodded and downed his drink. "No problem. I was just going anyway." He nodded in Juliet's direction. "Good luck to you, Miss Spider." The guy sauntered into the hotel lobby.

Her father moved for the street entrance. He stopped at the door and looked back. "I'm here, Juliet, if you ever need me."

Then he turned and walked out.

35

Larimar Springs' legal situation ramped up when Leo Paternoster filed seven more cases the week of Christmas. Trolling for victims via standard advertising was considered crass in most legal circles, but a well-connected friend working for the *Express-News* had proven very helpful to the ambitious plaintiffs' attorney. Especially when a well-timed feature article with an extensive interview appeared on the front page.

Mr. Lucier proved to be quite the taskmaster, and never more than when the process of collecting documents began.

"I'm fairly old school," he warned. "I don't use paralegals. I learn the intricacies of my case by poring over the documentary evidence myself."

In a document-heavy case like this, he used the services of a discovery vendor who would forensically scour all the relevant servers and extract responsive emails and files. In addition, they would create digital images of any paper files, and load disks would be provided to opposing counsel. "After I've completed a thorough privilege review," he explained.

The effort to respond to what seemed like mountains of requests for production felt overwhelming and left Juliet's head spinning. Unfortunately, there was no way out of the task.

Boxes of files retrieved from off-site storage were stacked nearly ceiling high in a room temporarily dubbed the War Room. Long folding tables lined the walls where she and Malcolm Stanford spent long hours sifting through the contents and creating an inventory, carefully following Mr. Lucier's written instructions.

When she expressed appreciation, Malcolm simply said, "I'm as anxious as anyone to get to the bottom of all this."

Another person who hadn't changed his colors was Greer. He showed up at her condo on Christmas Eve, his voice thick and smelling of alcohol. He carried a bottle of champagne and a grin. "Hey, truce?" he said when she opened the door. "Neither of us should be alone at Christmas."

Even the sight of an alcohol bottle caused

an involuntary shudder. After that night at the Menger, she'd been so sick she'd spent the next morning with her face resting on the bathroom floor.

She shook her head. "Look, Greer, this isn't a good idea." Despite her former beau's pitiful face, she stood firm. "Go home."

She waited for his flash of anger. Instead, he simply slumped against the door frame. "Okay," he said, his voice slightly slurred. "I suppose it was stupid of me to just show up like this." He held out the champagne. "Regardless, this is for you."

She took the bottle from his hand, more to hasten his departure than anything.

Greer leaned and stroked her cheek. "Well, merry Christmas."

She pulled away. "Maybe you'd better let me call you a cab."

Greer grinned. "Don't need to." He pointed down the hallway. "Already got one waiting downstairs."

As soon as he turned for the elevator, Juliet shut the door and leaned against it, knowing if the cad had shown up several hours earlier, she might have been tempted to be stupid and invite him in, just to turn off the painful memories playing in her head. Memories of her mother's salt-crusted

prime rib roast and her crème brûlée —
served every year. Or the traditional gift
opened on Christmas Eve — flannel pajamas always decorated with reindeers or
snowflakes.

She'd protested the ritual, but the antics
made her father grin, especially last year
when he'd taken her mother in his arms and
teased, "Want Rudolph's red nose to guide
your sleigh?" She laughed and slapped him
away. "Not on Frosty's corn cob pipe."

There was no question Juliet had made a
complete fool of herself in front of him at
the Menger. No doubt he was glad to spend
Christmas alone this year, happy not to have
to put up with his hostile offspring.

And she didn't have to put up with Greer
Latham just because he found himself all
alone on Christmas Eve.

The doorbell rang. She sighed and moved
to answer it, bracing herself for a second
encounter with Greer. If the guy was anything, he was a salesman — never taking no
for an answer.

But instead, she pulled the knob to find a
guy in a FedEx uniform and a Santa cap.
He grinned and pointed to a large box
loaded on his hand truck. "Looks like
someone's been a good girl this year."

Puzzled, she took the box from his hand

and thanked him. After wishing him a merry Christmas, she shut the door and set the package on her kitchen counter, took a kitchen knife and sliced the strapping tape, then carefully lifted the flaps and peeked inside.

The box was filled with green Styrofoam peanuts surrounding a white container made of thermal material meant to refrigerate during transport.

She lifted her brows, now very curious.

Her fingers carefully lifted the lid, freeing it from the bottom portion of the container. Immediately, her face broke into a huge smile.

He didn't.

Inside, the container held layers of large strips of fried pastry dough, drizzled with rich dark chocolate and smothered in white powdered sugar. Grinning, she inhaled the faint vanilla scent.

Cyril had sent her bugies — all the way from Italy.

In the hours following, she enjoyed nearly all of them, nibbling on the messy treats and drinking cups of French roast. The perfect accompaniment to hours of the televised musical *White Christmas*.

The thoughtful gesture got her through the holidays.

That, and attending Christmas Eve service at her mother's church.

She hadn't been back to Talavera Community Church since her mother's memorial service, despite many emails from Pastor Roper inviting her to services. She almost had a panic attack walking from the crowded parking lot to the sidewalk lined with luminarias. Perhaps she'd made a mistake in believing she could do this, she told herself. But once she was inside, the overwhelming masses of potted poinsettias and lights, mixed with the smell of real pine, caused a certain peace, as if her mother, who adored Christmas, walked alongside her.

Hoping to remain inconspicuous, she slipped into a pew at the back of the sanctuary several minutes after the service started, positioning herself behind a geriatric couple with white hair and matching hearing aids. As the choir sang "Away in a Manger," the woman leaned her head against the man's stooped shoulder. The sight warmed Juliet's heart, and she couldn't help but wonder if that might've been her own parents if things had turned out differently.

If her father hadn't strayed.

If she hadn't held so tightly to her anger that day.

Pastor Roper stepped to the podium and read the account of Mary and Joseph and the birth of baby Jesus from the Gospel of Luke. When he'd finished, candles were passed and the room dimmed.

Across the aisle, a young boy about nine or so, dressed in slacks and a white button-down with a tie, helped his little sister light her candle. Their mother smiled her approval as the choir sang and the orchestra played "O Holy Night."

The words rang out in the hushed room. *Till he appeared and the soul felt its worth.*

That was when she saw him. Second pew from the front. Holding a lit candle with his head bowed.

Her father.

36

On the first Monday following the New Year, the executive team gathered in the conference room with Mr. Lucier for their weekly litigation meeting.

"As far as I can determine, every single box falls within the time frame included in opposing counsel's requests and your memo," Juliet reported.

"Why aren't we fighting to narrow what we have to give them?" Greer asked.

Their attorney straightened his red tie and grinned. "Paternoster hopes we'll focus on all this paper instead of the upcoming depositions, but my approach is to turn the tables. Give them even more than they ask for. Their side has to review all this as well. Granted, he'll use a team of paralegals, but the process is expensive. And we'll shut down any argument that we haven't been cooperative if they try to raise an issue with the judge."

He turned to Dale Frissom. "You've collected the production records and the employment files I asked for?"

Dale nodded. "And then some."

There was a light knock and Mr. Lucier's assistant opened the door. "John, you're going to want to see this."

He waved her in and took a set of papers from her hand while sliding his reading glasses in place. His face drew into a scowl as he scanned the documents. When he finished, he looked over top his readers at Alexa. "Well, we have another plaintiff."

Alexa frowned. "Who?"

"Tavina Mosely."

Juliet shouldn't have been surprised at the news Tavina had looked to legal means to seek damages. After all, she'd lost her little boy because Larimar Springs marketed a product that contained a deadly form of E. coli. Her actions were completely understandable.

Still, she'd naïvely held out hope her trusted assistant would hold off and let Alexa fully recompense her outside of formal litigation, and that once Juliet was president, Tavina might rejoin the company and let Juliet help build her career.

Joining in legal action against the company

had many ramifications, including putting Juliet's ideas for Tavina's professional future at risk. Alexa would likely never consent to rehiring her now. A boundary had been crossed, trust breached.

Sadly, Tavina's decision to sue made clear that notion went both ways.

Juliet now understood why Tavina's mother had quit answering her phone calls to check on Tavina.

To make matters worse, Angela Silva, the temp from American Staffing, had given an interview to the *Express-News* telling what was going on *inside* the company during the first weeks of the outbreak. The story painted Alexa and her team as high-strung and nearly incompetent managers, mired in their own personal aspirations that kept them from properly responding to early reports of illness. "For example, my impression was that the quality assurance director, Dr. Ryan, was far more concerned with her, uh, shall we say *interpersonal* relationships with some of the team members than those falling victim to this horrible illness."

Alexa threw the newspaper across her office, exhibiting Juliet's exact reaction. "How dare someone I employed — even temporarily — turn on this company?" She punched out their attorney's number on the phone. "Did you see this morning's head-lines?" she demanded when he answered.

Over the speakerphone, he advised he had. "You can also bet she's talking off record to Paternoster."

Alexa huffed. "I want you to sue her. And American Staffing. She was under an employment contract that had a confidentiality clause, for goodness' sake."

"I will," he responded. "But now is not the proper time. When we finish settling these cases, we'll be better able to attribute the damage she's caused. In the meantime, I've asked the judge for a restraining order shutting down any further contact she might have with the media. I've also been in contact with the staffing agency's attorney, and he assures me his client is appalled at her actions and will take any appropriate measures to hinder her behavior. They'll file a countersuit against her, I'm sure. Even so, I'm afraid the harm is done."

Alexa looked at Juliet. "What more can she say?"

Juliet snuck a glance at Greer before shaking her head. "Nothing that I'm aware of."

After Alexa hung up with Mr. Lucier, she turned to Dale. "Doesn't your HR manager vet these contract employees?"

Juliet almost felt sorry for Dale as she

watched him scramble to assure his boss all proper precautions were utilized. Regardless, nothing he said seemed to make a difference. Alexa was testy, and growing more so as the days went by.

The frazzled CEO had skipped taking any time off for the holidays, sending her husband and son on to Sun Valley for a ski trip without her. With so much at stake, she spent nearly every waking moment at the office and expected the same of her executive team.

Even with the recent rapport Juliet had established, on one occasion Alexa had even fussed at her when she'd brought up the subject of the PCR thermal cycler that had been placed on hold in budget meetings last fall. "Alexa, now that we've started production again, I recommend we incorporate the equipment into our program as early as possible as an added layer of safety."

"If you're going to be president of this company, start acting like it and make some independent decisions," she snapped. "You have a budget. Use it as you see fit."

Juliet's breath caught. "Certainly," she responded. "I'm glad you have that level of trust in me."

The following week, the situation worsened and Juliet's concerns increased when she overheard shouting coming from Alexa's open office door late at night.

"I don't care what it takes, John. Before this outbreak, I had this company poised to go national, and with the help of Montavan, our ten-year plan could include an international market. Now do whatever you have to do to put this nonsense behind us so we can move forward. And do it without breaking the bank." Her voice was unyielding. "In case I need to spell things out and make my position more clear, I hired you to negotiate these settlements in our favor — as quick and low as possible. Understood?"

There was a short pause. Not one to skulk outside someone's office listening to a private conversation, Juliet couldn't seem to move away.

"What do you mean a mess?" Alexa screeched.

Juliet startled at the sound of something crashing against the wall.

"Yeah, you do that. I'm paying you enormous sums, now fix this." The phone slammed, followed by slammed drawers.

Juliet turned and moved silently back to her office, pondering what she'd overheard. The position was definitely counter to Alexa's public stance, and most certainly what she'd told Juliet privately.

She fingered her neckline. The acid in Alexa's voice left her unsettled. Either her boss was coming completely undone — or Juliet had been fished like a largemouth bass, lured with a tangled line of malarkey and empty promises.

Anxiety knotted her gut. She hoped Alexa could be trusted.

37

By April, the litigation gravy train (a term often used by Alexa in their weekly meetings) was moving down the track full steam.

In addition to numerous additional victims filing complaints, Water Circus cross-complained against Larimar Springs, alleging breach of warranty and of contract, as well as negligence and negligent interference with economic relations. They asserted that Larimar Springs had delivered contaminated bottled water to Water Circus and that this conduct had exposed Water Circus to liability and lost business after the E. coli outbreak.

Courtroom battles were mounted over discovery disputes, with the judge generally favoring plaintiffs and allowing broad reach in every instance.

As Mr. Lucier predicted, the court stayed the motion for class certification, instead administratively consolidating the cases for discovery and liability phases, promising to bifurcate the matters when it came time to determine damages.

The judge also warned he would be strongly urging mediation as early as practical.

In a very short time, everyone on the executive team became immersed in Litigation 101, and also realized the company's financial exposure was fast climbing past their primary liability coverage and would tap into their excess coverage, prompting yet another layer of attorneys to the mix.

Worse, Juliet knew Alexa had more to think about than resolving the company's legal issues. She needed to restore credibility among their customers. Now that the insurers held the purse strings, she no longer had the final say when it came to legal strategy, creating a tension-filled situation.

For example, Alexa hit the roof when Ellen Shaffer reported she and her public relations firm were getting calls from reporters wanting to know why the company was going back on its word to pay for the victims' care.

Despite knowing she'd catch the ire of Mr. Lucier and the insurers' legal counsel, Alexa instructed Ellen to issue a release in which she stated, "Larimar Springs wants desperately to do what is right here. And the right thing is to own up to our responsibility and pay for the expenses incurred when these poor people were in the hospital and needing medical care. Unfortunately, the legal system prohibits our ability to freely exercise that desire."

"What were you thinking?" Mr. Lucier demanded when he found out. His neck bulged with blue veins. "You might as well have sent the judge a 'kiss my heinie' letter with his ruling stapled to the back."

Despite the circus-like atmosphere created by all the legal wrangling, Alexa never succumbed to another outburst like the one Juliet had overheard outside her office door. That was not to say she didn't remain wary and on the lookout for fissures in her boss's censured exterior.

Juliet's future career would be iced if Alexa failed to keep it together, failed to keep the company running despite the giant boulders blocking the road to financial recovery, or failed to follow through on her intention to make Juliet president.

After she'd headed up the quality control effort at a company responsible for an outbreak of this magnitude, little doubt there'd be no other corporate ladder for her to climb. And without that promised promotion, her effectiveness at Larimar Springs would limp along crippled, at best.

Through it all, and despite the rogue actions of his client, John Davison Lucier promised that everything was still going according to plan and cool heads would prevail. Even the greediest plaintiffs' attorneys would agree that the expense of protracted litigation with costly experts and a lengthy trial would never net the financial rewards they'd enjoy via a successful mediation and settlement.

Sadly, that juncture remained in the distance until discovery wound to a close and a few key depositions were taken — to satisfy the legal minds that nothing had been left on the table in terms of punitives. After finding no smoking guns in any of the documentary evidence, even Leo Paternoster knew a more limited approach held wisdom.

That didn't stop the shrewd attorney from noticing up Alexa's deposition, with several more to follow, including Juliet's. Clearly, his intent was to leave no stone unturned prior to accepting any settlement offer.

On the morning of her deposition, Alexa showed up at the court reporters' offices dressed in a tailored Yves Saint Laurent suit, taupe colored with a subtle hint of gray woven into the fabric. Creamy silk ruffles peeked out at the collar, accented with a gold and pearl necklace and a thin yet simple sculptural gold cuff on her wrist. On her feet, she wore red-soled Christian Louboutin patent leather pumps, not for the video camera audience, but a statement for those in the room.

Usually, Alexa pulled her hair back into a woven knot at the nape of her neck, but today she stepped away from her norm and left her blonde hair down in a soft bob, with her lips painted bright scarlet, following Ellen Shaffer's advice. "The combination will signal like a red flag that you are emotionally connected to the victims in this case, yet fully in charge in every business sense."

The deposition would take place in a large conference room at the court reporters' offices located on an upper floor of the Omni Hotel. Allowed inside the deposition room would be the stenographer and videographer, along with the deponent and one attorney from each side, with their respective paralegals. Everyone else, including Juliet, would be in an adjacent room watching a live feed of both the video and a synchronized electronic transcript of the testimony. The judge would be on standby to resolve any significant disputes beyond the standard objections often made for the record by counsel during these proceedings.

Alexa was seated at the end of the table, centered in front of a photo backdrop. The court reporter clipped a microphone in place while Mr. Lucier sat opposite Mr. Paternoster and his paralegal, a young guy with blond hair and an infectious smile. Earlier, he'd wheeled in a couple of banker boxes on a hand truck and had been introduced as Seth Jinks. "This guy here has been with me over five years and is better than three associates put together," plaintiffs' counsel claimed.

Alexa poured herself a glass of water and took a sip. She leaned back and gave those in the room a comfortable smile, as if giving deposition testimony was an everyday occurrence.

"You ready?" the court reporter asked.

She nodded, cleared her throat, and directed her attention to Mr. Paternoster, waiting for him to begin.

He too cleared his throat. "Good morning. Could you please state your full name for the record?"

"Alexa Andora Carmichael. I'm the chief executive officer and current president of Larimar Springs Corporation, and I'm also the majority shareholder, holding 75 percent interest."

Mr. Paternoster lifted his chin. "Please limit your responses to the questions I pose."

Juliet noted a twinkle in her boss's eyes and knew she would never subordinate to his wishes. She also knew Mr. Lucier had spent hours preparing Alexa for her testimony. Everything had been well-rehearsed, including this tactical approach.

Primarily, Alexa needed to adamantly stay consistent on two things. First, that she had no knowledge of the bottles of water tainted with E. coli found in the warehouse prior to the CDC's alert. Second, that as the top corporate official, she had taken every precaution to put the people and procedures in place intended to eliminate a risk of this sort. If Alexa stuck to those themes, opposing counsel could do very little to make a case for punitives.

Leo Paternoster's mission was as straightforward — to establish she *should* have known and acted to protect his clients.

The first hour was taken up with preliminary questions — the history of the company, Alexa's background, her education and work history.

After a quick break, the questions became more focused.

"Now, Ms. Carmichael, let's go through your corporate structure." He buried his attention in the papers before him.

"The structure is simple. The entire executive team reports directly to me."

Mr. Paternoster looked up. "Would you care to wait for a question?"

Alexa reached for her glass and smiled. "Certainly."

He looked across the table at Mr. Lucier as if to elicit his help. Mr. Lucier simply stared back, his face void of expression.

Mr. Paternoster leaned his arm on the dark wood table. He drew a deep breath. "You've stated the entire executive team reports directly to you. Please identify the members of the executive team and state their general areas of responsibility."

Alexa nodded. "Greer Latham heads up our marketing and sales effort. Fred Macklin is our chief financial officer. Dale Frissom is the director of operations, which includes human resources, bottling, warehousing and distribution, and purchasing. And last spring, Dr. Juliet Ryan replaced Robin Ford as our quality assurance director. She supervises all the testing and lab operations. As I earlier stated, each of these individuals reports directly to me as the chief executive officer."

Mr. Paternoster thanked her. "Now, for the record, please identify which of these individuals was terminated as a result of the outbreak that is the subject of this litigation."

Watching the large monitor from the adjoining room, Juliet held her breath. Opposing counsel had taken off the proverbial gloves and was ready for a fight.

Alexa straightened. Nothing in her expression changed as she smiled and gave her response. "No one employed by Larimar Springs was terminated as a result of the outbreak."

Mr. Paternoster leaned back. His eyebrows lifted. "No one?"

"No one," she repeated.

"Not one single person on your executive team was held responsible for making dozens of people sick?" He wasn't ratcheting up for a jury, so clearly he wanted to ruffle his deponent.

Mr. Lucier, who had yet to say a word on record, scribbled something on the lined pad in front of him. "Objection. Argumentative. Assumes facts not in evidence."

Mr. Paternoster smirked. "Withdrawn."

Alexa took another drink of water and repositioned herself in the chair.

"Ms. Carmichael, prior to fall of last year

when you learned Water Circus patrons were falling ill, what did you know of E. coli O157:H7?"

"Despite the almost nonexistent occurrence of outbreaks connected to bottled water, it was common knowledge in food industry circles that particular bacteria could be virulent and make consumers ill. I was aware of regulations and safety standards that required certain precautions. I hired a highly educated person who was an expert in this field and gave her full support."

"You're referring to Dr. Juliet Ryan?"

"Yes. Dr. Ryan was charged with making sure Larimar Springs was compliant with all health regulations. She was also the one assigned to be the liaison with government officials once Larimar Springs had been identified as the source."

"And which of your executive team members was charged with knowing pallets of bottled water tainted with the deadly O157:H7 pathogen were being shipped to Water Circus and would be distributed to consumers?"

Once again, Mr. Lucier injected a comment onto the record. "Leo, I'd like to direct you to my client's responses to your interrogatories and requests for admission.

We've clearly stated in the record that Larimar Springs produced, stored, and later distributed bottled water containing E. coli. As noted, these events happened while Dr. Ryan's predecessor, Robin Ford, was employed by Larimar Springs. During that time, Ms. Ford grew ill, and the company remains baffled as to why these pallets physically remained in the warehouse while not showing up in the electronic inventories. We can only conclude this to be an error by someone no longer employed by Larimar Springs."

Mr. Paternoster clicked his pen several times. "Thank you for your testimony, counsel. If you don't mind, I'd like the deponent's take on the matter."

Turning from Mr. Lucier, plaintiffs' counsel directed his attention at Alexa. "Your attorney has gone on the record stating the company was" — he checked the live feed on his laptop monitor — "uh, yes — 'the company remains *baffled* as to why these pallets physically remained in the warehouse while not showing up in the electronic inventories.' " He looked back at Alexa. "Is that your testimony here today? Do you personally remain baffled —"

She didn't wait for him to finish. "I am not only personally baffled, but I'm appalled that this happened." Her eyes teared. "Unfortunately, the person I had assigned to identify and thwart any potential for our product to fall below the government standards was struggling with her own serious health issues at the time. She assured me necessary precautions had been taken. I trusted her."

Alexa rushed to add, "We had no reason to suspect —" She faltered. "I mean, there was no way for us to know until all this." She lifted the glass and took another drink. Her voice choked with emotion. "If I could turn the clock back, I would. I can't."

Mr. Paternoster rubbed between his brows. "That was a nice little speech, Ms. Carmichael. Now —"

Ignoring the fact opposing counsel was posing another question, she continued. "Currently, I have the future of nearly three hundred people who work for this company to consider. I have faithful employees nearing retirement, people sending children off to college." Her chin quivered. "Many people fell ill, and some even died as a result of this unfortunate accident," she said. "Even the tiny son of one of my own employees didn't make it." Her eyes filled with determination. "No one at Larimar Springs *let* this happen. And now it's my job to make sure these victims have all their medical expenses paid, while keeping the company financially viable so the people employed by my company remain financially secure."

Juliet frowned. The spiel sounded oddly familiar.

Attorneys sitting in the room with her furiously scribbled notes in their leather portfolios. One tapped out a text on his phone.

On the big monitor, Alexa tucked her hair behind her ear. And that was when Juliet's breath caught. She leaned forward and stared, heat surging through her body.

Hanging at Alexa's ear was a gold earring.

The same earrings she'd seen on Greer Latham's bathroom counter.

38

Juliet's hand flew to her mouth. "No," she muttered into her palm.

One of the insurance adjustors scowled. "Shhh."

Shaking her head in disbelief, she scooped up her pen and notebook, grabbed her purse, and stood.

"Excuse me," she whispered, making her way past the attorney sitting to her left. Another attorney sitting in the row behind threw up his hands. "Hey, sit down," he scolded, not bothering to keep his voice lowered. "You're blocking the monitor."

She gave him a vacant look and turned for the door, fully aware everyone in the room, including Greer, now watched.

Her hands pushed through the doors, and she quickly glanced up and down the empty hallway.

How could she have been so stupid?

She moved in the direction of the lobby,

questions swirling inside her mind. But one topic parked itself front and center.

When exactly had Greer gotten romantically involved with Alexa?

A ball of anger slammed against the pit of Juliet's stomach. It was highly likely that snake with the gorgeous blue eyes had been playing her, maybe the entire time.

She marched to the elevator and punched the button, her mind rehearsing all the times she'd felt professional tension, knowing somehow that Greer never quite had her back when it came to their boss.

The elevator doors opened and Juliet moved inside, then leaned against the back wall.

And what about her boss? Alexa was considerably older, married — had a teenage son. Were all those happy faces in the frames in her office a pretense?

All the mentoring, the phony discussions, concerns, and promises. All suspect. Everything out of Alexa's mouth could have been a lie.

An arm suddenly burst through the closing doors. Startled, she looked up.

"Juliet? Where are you going?"

"Greer, I guarantee this isn't a good time."

He scowled. Ignoring her warning, he moved into the elevator beside her, letting the doors close behind him.

Unable to keep the disdain from her voice, she squared her shoulders and repeated herself. "Perhaps you didn't hear me clearly. I believe I said this isn't a good time."

In a remarkably stupid move, he touched her shoulder.

She flinched and pulled away. "Keep your hands off me." Her eyes narrowed. "What kind of game are you playing?"

He laughed lightly, as if she was teasing him. "You're going to have to quit being so subtle, Juliet." He took a deep breath, pulled at his cuffs. Then, as if speaking to a child, "You can continue to make me guess what this is all about." He widened his eyes innocently. "Or you could just explain."

"How dare you take that condescending attitude with me?" She couldn't help herself — her face flushed and she rushed on. "Did you ever stop to think I might find out about the two of you? About you and Alexa?"

His face turned to cement. Except for his jaw, which twitched wildly. "How —"

"Men are so stupid."

Of course, Greer was instantly on that remark. "Oh, I see. You're going to act out the junk with your dad. But I'm not your father. Although it was never explicitly expressed, I believe we had an understanding."

The elevator stopped and the doors opened to the lobby. "Is that what we had? An understanding?" She brushed past him and marched across the tiled floor. She pushed through the front doors, aware he followed close behind.

Outside, a white mist of clouds floated across the sky, obscuring an airplane that droned overhead. Despite the air growing sticky hot already, she felt a shudder run down her spine.

She'd shared too much. Let him in her head too far.

That creep knew her tender places — the ways she hurt inside.

She hurried and climbed inside her Jeep, tossing her bag and the notebook on the passenger seat. Weary, she rubbed her face, knowing Greer followed and stood near. "Look, just leave me alone." She moved for the door to pull it closed.

Greer stepped in the way. He shook his head in disbelief. "You broke it off — remember?" Incredibly, he said it as if she had pushed him into a relationship with someone else. With Alexa.

Except the timing was a bit off.

Her fists balled in rage. "Do you think I'd

still want to be with you after finding another woman's earrings on your bathroom counter? What — was I supposed to maybe wear them the next time we went out to dinner?" A self-satisfied smile played on her lips. She had him. "Better yet, to an office meeting so your boss would find out about *me*?"

Greer looked at her intently — and said nothing.

Juliet stared back at him, understanding dawning. "Oh," she said, stripped of her dignity. So she *had* been played a fool the entire time.

She sensed Greer's mind at work, knew he was mentally calculating the damage done and how he would react. More importantly, how he would protect himself — even if it meant throwing her into jeopardy.

She too was estimating what all this meant to her personally — and professionally.

An argument could be made that she was the victim of an outrageous betrayal. Her career had been washed out at the hands of two conniving, disingenuous co-workers. One of them her own boss.

While she'd been maneuvering the outbreak, they'd likely been pulling up the sheets, laughing at her the whole time.

Her inclination would be to cling to the

pretense that she'd held no part in any of this. She had every right to be angry and place the blame squarely on these others.

But in the back of her mind, she heard her mother's voice. "Oh, sweetheart, what empty place inside makes you keep trying so hard? You knew what you were doing was wrong. You even saw the signs and ignored them."

It was true.

She'd so wanted her life and work to matter. But she'd somehow ended up nothing more than a tired cliché, an ambitious woman so focused on getting ahead she ended up losing herself along the way.

The implication of it all was so powerful, she felt like that tiny spider all over again — being swept away. So swept away she barely comprehended that the outcome of all her striving was as inevitable as the tide.

39

Juliet was back at the office when the first text arrived. She walked through the lobby and pulled her iPhone from her bag, expecting to see Greer's name on the face. Instead, she was surprised that it was Alexa.

I'd like to meet for dinner. Six o'clock at La Margarita in the Market Square?

She hadn't even clicked off when a second message appeared, this time from Greer.

I know you're angry, but we need to talk. Meet us at La Margarita at six.

She didn't respond. Let them wonder whether she'd show up or not.

Lindsay glanced up from the receptionist counter. "Juliet, what are you doing back? I have you out all day attending Alexa's deposition."

"They no longer needed me," she said, walking past and down the hall to her office. The statement was true. She was no longer necessary to this company, not really.

Even if they wanted her to stay, she couldn't work alongside people she didn't trust.

No doubt she'd learned a valuable lesson. Going forward, she'd be wary of every motive, every promise made. No longer would she trust that people in charge always had her best interests, and those of the company, in mind when they made critical decisions.

Her father would have a heyday with this. Hopefully, as soon as the litigation wrapped up and these cases settled, she could resign and quietly move out of state. The less fuss the better.

Her career had been burned, and the acrid smell of smoke would follow her. But somehow she'd find a way to start over.

In her office, she tossed her purse and notebook on a chair and moved behind the desk. She flipped open her Mac and scrolled through her emails. There were two from Cyril, one thanking her for all she was doing to get Larimar Springs through the litigation, and the second simply one line.

Italy is beautiful in the spring. Ready for a visit?

Strolling the Tuscan countryside with a gentleman like Cyril sounded appealing. Unfortunately, she'd learned her lesson. No more office romances. Period.

Without bothering to respond, she scrolled

past and opened a communication from Dr. Breslin. He'd attached the CDC's final report summarizing the etiology of last fall's outbreak. Her eyes drifted to the morbidity factor, and she swallowed — hard.

All those years in school and internships, absorbing the necessary training so she could make a difference . . . Book knowledge proved worthless when common sense had failed her. No university course taught that you could be gullible and working in a den of thieves.

She glanced at her white lab coat hanging on the back of her office door. With her position here, she'd been poised to bring all that training to bear and maintain the trust the public placed in Larimar Springs products. Maybe even prove to her father that this time he was wrong. Her state-of-the-art quality assurance program would see to it that no unsafe product ever got in the hands of a consumer.

How could she have known the cards had been dealt before she'd ever been invited to the table, and that those seated across from her had already gambled it all? She'd been destined to fold before she even got a chance to wager her skills.

She'd like to call Alexa and Greer's bluff — provide deposition testimony that would establish her father had been right. This company had tightened her budget when it most counted, had focused on profits and mergers and neglected leadership when Malcolm Stanford brought Alexa his concerns.

Of course, Lucier would consider her a loose cannon and would now settle before ever allowing her in a deposition chair.

She scowled, lost in thought.

Suddenly, she closed the lid on her Mac. Her QA supervisor did have concerns, and he'd timely communicated those issues to the head of the company, who seemed to have simply brushed them off.

Yes, Alexa Carmichael had been immersed in courting international investors and, ultimately, in her negotiations with Montavan International. Juliet had taken Alexa at her word when she'd been told her boss had no actual knowledge of product tainted with deadly pathogens.

She'd believed her boss, while at the same time Alexa had looked her straight in the eye and promised to make her president, bypassing the man who had handed her Larimar Springs' single largest customer — the same man she was secretly sleeping with.

That same man had locked Juliet out of the building and lied about the reason.

Juliet was a fool if she believed Alexa was trustworthy and had told the entire truth about these events. Or if she trusted that Greer did not know more than he let on.

A lot of good people worked for this company, and a lot of good people had been hurt in the outbreak. She didn't have a lot to go on at this point, but at a minimum before moving on she needed to investigate and find out the truth. For everyone concerned.

With a sense of determination, she grabbed her lab coat and headed out the door. "I'll be in the QA lab," she told Alva, who looked up from her Selectric typewriter and nodded as Juliet hurried by.

In the lab, she found Malcolm backflushing the reagent dispenser. "Could I talk with you for a few minutes?" she asked.

Giving her a wary look, he turned off the switch. "Sure, Dr. Ryan. What's up?"

She pointed outside. "Let's talk in private."

They sat at a table in the courtyard, often used by employees on their smoke breaks. Something Juliet could find pleasure in right now, given her heightened nerves.

Malcolm seemed nervous as well.

"Let me quickly put your mind at ease," Juliet began. "This isn't about you or any problem with the lab. You are doing a fine job. The company is lucky to have someone with your integrity aboard."

The man sitting across the table visibly relaxed. "Thank you, Dr. Ryan. I appreciate that." Behind his black-framed glasses, his eyes turned earnest. "Over these past months, I've grown to respect your diligence. Especially given the difficulties this company has faced."

"Thank you," she said, knowing Malcolm Stanford's respect was not easily granted. She thought back to Tavina in the hospital room and seeing the flowers he'd sent. He'd also braved conveying concerns to the highest level in the company, likely done with a lot of forethought. She believed she could trust him.

"Malcolm, I want to be candid here. Did you place an envelope on my car window?" She watched for his reaction.

He lowered his head and stared. "A what?"

"Months back, in the middle of the outbreak, someone taped an envelope to my car window while I was parked in the hospital lot." She'd never told anyone about the envelope. She swallowed, hoping she'd not made a tactical error disclosing the information now.

Malcolm shook his head. "No, I don't

know anything about an envelope. What was in it?"

Her hand moved inside her purse, and she withdrew the analysis report and slid it across the table.

He examined the test and frowned. "What's this all about?"

She rubbed her chin. "I was never able to figure it out." She pointed to the line reading *Total Coliform Units — MCL.* Then she pointed out that the date was in the same time frame as the outdated pallet found in the warehouse. "Look, I haven't shared this with anyone. But obviously, there's something going on with this report. Someone wanted me to see it." She leaned back and sighed. "I spent one whole night at the office, without anyone knowing, scouring lab records. I found nothing out of line. Everything in our system confirmed that the MCL counts on the test report left in that envelope matched up."

"And you checked to see if the right coefficient values were utilized in the calculations?"

She nodded. "Everything checked out. I even audited tests conducted well before the date on the pallet." She folded the test and slipped it back inside her bag. "Alexa let it slip that you came to her with some concerns about the same time my predecessor resigned."

Malcolm frowned. "Resigned?" He let out a nervous laugh. "Who told you that? Robin Ford was terminated."

40

Juliet paced her kitchen, waiting for the teapot to boil, knowing she was in more hot water than she'd earlier recognized.

Alexa Carmichael hadn't only deceived her by hiding her relationship with Greer, knowing Juliet was also romantically involved with him, but she'd lied. Clearly, she'd characterized Robin Ford's departure as voluntary, predicated by a medical situation that left her unable to fulfill her duties.

After pulling out the box of chamomile tea bags, Juliet slammed the cupboard counter. She'd fallen for every bit of untruth Jezebel and Mr. GQ set in front of her — gobbled it up, hungry for their approval and accolades.

She tore open the tiny envelope and tucked the bag into a mug. The whistle blew. She startled and grabbed the handle on the teapot. "Ouch! Blast it!" She quickly withdrew her burning palm.

After slamming the faucet handle up at the sink, she placed her hand under the cold stream of water. With her head thrown back, she closed her eyes against tears that formed, unsure if pain or emotion had prompted their appearance.

She'd been so gullible, believing everything and anything they'd told her. Even when things weren't quite adding up. Even when a small voice inside told her something wasn't quite right — like the night she'd been locked out of the building.

Letting the cold water run across the blisters already forming, she replayed what Malcolm had told her back at the office.

Her QA supervisor had liked Robin Ford, saying she was young but very bright and a hard worker. Malcolm was her first hire, and they'd worked closely to establish well-thought-out lab procedures.

"She wasn't nearly as highly trained as you, Dr. Ryan," he'd explained. "But I admired the effort she made to do her job well. I enjoyed working with her. In many ways, we were a team."

The comment jabbed. Making the mistake so many managers promulgate, instead of joining with her lab staff and creating an aggregated effort, she'd elevated herself above them in an effort to feel secure. A critical error in judgment, for sure. Perhaps if she'd signaled she was more available, Malcolm might have felt free to voice concerns and she'd have clued in to problems earlier.

What if together they could have prevented, or at least reduced, the number of people who fell victim to the outbreak? What if the tainted product had been discovered on their own, instead of the CDC officials alerting them to a problem? Tavina's little boy might still be alive, and the entire company wouldn't be in jeopardy.

Not that she cared if Alexa lost her financial holdings, but Juliet agreed with her boss's statement that a lot of good people were employed by Larimar Springs — vulnerable employees who would be hurt if their financial security was suddenly ripped away.

Her hand finally grew numb under the cold water, prompting her to close the faucet. She moved the still steaming teakettle to a cold burner and left the cup empty on the counter.

No amount of chamomile could soothe her conscience.

She moved to the sofa and tucked her legs up underneath, then settled her Mac on her lap, carefully typing "Robin Ford phone number" in the Google search window. Her eyes scrolled the results, settling on a site that looked promising.

She clicked and opened what appeared to be a phone directory. Granted, if she waited until tomorrow, she might be able to access records at work that would provide the contact information she needed, but this was urgent. She didn't want to wait.

Of the twelve numbers provided, there was little way to know if any of them belonged to the woman she hoped to talk to without calling each one.

And what if the woman didn't have a landline and used a mobile as her primary phone? In that case, Juliet might not have access to the number.

Of the list, four were no longer in service. The first several remaining numbers were not matches. Moving on, she dialed the seventh number — shown listed to Oliver and Robin Ford in Gruene, a popular tourist destination less than an hour north of San Antonio.

Malcolm said Robin had suffered through a series of fertility treatments before becoming pregnant. "Despite employment laws, I never got the impression Alexa was too keen on mixing career and family. Robin confided that Alexa was giving her a hard time about missing work." He shook his head. "Funny how often women fail to be supportive of other women when it comes to their professional lives."

He'd gone on to say that shortly after her first trimester, Robin encountered severe difficulties that required her doctors to put her on full bed rest. His own daughter had encountered something similar, and the condition was nothing to fool with.

Unfortunately, her medical situation hit about the same time they started seeing abnormal microbial counts.

"There were a couple of days she still made it in, despite the medical warnings," he said. "We both worried the Edwards Aquifer might be having a similar situation that was encountered a few years back when discharge back into the system from the San Antonio Zoo presented increased and dangerous fecal matter in the water system." Malcolm rubbed his hand through his thinning black hair. "Robin's husband showed up at work and scolded her. Made her stay home, as he should've. In Robin's absence, I took my concerns to Alexa."

Juliet nodded. "And?"

"And I was told in no uncertain terms she'd already resolved the issue directly with Robin." Malcolm turned sad. "I'll always regret not forcing the issue. But something she said left me nervous." His eyes filled with regret. "Frankly, I was scared — even too scared to call the CDC and turn her in. There just wasn't enough evidence to prove anything — you know?"

She'd nodded and patted his arm, promising she understood. She'd assured him she was going to push to find out whatever she could. Which is why she now sat with the phone glued to her ear.

The phone rang again. Juliet sent up a quick prayer, hoping somehow to find and talk to the former quality assurance director. Getting the account directly from her was the only way to fill in the blanks and know the full story. Especially given the questions in her mind, and knowing she'd likely never get the truth from Alexa or Greer.

Together, she and Robin Ford could join forces and take what proof they could piece together to Dr. Breslin.

"Hello?"

The man's voice on the other end sounded about the right age. A baby cried in the background, which was a promising sign she might have the right party.

She cleared her throat. "Hello, I'm trying to locate a Robin Ford, a woman who used to work at Larimar Springs Water Corporation."

"Who is this?"

Taken aback at his gruff response, she tried to explain. "Uh, my name is Dr. Ryan. Juliet Ryan."

"What's this got to do with Larimar Springs?"

"I'm the director of quality assurance," she told him, hoping the man on the other end of the phone could hear her over the baby crying. "I'm trying to locate the woman who worked in that position before me. I'd really like to talk to her."

"Yeah, my wife used to work there. I heard all about the outbreak. I'm really sorry for all those people, but frankly, I couldn't think of a better company to have something like that happen to."

His response didn't entirely surprise her. Obviously, his wife's termination had left bad feelings. Treading carefully, she tried again. "There are some things that — well, to be honest, I'm wondering about a few of the events surrounding your wife's departure from the company."

"Departure?" he huffed. "That blonde witch fired my wife. Just for trying to do her job." He paused to try to quiet the baby. "The stress over all that is what did her in."

Juliet closed her eyes. She knew this would be delicate, but he wasn't making her intentions any easier. "I — I understand. Really, I do. But, if I could just talk to her. Is she there?"

"Is she here? Are you serious?"

"Excuse me?"

"For goodness' sake, because of what was going on with that company, my wife became severely hypertensive and suffered seizures. Her entire system shut down. We nearly lost the baby."

She swallowed, thinking of little MD hooked up to all those machines. "I'm so sorry to hear that. That had to have been extremely difficult." She quickly glanced at the computer screen for his name. "Oliver, if this wasn't really important, I wouldn't ask, but I really need to talk to Robin."

"Yeah, me too," he said in a solemn voice. "But you're not getting what I'm telling you. My wife is *dead*."

41

Juliet hurried through the crowded walkways of Market Square, taking special care not to trip in her heels on the terra-cotta Saltillo tiles. Overhead, brightly colored paper flags and strings of lights swayed in a breeze filled with the scent of tamales and grilling onions.

Her stomach growled. Had she even eaten today?

La Margarita was just ahead, with blue and white patio umbrellas lining the outdoor courtyard. When a woman pushing a stroller stopped and bent to check on her child, Juliet ducked around a lamppost and swiftly made her way to a wooden podium stationed at the entrance of the restaurant.

Out of breath, she brushed her hair into place. "I'm Dr. Ryan. I'm meeting Alexa Carmichael and Greer Latham. They should already be seated."

The man with dark hair and a moustache

glanced over his list. "Ah, *bueno.* Yes, this way, please." He motioned for her to follow and led her inside the iconic establishment with its massive bar and exposed brick interior.

Alexa and Greer were tucked at a table near a window at the back. They both waved as they spotted her walking to the table, as if she was a friend and this was a social event.

As she took her seat, Alexa gave her a wide smile. "I'm so glad you agreed to join us," she gushed, sounding as upbeat as the mariachi band playing across the room.

Greer held a more wary approach. "Juliet," he said, acknowledging her with a simple nod as his manicured hand circled the large glass on the table in front of him. His eyes stared at her over the rim as he took a long sip of his frozen margarita. An identical glass stood empty on the table, except for a straw leaning against a crusty salted rim.

"I swear, these are the best margaritas in San Antonio. They add Grand Marnier to only the finest brands of tequilas. We nearly ordered one for you as well," Alexa rambled, looking uncharacteristically nervous. "But we thought it might melt before you arrived." She raised her arm to signal the waiter back to the table.

Juliet shook her head. "No, nothing for me." Alexa's use of the word *we* — as in *us, me and him, a couple* — didn't go unnoticed.

A young woman in a brightly colored full skirt and white peasant blouse placed a basket of tortilla chips on their table. From a pitcher she carried in her other hand, she poured salsa into individual molcajetes and scooted the little-legged bowls in front of each of them.

As soon as the waitress moved away from the table, Juliet wasted no time. She glared across the table. "Why did you two want to meet?" *Let them put their cards on the table first,* she thought.

Greer set his glass on the table. "A few issues have become a bit convoluted lately. We hoped to straighten things out."

There was a flinty look of determination in his eyes, an intention to defuse any trouble she might cause. Did he think she could be easily manipulated?

She nodded slowly. "Oh, I see. You need to straighten *me* out."

Greer's jaw twitched. "Don't twist my words. I think you'd be the first to admit, personal lives are separate from professional. This isn't high school."

She winced at his bold put-down. "Look, Ken. Barbie has moved past caring about Midge. What's going on here is much bigger than your personal improprieties."

Alexa flashed a stern look his direction and placed her hand on Juliet's arm. "I think what Greer is trying to say is that Larimar Springs has valued and continues to value your expertise. Your position at the company is secure, despite what you might recently believe."

Out of the corner of her eye, Juliet spotted a family eating at the next table over — a black family with a little guy about MD's age. He was giggling as his mom wrestled him back into his booster chair.

She took a deep breath. "Let me spell out what I've recently come to believe. The two of you have some kind of game going. I don't know why you hired me exactly, or how you thought I'd never find out about your *personal* relationship — or whatever term you might want to use — but I'm not one who appreciates being exploited." She turned to Greer. "And you, sir, are as greasy as that junk you slime on your hair to keep it in place."

Alexa's eyelids batted rapidly. "Let's not let emotion —"

Juliet rolled her eyes. "Oh, cut it, Alexa."

Her boss's eyes flew open as if Juliet had slapped her. Alexa leaned back in her chair as if to catch her breath.

Greer lifted his glass. "See, I told you." He downed a large drink of his margarita, then placed it back on the table so hard the glass made a thud.

Alexa flinched. She took a deep breath and fingered the neckline of her butter-colored tank. "Relationships — all of them — tend to be complicated. Right now, a good company filled with hardworking people teeters on how we move forward. Given that, I'd like to focus on the critical issues before us."

A waiter brought menus to the table, forcing a pause in the conversation. Across the room, the mariachi band finished, and the three men carried their guitars through the doors leading to the courtyard. Ceiling fans whirred overhead as they each buried their attention in the food choices.

When the waiter lifted a pen to his pad, Greer ordered beef fajitas. "And another margarita," he quickly added.

"The chicken lime salad, please." Alexa handed off her menu to the waiter.

"And you, miss?"

Juliet closed the menu and handed it to him. "Just iced tea. I'm afraid I've lost my appetite." She reached inside her bag and took out a copy of the analysis report that had been left in the envelope on her car, glad she'd never revealed anything about it before now. She unfolded the paper and handed it over to Alexa, watching her face carefully for a reaction. "You should see this."

Alexa scanned the columns of information. She looked up. "What is it?"

Greer snapped it from her hands. He looked it over and frowned. "A water test."

Juliet nodded. "The test from the tainted pallets. Only, look." She pointed at the coliform counts. "Everything is within range."

Greer tossed the report on the table in front of her. "Yeah, so?"

Alexa's face turned the color of uncooked chicken. She cleared her throat. "What are you implying with this?"

Before she could respond, Greer grabbed Juliet's wrist.

Shocked, she pulled away.

He rushed to apologize. "Look, I'm sorry. But you're making a big mistake."

"Are you threatening me?" she spat back at him.

He took a deep breath and leaned back in his chair. "No. I'm simply trying to make you stop and think. If what you are implicating is true — and I'm certainly not conceding that it is — and you take this idea public, you do know Larimar Springs will go down?"

Alexa held up her hand. "This is my fault. Like I told you in my office, I'm the one accountable here. I trusted Robin Ford when she told me there were no safety issues to worry about. I believed her."

A voice inside warned Juliet not to disclose everything she'd learned. But she couldn't sit here and tolerate any more lies. She glared at Alexa. "And I believed you when you said she resigned. In fact, what really happened is you terminated her."

"Who told you that?"

"What does that matter? What really matters is the two of you placed your own financial well-being above innocent consumers, who opened and drank from bottles of our water you knew were tainted with deadly pathogens." She leaned forward and pointed her finger. "Children were killed."

Greer glanced around. "Lower your voice. Yes, we made a critical error in judgment. The executive team was buried in work, profits were floundering, and we had to do something." He nodded in Alexa's direction. "She did everything she could, explored every option. If the deal with Montavan International had gone south, she would have lost it all."

"I couldn't take that chance," Alexa said, joining in Greer's argument.

The waiter showed up then with a large tray balanced on his shoulder. With his other hand, he positioned a bussing stand and set the tray down. He placed the salad in front of Alexa and the platter of sizzling fajitas near Greer. "Let me know if you need more tortillas, sir."

Greer lifted his empty glass. "I need another margarita."

Alexa scowled.

He frowned back at her. "What?"

When they were alone again, Juliet held up both hands. "Look, I'm not going to be a party to any of this."

Greer smirked and stabbed a piece of beef with his fork. "Don't kid yourself, Juliet. You are already involved."

"What do you mean?"

He pointed at her purse with his fork. "I don't know how long you've known, but seems to me you failed to take that little piece of paper directly to the authorities." He slid the fork in his mouth and chewed, talking with his mouth full. "What's that going to look like?"

Alexa nodded. "Or the fact that you were regularly spending the night with the company's sales director."

Her comment knifed.

"Or that you were having private lunches on the Riverwalk with Cyril Montavan and making plans to visit him in Italy," Greer said, pushing the blade in deeper.

"In fact, you met with him fairly regularly," Alexa added. She took a bite of her salad, the color returning to her skin.

Juliet's gut squeezed at the implication. They'd followed her. Had they also tracked her phone and email messages?

A slow, disheartening breath leaked from between her lips. She didn't know what she'd been expecting, but she'd been a fool to believe she could force their hand without them pushing back.

A little tremor raced down Juliet's spine, and she tried not to visibly shiver. Greer noticed and a calculating smile sprouted on his chiseled face. She knew that smile, knew what it meant. The salesman was about to close the deal.

"We've talked to John Lucier. Our attorney assures us that as a member of the executive team and an officer of Larimar Springs, and especially given your assigned duties as quality assurance director, you could easily be implicated in a criminal action. But don't worry. I'm sure all the lab rats, including your father, would visit you in jail."

A ripple of disgust moved through her. She looked at the man with all his empty margarita glasses, this stranger she thought she knew, who believed he could raise the threat of government prosecution and slap her down.

"You're one lucky pair, you know that? Greer hangs out in a golf club one day and runs into a highly trained microbiologist, the answer to everything. You simply threw the bait and waited for her to bite. Then you lured her under your sheets and into an interview with the boss you were already tangled up with, in more ways than one. Who else to keep your nasty secrets than the gal you set up to take the fall if this all went down?"

Her former boyfriend watched her, his eyes proprietary and cool, calculating how she'd tipped the balance of their carefully measured world, placing everything that mattered to them in jeopardy.

Her actions could sink their plans to expand, to eventually go global. Alexa Carmichael wanted to elevate Larimar Springs to rival Nestle or PepsiCo, competitor bottled water conglomerates that held over 90 percent of the industry in their control.

Now, Juliet held the power to topple everything. They knew it, and intended to make sure that if she made the decision to toss their ambitions in the fire, they'd burn her as well. And maybe even Cyril in the process.

A flicker of doubt, like reaching tendrils, wove itself around her righteous anger. She considered abandoning the notion she could resist them before any of this grew out of control, but she couldn't bring herself to fully swallow the barbed hook.

Even so, she glanced at her hands and was surprised to see them tremble. She thought of her mother, and the faith she often relied on. If ever Juliet needed God, it was now.

Please, you've got to help me here, Lord.

She stood. "I get that you're ambitious and have big plans for your company. What I'll never understand is how you could stand by and let people, even children, get so severely sick." She turned to Alexa. "You kept your secrets and Tavina's son died."

For the first time, she noticed tiny wrinkles at her boss's eyes, at her mouth. These were nothing compared to the fault lines in the woman's character.

"In the nights ahead, I'll be able to lay my

head on my pillow and sleep — even if it's in a jail cell. But will you?"

She shoved the chair back into the table and walked away.

42

Juliet raced to beat Alexa and Greer back to the office. She swiped her entry card, thankful it now worked, then hurried through the empty lobby and down the hall to the executive offices, surprised to see her assistant at her desk hunched over her typewriter.

"Alva? What are you doing here so late?"

Her assistant looked up. At the side of her desk were several piles of ledgers. "Quarter end is coming up and Fred needed some reports typed up." The older woman raised her eyebrows. "And you?"

"I — uh, I need to pack up a few things. Do you know where I could find some boxes?"

The CDC had copies of all the manuals on her bookshelf, all the important emails on her hard drive. At home, she had her file of the important audit documents from the suspect time frame. She'd only need to pack the personal items in her desk drawers.

Alva stood and waved her hand. "You go ahead. I'll find you some boxes."

Juliet thanked her and checked her watch. Likely she didn't have much time.

Minutes later, Alva stood at her door, her hands filled with empty shipping label cartons. "Are these big enough?"

"Yes, those are perfect. Thank you." Juliet took the boxes from her assistant. "Uh, I'm not likely going to be back."

With a sympathetic look, Alva rubbed at her chest. "Yes, I figured. I'm sincerely sad to see you go."

Juliet tried to smile. "I'm going to need you to alert Malcolm, tell him he can call me at home and I'll explain. I left my resignation letter, my security card, and keys to my file cabinets all on the top of my desk. Please give them to Alexa."

Alva nodded and promised she would. "Before you leave, do you need anything else?" Her assistant lifted her wrist. Keys dangled from the coiled band.

Juliet stared into the woman's eyes, liquid and serious. "What do you mean?"

A tiny grin formed on Alva's face. She rubbed at the back of her head. "Well, it's like this. Sometimes people place things in file cabinets or desk drawers they don't necessarily mean for others to see, not realizing both Muriel and I have master key sets. We can open all doors. All cabinets." Her brown eyes twinkled. It was a bold thing to say, but she looked extremely pleased with herself. "One day, I see this water analysis report in somebody's desk drawer. I think to myself, now why would a sales guy need a lab report?"

Juliet dropped the boxes to the floor, stunned. Of course — why hadn't she thought of it before? This time, it was her turn to smile.

"So, you're the one."

43

Juliet pulled her Jeep out of the Larimar Springs parking lot and turned right. Thanks to Alva's help, she'd collected her things and got out of there in under twenty minutes. No time to spare, really.

Out her driver side window, she viewed several medical complexes and a lot filled with storage units and rental vans. Several hundred yards from the on-ramp to I-90, she spotted Alexa's black Aston Martin.

As they slowly passed, both she and Greer gawked in her direction, their discussion no doubt turning trenchant as they realized she'd beaten them to the office and they'd missed the opportunity to stop her.

She pressed the gas pedal, wanting to put as much distance between herself and Larimar Springs as possible.

She'd entered the lobby doors of Larimar Springs for the first time believing she'd landed a job fit for a queen, never realizing the kingdom was filled with fire-breathing dragons. Or that she'd walk out months later nearly burned.

She glanced in her rearview mirror, making sure the dragons hadn't turned around to follow her. For now, it appeared she'd escaped the heat, but she wasn't naïve enough to believe there weren't still battles ahead.

Her phone buzzed on the seat next to her. She merged onto the freeway and clicked on her Bluetooth.

"Juliet? It's Sandy. For goodness' sake, where have you been? I've tried for weeks to get ahold of you."

"Sorry, life's been — uh, a bit crazy." Her mother's best friend had sent emails and left voice messages, and she'd meant to get back with her. Somehow, she'd always felt slammed with work and let time slip away. "I'm really sorry, Sandy. I meant to call back."

"No problem, honey. But hey — this weekend is Easter Sunday. I want you to go with me."

Normally, Juliet would make excuses and decline the invitation. But women like Sandy and her mother were true royalty. Despite what she'd earlier thought, there was wisdom in emulating their quiet strength.

"Sure, what time?" she asked.

"You'll go?" Sandy's surprise was evident, even over the phone. "Great. I'll pick you up at your place and we'll go together. Okay, then. Well, I'll see you at eight o'clock on Sunday."

"Sandy?"

"Yes, honey?"

Juliet let a smile form. "Thanks for asking me."

At home, she shot off a quick email to Cyril. Without going into detail, she told him she needed to talk to him as soon as possible and asked him to call her when he got a chance. No telling if he was in Italy or where, but hopefully he'd be checking emails.

She didn't know what to say exactly. But she didn't want Cyril hearing from Alexa or Greer that she'd left the company without her first explaining why. Given the delicate nature of the situation, she may not be able to disclose everything. He was fairly astute, and he'd be able to size up her departure and make his own conclusions. Eventually she hoped to confide fully — after Cyril learned he'd partnered with snakes.

With their professional relationship eliminated, who knows? They might even pick back up on building a friendship.

By Sunday morning, both the sky and her spirits had dawned brighter than in months. Despite her unpredictable future and the threats made against her, Juliet felt good about her decision to walk away from it all.

Once again, she believed her mom would be proud of her decisions — something she hadn't been able to claim for a while now.

On Easter morning, traffic was fairly light, until they neared the church. Baldera Road was congested with a line of vehicles extending for almost a quarter mile. Armies of church members in orange vests directed churchgoers into overflow parking areas with shuttles waiting to transport people to the main building, where Pastor Roper would be teaching in the sanctuary. Satellite dishes were positioned on the roof, ready to broadcast the services.

"I can't believe the crowd this morning," Juliet said while freshening her lipstick in a compact mirror.

Sandy inched her car forward. "Yes, lots of Chreasters."

She frowned. "Chreasters?"

Her mom's friend grinned. "People who only attend church on Christmas and Easter."

"Oh — uh-huh." She nodded and closed

her compact. "Go ahead and give me a hard time."

"Well, if the shoe fits," Sandy teased. "By the way, how long has it been since you've checked out New Beginnings? Your mom would be so pleased to see how many women are benefiting from what she started."

Juliet slipped the lipstick and compact back in her purse. "It's been awhile," she admitted, reluctant to disclose she'd never returned after her mom died last fall. It was just too hard.

"Yeah, your dad has a difficult time going too."

She looked across the seat. "You stay in touch with Dad?"

Sandy followed the directions of a man waving her to the right and turned the car into an empty parking spot. "Yeah, Bill and I occasionally have him over for dinner. He said he saw you awhile ago — at the Menger."

Embarrassed, Juliet unfastened her seat belt. She looked at Sandy. "I'm not sure what he told you, but that night wasn't one of my shining moments. In my defense, I had a lot going on. Hard things."

She got out of the car and joined Sandy as they headed for the shuttle parked several yards ahead. As soon as they were seated inside, Sandy turned to her. "He comes to church sometimes. Your dad."

She nodded, remembering she'd seen him on Christmas Eve. He came to feel closer to her mother, she supposed. She knew that was how she felt in this place.

"He's had a really hard time — since losing your mother."

She sighed and turned to her mother's friend, knowing what she was about to say might sound harsh. "Look, I'm glad y'all see each other once in a while, but past that I really don't care."

Sandy frowned. "Oh, honey. Of course you do. That man owns you."

She gave a nervous laugh. "I don't know what you're talking about."

The shuttle driver ground the gears and the shuttle lurched forward. Sandy clutched her purse tightly in her lap. "Are you kidding? Everything you do is based on pushing him away, not letting him back inside your heart."

"Thank you, Dr. Freud."

Sandy's eyes softened. "It doesn't take a genius to assess your relationship with your dad. If he turns left, you turn right. He stands, you sit — even if you don't really want to."

When Juliet said nothing, Sandy gave her a sad smile. "Honey, your mom and I talked often. She loved you so much but was so disheartened you'd never learned to —"

"What? Forgive him?"

"Juliet, you strive so hard to be the opposite of whatever he is. Problem is, you don't know who he is, which makes being you impossible."

Sandy's words wouldn't leave Juliet as they walked to the front entrance, as they shook hands with the greeters, and even when they passed through the foyer and found a seat in the crowded sanctuary.

As they waited for the service to begin, Sandy chatted about her husband's business trip and how she planned to pick him up at the airport later in the afternoon, but in the back of Juliet's mind, Sandy's earlier comments expanded, leaving little room to think about much else.

Sandy had given the famous Dr. Bennett Ryan far too much credit. Despite what her mother's best friend claimed, Juliet hadn't customized her life in opposition to her highly esteemed father. For proof, all you had to do was look at her career choice. She'd not been afraid to enter the profession and make her own way to shine.

If anyone was constantly in opposition, it

was him.

Her father had no right to judge her, given his history of improprieties and the way he'd failed to be there for her — for her mother. But had that stopped him?

Certainly not.

He felt entirely free to voice his opinions. There were better programs than the school she'd chosen. She never came home often enough, studied hard enough, bought the right car . . . and most recently, of course, her choice of employers was found lacking.

Never mind he'd ended up on the right side of that one.

He'd even claimed she didn't have a heart and soul.

If Sandy wanted to preach to someone, she might reserve her sermons for that man.

The music started and everyone stood. Juliet cleared her mind of her father, determined to focus on the large screen at the front and the lyrics displayed.

When peace, like a river, attendeth my way,
When sorrows like sea billows roll;
Whatever my lot, Thou hast taught me to
    say,
It is well, it is well, with my soul.

Without warning, her eyes burned with

unshed tears. The words of the song, one she'd often heard her mother humming while at the kitchen sink, peeled back her strong resolve, revealing a fragility she'd tried desperately to deny, even to herself.

Her mother had had that kind of peace, even when Juliet's father had failed her miserably. She'd died knowing it was well with her soul.

A lump rose in Juliet's throat. As hard as it was to admit, she couldn't say the same. For months, her life had been a series of waves, each one threatening to take her under. Some days, it'd been all she could do to stay afloat.

Right now, she'd give almost anything to feel anchored, to relax and let someone bigger than herself guide the boat.

She swallowed in an attempt to gain control of her emotions. Reaching to her right, she took Sandy's hand and gave it a squeeze. Sandy smiled and squeezed back.

With an intensity that couldn't be argued, Juliet both admired and adored her mother, wanted desperately to be more like her. Instead, she was stubborn and critical, just like him.

As difficult as it was to admit, at some

level perhaps her mother's close friend was right.

She needed a new approach.

44

After the service, the crowd spilled into the church foyer. Ahead of her, two men in suits shook hands and a young mother tried to corral a little boy with a yellow marshmallow chick in his fist, while another mother posed for a photo with her daughters, all of them in matching pastel dresses. Juliet overheard plans to meet for brunch and comments that the sermon had really been spot-on.

Juliet looked around at this place her mother had loved. The welcome desk with racks of brochures promoting Bible studies and midweek classes. The bookstore to the right of the front door, with Bibles and inspirational art displayed in the glass window. On the other side of the front foyer, a wall of glass overlooked an outdoor courtyard that featured a large cross surrounded by a bed of pink and white cyclamen.

Talavera Community Church had been

her mother's second home, and she now regretted the times she'd declined her mom's invitations to attend. It would have made her so happy.

Sandy's hand went to her back, as if she knew what Juliet was thinking. "I feel her too when I'm here."

Outside, she lifted her face to the sun, letting the warmth hit her skin. On this Easter morning, Juliet wanted to resurrect her life, to move past the ugliness she'd encountered at Larimar Springs. Her mother had been right to suggest she had a hole inside that could never be filled with career aspirations.

"Are you ready?" Sandy asked.

Juliet nodded. Together they walked to the shuttle that would take them back to where the car was parked.

Her phone buzzed, and she pulled it from her purse. A text — from Malcolm.

Have you seen the news?

Before she could tap out a response, a woman in a light pink dress approached. "Dr. Ryan?" she asked. "Aren't you that woman from the bottled water company?"

Not sure what this was about, she slowly nodded. "Yes, what can I —"

"How could you do that?" she demanded. "My grandmother spent two weeks in the hospital."

A man with light brown hair and glasses quickly stepped forward, placing his arms around the angry woman's shoulders. "Judy, not now. This isn't the time or place." He gave them an apologetic look. "I'm sorry," he said, and guided her away.

Sandy's hand went to her chest. "Wow, what was all that?"

Feeling a bit disconcerted, Juliet shrugged. "I — I'm not sure."

Her phone buzzed again. This time it was Alva.

You need to get to a television. Alexa and Greer gave a press conference, and it's been airing all morning.

At home, Juliet pointed the remote at the television and clicked. Holding her breath, she moved through the channels until the screen filled with two bright red words — BREAKING NEWS.

The news anchor appeared, solemn faced. "In a stunning new development, top executives at Larimar Springs Corporation, the bottled water company that distributed water tainted with the deadly E. coli pathogen that made several dozen ill and caused four deaths last fall, have revealed that their director of water quality knew of the suspect product prior to the outbreak and failed to notify them."

The screen changed to Alexa and Greer standing in front of the Larimar Springs building. Ellen Shaffer, dressed in a bright red sheath dress with lips to match, stood by their side.

Juliet's hand flew to her mouth.

Alexa spoke into the microphones first. "I recently learned that Dr. Juliet Ryan — our director of water quality who was charged with the responsibility of overseeing the company's comprehensive food safety program, including monitoring the microbiology programs established for contamination prevention — was not only aware of a suspicious test report but failed to report her findings to company officials and the proper authorities in a timely manner."

Ellen leaned into a microphone. "As the news release indicates, copies of the report have been given to Dr. Breslin at the CDC, and copies are now being handed out to each of you here today." She stepped back.

Reporters holding cameras and microphones bulleted questions at the three of them. Greer cleared his throat. "I think I can shed some light on that. Company security records show Dr. Ryan entered this building late one night while no one was here. She spent several hours inside, accessing company records." He pulled at his cuffs. "More recently, video from our lobby shows her carrying boxes out. All this was done outside of office hours, when no one was there to see her."

Alexa continued. "This suspicious activity, coupled with the report that she withheld, has led the company to terminate her. We've directed legal counsel to investigate further, and they are authorized to take whatever legal action might be appropriate. This is outside whatever criminal action might be instigated by health authorities."

Ellen raised a document and stepped forward again. "I have a statement from Dr. Breslin at the CDC, the official who headed up the original outbreak investigation team. Here's what it says:

"While it is premature to comment on the allegations concerning Dr. Juliet Ryan, the Centers for Disease Control is committed to public food safety.

"In 1938 Congress passed the Federal Food, Drug, and Cosmetic Act in reaction to growing public safety demands. Chapter III of the Act addresses prohibited acts, subjecting violators to both civil and criminal liability. Provisions for criminal sanctions are clear. Felony violations include adulterating or misbranding a food, drug, or device, and putting an adulterated or misbranded food, drug, or device into interstate commerce. Any person who commits a prohibited act violates the FDCA. A person committing a prohibited act 'with the intent to defraud or mislead' is guilty of a felony punishable by not more than three years or fined not more than $10,000 or both.

"As mandated, our agency will fully investigate and take any appropriate action."

Ellen thanked the reporters for coming, and the news anchor soon reappeared on-screen. "In a related story, the mayor of San Antonio says these allegations are serious, and he is deeply saddened to know the outbreak might have been prevented."

Stunned, Juliet clicked off the television.

"They — they lied," she said out loud. She tossed the remote on the cushion and stood, pacing her living room with her hand at her mouth.

What was she going to do? They'd turned everything around and made her actions appear sinister. Alexa and Greer had wanted to discredit her, and they'd taken proactive, if not deceitful, steps to eliminate any possibility she could follow through on her threats.

She'd been so stupid to believe she could handle this. How foolish to have met with them privately, with no witness to what she'd revealed and why.

Feeling panicked, she sank to the sofa. She could face criminal action and had no way to prove she wasn't culpable for the things they'd misrepresented and accused her of.

No wonder Cyril wasn't answering her emails. Likely they'd poisoned his mind against her as well.

Shaking uncontrollably, she wrapped her arms tightly around her chest and rocked back and forth, trying to make sense of this. Her breaths came in large gulps, and sweat beaded her brow.

She'd foolishly believed things couldn't get worse, that she had the upper hand. She now knew that reasoning was severely flawed.

The situation had definitely taken a turn for the worse. Alexa and Greer had stopped at nothing to neutralize her, to take her down. They might as well have physically kicked her in the gut. She could barely breathe.

She was in serious trouble here.

And sadly, she had nowhere to turn.

45

Juliet's fingers moved to the handle on her car door. After taking a deep breath, she unlatched the door, grabbed her bag, and moved to get out, placing her running shoes squarely on the pavement.

With her bag flung onto her shoulder, she gently closed the door and surveyed the arthritic-limbed oaks lining the street, the manicured lawns and carefully tended flower beds. The mounds circled in decorative stone were filled with oxblood lilies with their spiky red blooms, and large yellow-to-orange African marigolds that measured nearly five inches across, a favorite of San Antonian gardeners.

The warm air carried a slight aura of mown grass, and the sky overhead was dappled with lavender. A graceful prelude to morning.

She followed the cement pathway that wound to the steps leading to the brick landing, wishing she could stand there for hours, absorbing the peace of it all, but her chest was too tight to truly absorb such beauty.

Before her stood a large arched wooden door, surrounded by coping made of southwestern tiles decorated with a blue and white design. To the right was a small adobe banco, its mission-styled bench seat trimmed with similar tiles.

With a deep breath, she considered perhaps it wasn't too late to turn around, to just return to her car and drive away.

She fingered the open zipper on her running jacket, knowing she really had no choice.

Unable to steady her trembling hand, she placed her finger on the doorbell. She pressed . . . and waited.

Her heart thumped in her chest. After several long seconds of standing there fidgeting, she considered pressing the bell again when she heard noise on the other side. Suddenly, the door opened.

She saw him then, standing there in pajamas and a robe. He inventoried her rumpled clothes and hapless ponytail, her sleep-deprived face with no cosmetics, and frowned.

She swallowed and forced herself to look

him in the eye.

"Dad, I need your help."

46

Her father invited her in and she moved through the door, taking in the familiar décor she hadn't seen in months. Her mother's bookcases, her wedding photo in a frame on the table by the sofa, the tiny wooden cross hanging on the wall near the entry to the kitchen.

And her slippers.

Her father cleared his throat, noticing that she saw them. "Uh — please, sit down," he said with a formality you'd use with a guest. "Can I get you some coffee?"

She nodded but remained standing. It felt unnerving to be here in this house with him after so many months. It was overwhelming, so many memories . . . and regrets.

He picked up on how she felt. She could tell from his apprehensive smile before he headed for the kitchen.

She supposed he'd seen the news, watched the press conference. Did he believe them?

she wondered.

He quickly returned with a mug in his hand. "I haven't changed much around here," he said, as if hoping that might earn him points. "Guess I just liked the way she had it."

She nodded again and took a sip from the steaming cup. "The flower beds look nice," she offered. "Are those African marigolds?"

His eyes sparked with pleasure. "Yes, your mom liked those. Planted them every year." He motioned her to sit down.

This time she sank into the sofa, leaning back against the afghan her mother had crocheted. If she closed her eyes, she could still smell her presence. Her father sat in an armchair next to the window overlooking the golf course.

"I have to admit, this is a surprise." He smoothed his pajama bottoms. "If I'd known you were coming, I'd have dressed up a little more." His attempt at humor fell flat.

They sat in uncomfortable silence for several seconds, neither of them acknowledging why she'd shown up at his door — though the issue permeated the empty space between them like the proverbial elephant in the room.

Her father set his coffee mug on the table. He leaned forward and rubbed his chin.

"Look, JuJu, I need to say something."

She stiffened.

His eyes probed her own. "I'm so sorry about that day. Wish I could take it all back." He shook his head. "I've asked myself a thousand times why I reacted —"

"I wish Mom were here."

It was out of Juliet's mouth before she could censor herself. What a stupid thing to say. Callous. He was trying to apologize.

She faltered. "What I meant to say is how much I wish she were sitting here with us, but I know what she'd say." She looked at him then, with genuine sorrow. "Look, Dad, I've been angry with you for so long, anything else just seems awkward."

His eyes softened. "I know what you mean. I picked up the phone so many times to call you but just didn't know what to say. Or if you'd even talk to me."

She swallowed the knot in her throat and forced a laugh. "Ha, what would give you *that* impression?"

He grinned at that.

She slid their wedding photo from the table, letting her fingers trace her mother's face. "She really loved you, you know."

"Your mother was a good woman. Carol was far better than I deserved."

Juliet screwed up her mouth as if to say,

"You're joking, right? Of course you didn't deserve her." But her father wasn't joking. She needed to learn to let all that go.

Somehow.

"You look so much like her, Juliet. It nearly takes my breath away."

She didn't know what to say to that, so she didn't say anything at all. Instead, she stared at the floor and fingered her hair, trying to summon the courage to admit why she was here.

"Dad," she managed. "I — I'm in trouble."

"I saw the news."

She looked up, miserable. "They twisted everything. Made all my actions out to be something sinister, when in fact I'd confronted them about what I'd uncovered." Her voice snagged, and tears sprang to her eyes. She struggled to get control of her emotions even as her father moved to her side and placed his arms around her shoulders.

His touch created an ache so deep it felt bottomless.

As if she were ten years old, he lifted her chin. "Don't worry, JuJu. Everything is going to be all right."

She opened up and spilled about the envelope left on her car, how she'd recently learned it was from Alva Jacobs. "She had a set of universal keys, and she wasn't afraid to use them," she told him. "She found the analysis report in Greer Latham's top desk drawer, laying on top of his pencils. The way she figured things, the company's top sales executive wouldn't have reason to tuck a lab report away like that, unless there was something suspicious going on. Especially after she overheard yelling and saw Robin Ford, the former QA director, storm out of Alexa's office. So she made a copy and hid it away."

She dug in her purse and handed her father the report.

He examined it carefully. "Everything's within range," he said, scowling.

"I know. The same night I found that on my car, Dr. Breslin alerted me about the outdated pallet in the warehouse."

"The tainted product."

She nodded. "I audited everything — thoroughly examined all our systems. Everything checked out." She pointed to the paper in his hand. "As you can see from that report, none of the microbial counts were off. Even when they should have been."

Her dad tapped his nose in thought for several seconds, then dropped his hand and looked at her. "And you confronted Alexa

Carmichael?"

"Yes — which led to the damaging news conference."

Her father slowly nodded.

"There's no evidence to counter what they say happened — or about me," she said, feeling panicked all over again. She'd come to him for help, but how was he going to fix this mess?

"Who else knows about this?"

"Malcolm — oh, and Robin Ford's husband." She explained how she'd found the number and called, and what she'd sadly learned. That her predecessor was dead.

That news seemed to alarm her father. "You know where this guy lives?"

"I don't have an address, but somewhere in Gruene."

Her father grabbed his coffee mug and stood. "Well, I want to talk to him."

"I don't think he will. He's really angry at the company."

"You underestimate me." He turned for the kitchen, calling over his shoulder, "I'm not going to offer the poor chap any choice."

47

By ten o'clock, she'd showered and her dad picked her up at her condominium. "Nice place, JuJu," he said, looking around. "Great view."

She waited for the critical comment she knew would follow, and her father didn't disappoint. "But your air conditioning bill must be atrocious with those windows."

She shrugged. "Not really."

Within fifteen minutes, they'd packed her company files, Oliver Ford's address, and their tenuous truce into the car and headed north.

After pulling through a McDonald's for breakfast sandwiches and coffee, her father turned to her. "I thought we'd take the back way to Gruene."

She unwrapped her Egg McMuffin and checked to make sure the cheese had been left off like she'd requested. "The freeway's faster."

"Not really," he said, rolling up the window. He eased his car through the egress into traffic and merged into the left lane.

She unwrapped his egg biscuit. "How can you say the freeway's not faster? It's closer and the speed limit is much higher."

Her father's grip on the steering wheel tightened.

"It doesn't matter, I guess," she conceded, handing over his breakfast sandwich. "You're driving."

They passed a tattered strip mall, the kind that had once been filled with promising new retail shops but over time had become worn, now many of them empty and boarded up.

"So, how are things at the university?" she asked between bites, in an attempt to fill the silence.

"Eh, administration's focus has turned to technology. They want every lecture in electronic form with digital illustrations. My presentations are now turned into webinars, and students log in from home and watch whenever it's convenient." He juggled his sandwich while changing lanes and gave her a halfhearted grin. "They built me a Facebook page and want me to start interacting more with the public, advocating for the university and their fund-raising efforts. Oh, and I'm supposed to start nailing some of my articles to some board on the internet," he said. "Whatever the Tom Pete that's all about."

"Pinterest."

"Huh?"

"Pinterest," she repeated, scrunching her wrapper and throwing it in the empty bag at her feet. "I can help you if you want."

He shook his head and handed her his empty wrapper. "Nah, I've got some interns willing to step up. If I play my cards right, I can push all those time-waster projects into their laps."

Even though her first thought was, *Yeah, what's new?* Juliet was determined to keep her cool. The interns could be of the male persuasion, she tried to tell herself as they made their way through the outskirts of town and the scenery became more rural.

Perhaps it'd be best to change the subject.

She handed him the coffee. "How do you like your Jetta?" He and her mother had purchased a hybrid Volkswagen early last fall, mocha-colored with a cream top. Her mom wanted the light blue one, claiming this car made her feel like she was driving around a cup of hot chocolate topped with marshmallows. But in the end she'd let him have his way.

Her father took a quick sip, then launched into a diatribe about global warming, claiming an overwhelming majority of climate scientists agreed that human activity, and primarily cars run on fossil fuels, were to blame.

She listened, staring straight ahead at the sun-dappled winding, narrow road, knowing from memory that up ahead were blind curves and drop-offs that could send a car flipping end over end down a jagged limestone crag.

"These vehicles run better too. With 170 horsepower, this baby tops off at nearly fifty miles per gallon." His face turned indignant. "So, when are you going to get rid of that gas-guzzling Jeep of yours?"

"I think I need to get employed again before I consider buying another car," she said, maneuvering the conversation carefully.

This served as an invitation for what she knew would eventually come.

"Look, JuJu, I'm sorry you're in this mess. But in some ways, it's just as well." He reached over and manually turned on the radio, ignoring the automated button she knew was next to his washer switch. Despite what the manual said, he always had to do things his way. "You knew working for a profit-driven enterprise held risk. Your talents are far better utilized elsewhere."

His tired attitude was a living, breathing, hurtful thing. She wanted to let his comments pass without argument, but couldn't. "I did a lot of good at Larimar Springs," she pointed out. "I upgraded the lab and incorporated state-of-the-art processes. I utilized my expertise and educated a team of lab technicians, instituting a culture of heightened awareness of the need for food safety." Reciting her accomplishments emboldened her confidence, her self-worth. She barreled on, letting her comments pick up steam. "Despite the outbreak, many believe my contributions raised the bar. And I'd hate to think what might have happened in this community had I not been the one at the helm when it all broke loose. Many more people would've likely fallen victim, that's what would have happened."

She wanted him to answer, felt herself needling him to further her point. But he said nothing in return. Even so, she knew what he was thinking.

She'd been a terrible disappointment on many levels. Her career choice, certainly. Likely the way she'd handled everything with the investigation team. She even drove the wrong car.

Some things would never change. She could frost this rock, but the stone would never be a cupcake.

Her father nosed his vehicle up against a line of cars trailing a slow-moving tractor that pulled a flatbed loaded with bails of stone, the kind used in landscaping. He lifted his wrist and checked his watch. Looking frustrated, he laid on the horn.

Her hands balled into fists. "They can't move any faster."

As if she'd said nothing, he honked again and swerved into the oncoming lane in an attempt to get around the cars that stalled their progress. That was when she saw he was no longer wearing his wedding ring.

In angry silence, she turned and stared out the window at the brown countryside, with only an occasional splotch of green from cedar trees too misshapen to ever be considered as Christmas trees.

Oblivious to her darkening mood, her father punched the gas and passed the line of cars, swerving back into their own lane at the last minute, just missing an oncoming motor home.

She gripped the dash.

"JuJu, you may have hoped to make a difference," he continued before she could yell for him to be careful. "But a couple of bad apples motivated by greed can spoil the pie."

Something inside her head snapped. She'd experienced all of this a hundred times, a thousand times.

She pointed up ahead, to a lane leading to a million-dollar house perched on a distant ridge with hill country stone turrets to capture the view. "Dad, pull over."

He glanced at her, confused.

"Just pull over," she repeated.

He quickly glanced in the rearview mirror and did as she asked, pulling the car several hundred yards up the lane to a massive iron gate mounted in stone columns. "Are you sick? Do you need some water?"

Without answering, she barely waited for the car to come to a stop before she bolted out the door and ran as hard as she could in the direction of the stone fence bordering the property. When she reached the stone border and could go no farther, she folded at the base of a scrub oak and buried her face in her hands. In the distance, she heard cars passing out on the highway.

Seconds later, her dad came up behind her, heaving and out of breath. "JuJu? What's wrong?"

She angrily shook her head. "Quit calling me that!"

"Calling you what?"

"I'm thirty-three years old. I graduated from Cornell University with honors. I hold a PhD in epidemiology and public health, and up until just recently, I garnered great respect for my work on prevention and control of foodborne illnesses." Her fist pounded the hard dirt beside her. "My name is Juliet. *Doctor* Juliet Ryan."

She fell to uncontrollable sobs, great wracking heaves of sobs. It was all too much — too many hopes and regrets and deep disappointment. Her heart was raw and exposed, sitting in the ashes of her burned dreams. Worse — her father's lack of faith in her wounded as deeply as any sword thrust in her gut.

She sensed more than saw her dad sink to her side. He sat quiet as she cried herself out.

Finally, her lungs filled with ragged breaths, and she rested her burning eyes against her arms.

Birds sang overhead. Any other time, she'd marvel at the idyllic sound. Today, she simply lifted her face and brushed her nose with her hand.

She glanced over at her father then. He stared out at cars passing on the highway, his eyes red-rimmed. A pained look etched across his face.

"I know I failed you, Juliet. And I'm sorry."

Tears filled her eyes again. She let his words sink in. Oddly, the apology she'd long waited for only served to highlight her own shortcomings.

Her father wasn't entirely to blame for their broken relationship. He had a way of nailing her vulnerabilities to the wall, and frankly, she didn't like looking at them. Sandy was right. He couldn't hurt her like this if she didn't care what he thought.

She gave a slight shrug. "Being so angry at you was fairly constructive, I suppose — I got a lot done. You were also my scapegoat anytime things went wrong. I could blame you — it was all your fault."

She reached and took his hand.

His face turned earnest and unguarded. "I get up every morning and pray I can get through the day without somebody." He swallowed against tears filling his own eyes. "I need you, kiddo. If you only knew how much."

Her throat knotted. She leaned her head against his chest and whispered, "That's the first time I've ever heard you say that."

He squeezed her hand. "And I'm sorry for that too."

48

The remaining drive into Gruene went fairly smooth. Despite the longer route and unplanned stop, Juliet and her father arrived nearly an hour early. Her dad parked in a lot off the main highway running through New Braunfels, a trendy area of Gruene, populated with historic buildings renovated into gift shops and restaurants.

"We have some time to kill. You up for a scoop of Blue Bell at the old General Store?" he asked.

She shook her head. "I don't think I could eat anything right now." Now that the friction with her dad was somewhat resolved, her mind seemed bent on the risk they'd taken in coming to meet with Oliver Ford.

"Worrying about this meeting isn't going to change a thing. Let's go at least check the place out," he urged. "Maybe buy some of that honey butter your mom used to love."

He was right. Feeling anxious about Oliver Ford, and whether or not he'd be open to helping her, was not productive.

Even so, she found it difficult not to fixate on how likely he was to not want to help. Oliver had been reluctant to meet when she'd called, as she suspected he would be.

"Look, like I told you, I've moved on," he'd said. "After what that company did to Robin, I don't even want to think about those people."

She assured him they were not on opposing sides. What they'd done to his wife, they were attempting to do to her. But with added criminal implications.

"Please, just let me come talk to you," she pleaded.

Thankfully, he'd given in and they agreed to meet for lunch at the Grist Mill, a restaurant situated on a bluff overlooking the Guadalupe River.

While her dad locked the car, she glanced up and down the street leading into the quaint district popular with tourists. Across from the parking lot, a man took a photo of his wife and young children posing in front of a sign that said WELCOME TO GRUENE.

Juliet pulled her bag onto her shoulder, amused by the puppy dog look on her father's face. "Okay, I'm game. Let's go," she told him. Besides, what else were they going to do until it was time to head to the restaurant?

A brick sidewalk lined with lantanas, salvias, and pretty yellow columbines growing along a low split-rail fence led them to the General Store. Several motorcycles were parked out front, a strange juxtaposition to the historic façade with its turn-of-the-century feel.

"Whoo-ee. Will you look at those Harleys?" Her dad slowly circled the bikes, admiring the custom chrome work.

Juliet moved to a wooden bench to the right of the front entrance, watching as he inspected the saddlebags.

He whistled. "You don't see a lot of these twisted spokes. Gives the bike a great look."

She tried to smile, wondering why he didn't seem at all worried by what she faced.

He noticed her frowning. "What's the matter?"

She brushed the top of her slacks. "What if we drove all the way here only to find out the guy has nothing?"

He crouched to get a better look at the wheel base. "If the former director raised suspicions with those folks and nothing was done in response, you can be sure she kept backup to prove her allegations." He stood and turned to her, his eyes twinkling. "You know, I think it's time I break down and buy me a hog. Maybe take a road trip."

"But what if she didn't? Or what if her husband tossed out anything she might have had? That's entirely possible, you know."

He grinned and joined her. "What if we go inside and get your mind off all this?" He offered his hand.

She stood and followed him inside.

The place was just as she remembered. Wooden floors and shelves cluttered with souvenirs and trinkets, vintage metal signs, specialty foods, and — well, junk, really. As a little girl, she'd visited with her parents and pretended she was Laura from *Little House on the Prairie,* finding it easy to imagine mean old Nellie Oleson sitting on one of the bright red bar stools at the long soda fountain.

"Hey, remember these?" Her father held up a package of whoopie pies. He tucked the package under his arm and grabbed two more. To that, he added several packages of Black Jack gum and pecan pralines, and a large jar of jalapeño salsa.

"Are you thinking you're going to go hungry?" she teased, handing him a basket.

He wandered off down the aisle while she buried her attention in a book rack, picking up *A Field Guide to the Hill Country* and thumbing the pages.

She'd been there about ten minutes when three guys in leathers with blue bandanas on their heads wandered past. "You want some water?" one of them asked.

Overhead, a ceiling fan slowly turned, stirring up the air.

"Nah, I don't drink that garbage. Ain't you been watching the news 'bout that lady and the bottled water with those microbugs in it? That's what killed all those kids over in San Antone."

"Yeah?"

The first one nodded. "They oughta hang that gal up by her toenails for withholding that information, if you ask me."

Suddenly, her father was at her side holding a brown sack. Without a word, he took her elbow and maneuvered her toward the front door.

Outside, she was visibly shaken, and he knew it. He dropped his hand from her arm. "C'mon, I think it's time we go have that meeting."

The Grist Mill was a short walk. The hostess leaned on the wooden podium at the entrance to the old cotton gin, now converted into one of the most popular restaurants in southern Texas. "Do you want to be seated now? Or wait for your other party?"

"Now would be fine," her father told the pretty blonde.

Juliet waited for some unspoken exchange, a stolen look of mutual appreciation that would pass between them. Failing to see anything bothersome, she took a deep breath and followed the hostess to an outdoor table on a wooden deck nestled under the shade of towering oak trees and overlooking the river.

The air was filled with the smell of mesquite wood smoke and grilling meat, and the sound of people's voices. A Kenny Chesney tune softly played overhead, piped through outdoor speakers.

Once seated, she reached for her water glass. "Do you think he'll actually show up?"

Her father didn't have to answer. Several yards away, the hostess pointed a guy who looked to be in his thirties to their table. He came toward them, looking even more nervous than she felt inside.

He wore ratty cowboy boots and faded jeans, a belt with a large silver buckle, and a plaid shirt. His shirtsleeves were rolled up, and he was wearing a baseball cap. As he approached the table, he slipped the hat from his head and twisted the bill in his hands.

"Uh, you the Ryans?" he asked.

Her father stood and extended his hand. "You must be Oliver. I'm Dr. Bennett Ryan and this is my daughter, Dr. Juliet Ryan."

His eyes turned amused. "Bet that causes some confusion." He took the seat closest to the railing overlooking the water as a waitress stepped to the table and passed out menus.

Juliet fingered her utensils. "Thank you for meeting with us, Oliver."

"Yeah. No problem."

They sat in uncomfortable quiet a few moments. She tried making small talk. "I saw photos of your little girl on Facebook. What a doll."

Immediately, she kicked herself. He'd know she'd been checking up on him. Like a stalker. Never mind she wanted to know everything she could about her predecessor and her husband, who possibly held the key to clearing her name.

Fortunately, her question pulled a smile. "Her name is Amy. She's a beauty, even at this age. The epitome of her mother. Especially her happy temperament. Oh, except that first day you called when you heard her crying in the background. She wasn't terribly happy that afternoon."

He blinked, and everything about him draped with sadness. His face, the way he held his shoulders — but mostly his eyes. His eyes revealed the deep loss he'd experienced.

It was then she knew the cost of meeting with her and reliving the details of those months. She sincerely wished for some other way beyond asking him to dig into his wounded heart to help her.

Her father saw it too. He glanced in her direction. "Daughters are indeed special."

The waitress returned to the table with a pen and tablet.

"Did you change your mind and decide you were hungry?" her father asked.

She shook her head. "Just a small salad, please." She lifted her menu to the waitress. "With ranch on the side."

Her father ordered the GristBurger, a half-pound patty covered in a special queso sauce. And onion rings.

Oliver handed off his menu. "Same for me."

Her dad casually leaned his arms on the table. "You live here long?"

"About two years. Robin and I moved out here just before — well, before everything."

They learned he owned his own residential

construction firm. Business had been good with the booming growth in the area. "There's been nearly a 50 percent increase in new homes over the last ten years," he said. "The schools are good, and you can't beat the locals. Neighborly folks. Last year, we made Sperling's List of Best Places to Live."

Juliet listened to their chatter, nodding at all the appropriate times. Under different circumstances, she might actually enjoy herself. But no matter how she tried to ignore the noise inside her head, she couldn't quit thinking about how the guy sitting across the table might be her last hope to prove Alexa and Greer had lied.

She wasn't the sort to dwell on the unfair side of life, believing that with enough grit and hard work, you could counter any negativity and come out stronger for it. But lately, everything had spun out of control. And even though she faced nothing like Oliver's painful journey, the situation was making her feel crazy.

She glanced down at the river below the deck. By summer, it would be packed with people floating the current on tubes and in rafts. In the same token, by summer her entire career and even her freedom could be sunk. Oliver Ford would be the one to determine how far and how fast.

Their food came. Her father reached for the ketchup and squirted a large mound next to his open bun. He offered the bottle to Oliver. "So, when did your wife know she wanted to go into food safety as a profession?"

Oliver became pensive and picked up an onion ring. "I don't think it was ever really a decision on her part. Her degree was in policy and management, focusing on organizational development, which proved fairly useless in the marketplace. She became a corporate consultant. That's how she met Alexa Carmichael. Alexa was impressed with a motivational workshop Robin gave at some women-in-business thing and offered her a job."

Juliet cringed at hearing how little regard had been given to selecting a candidate with the proper qualifications to oversee a food safety program. Nudging a piece of lettuce around on her plate, she posed another question. "When did Robin first feel things going south?"

Oliver swallowed and wiped his mouth with his napkin. "Well, probably the first I heard her complain was when she wanted to hire Malcolm Stanford. Clearly, the guy was qualified, but his salary requirements were at the top of the range, and Alexa urged her to pass for another. Robin held her ground, which in hindsight was likely the beginning of her undoing." He looked at her dad. "Not a good idea to cross Alexa Carmichael."

Yes, she now knew that sentiment to be true.

"Robin knew fairly early she needed someone running the lab who had the necessary scientific background she lacked. Alexa's argument was that the number of outbreaks in the water industry was next to nil and that the entire effort was fairly perfunctory. If you want to know the truth, I think she just wanted to be able to print some fancy language on their marketing materials about how careful the company was to meet the standards — blah, blah, blah."

Juliet looked over at her father. Their eyes met. She knew what he must be thinking. For the first time, she was beginning to understand his soapbox stance against corporate attitudes when it came to this important issue. She'd been naïve enough to believe Alexa when she said product safety was her number one priority. She hated to consider there might be more executives out there sending these same mixed messages.

Her father turned his attention back to Oliver. "And at some point, your wife became concerned about some test results?"

"Gravely concerned. By that time, she'd attended some food safety conferences and had studied industry publications." He looked to her father. "Some authored by you, Dr. Ryan."

Normally, a compliment directed at her father would've sparked resentment on her part. But now she found herself feeling pride. Likely her father's notoriety had moved Oliver to meet with them. And she was grateful.

"My wife knew any food product held some risk, and that proper precautions had to be taken to keep the public safe." He pushed his plate back, apparently no longer hungry. He looked at her dad, then back at her. "Granted, all this is fairly over my head, but I know what she told me."

"Which is?" she urged.

"Malcolm warned her some tests were coming in with suspicious counts. Robin did some research and concluded there might be a problem where they were sourcing the water. She reported that concern to Alexa."

Juliet laid down her fork. "I was told

Robin experienced some issues with her pregnancy about that same time and often missed work."

Oliver shook his head, looking disgusted. "I can assure you my wife missed very little time at work. In fact, I begged her to stay home and off her feet. I wanted her to follow her doctor's instructions." His eyes filled with pain. "Instead, she stormed ahead and worked herself to the bone trying to get support for addressing what appeared to be a risky proposition. She wanted to halt production for several days, until she could invite someone more qualified to help her further assess the situation."

Her father's eyebrows drew into a frown. "And?"

"And she met with unbelievable resistance. Two days later, she was terminated over the phone. She was never even allowed back in. The company packed her things and had them delivered to the house."

The statement caused Juliet's breath to catch. This information was not what she wanted to hear.

Her fingers worked the skin at her throat. If the company sent everything home without giving Robin a chance to collect the important records, this meeting was for naught. She was in real trouble.

In the very near future, she expected to be called to testify at administrative hearings before the CDC officials. There would be prosecutors present, ready to pounce. Right now, all she had was testimony, hers and others. Without some proof to back up her innocence, she'd be paddling a treacherous current with bare hands.

Her father knew it too. "Robin didn't have a chance to stow away any proof to back up her allegations?"

Oliver leaned back, looking at both of them with eyes still somewhat wary. "Like, what kind of proof you talking about?"

Her dad pushed his plate back. He leaned his arms over the table and gave Oliver an earnest look. "Look, I'm not the kind of guy who likes to dance around issues. My girl here is in some real trouble. We need any of your wife's handwritten notes, any logs or emails . . . anything that would help back up our position and clear Juliet's name. And Robin's," he skillfully added. "What we really need is information relating to the tests Robin was concerned about."

Juliet pulled a copy of the analysis report from her bag and handed it across the table to him. "I audited the company records. Oddly, nothing was out of order. All the counts are within standard. How can that be, given what you are telling us?"

Oliver examined the analysis report, his face darkening. He handed the paper back and turned to her father. "So, what happens if you find proof?"

"We'll take them down — Alexa Carmichael and Greer Latham, and anyone else found to be a part of their neglect and greedy schemes."

Juliet bit at the inside of her cheek. She prayed Cyril Montavan was not a part of any of this. She didn't think so, but then she'd severely miscalculated Greer Latham's character.

Her father drew a deep breath. "And we'll clear your wife's reputation in the process. No telling what lies they've spread, and to whom." He leaned back, apparently hoping his last comment had sealed the deal.

Oliver's hand reached in his back pocket and pulled out his wallet. "Then I guess you'll be needing this." He extracted a folded-up paper, opened it, and placed it on the table in front of her father.

Juliet saw a smile dawn on her dad's face. He nodded. "Yes, that's exactly what we need," he said. Now grinning, he handed it to her.

The analysis report was shocking. The counts showed that the water was clearly adulterated with high levels of Shiga toxin–producing E. coli. Given the sanitary measures in place inside the company, the contamination likely came from the extraction site. Although rare, runoff from nearby land surfaces sometimes found its way into an underground spring, exposing the water to deadly pathogens originating in animal feces. Media around the country reported findings in underground springs located near zoos or running through cattle pastures.

At these high levels, no process could guarantee 100 percent elimination of the deadly pathogens. Which was why Larimar Springs should have pulled the product from distribution.

More importantly, the date of the report matched the period of time Alexa was courting Cyril Montavan's capital infusion. The crafty owner of Larimar Springs had taken a chance, not wanting to risk even the slightest hint of a problem with their source water during critical negotiations with her financial benefactor. She'd taken steps to eliminate Robin from the scene, cutting possible exposure of her decision to place her financial interests above consumer health.

Greer had discovered Juliet that day at the

golf course and delivered her résumé to Alexa, who quickly extended an offer of employment. She'd wanted someone with high credentials to cover her tracks, leaving Montavan International and the public with the mistaken impression that the company placed product safety high in their company priorities.

Sadly, the pallets were stored in the warehouse, waiting for an opportune time to destroy the bottles of tainted water without anyone finding out. In the mayhem of increased production requirements for the expanded Water Circus account, the product was distributed.

Alexa's decision had set up the perfect storm. And in the aftermath of that hurricane, first Robin's and then Juliet's career was strewn and left in pieces. Lives of families were shattered. Including Tavina's.

And Oliver's.

She held the report in her shaking hand, knowing it also proved someone inside the company had created an altered version. She wasn't an attorney, but that would likely prove intent. Nothing about any of this was an accident.

"The original is in my safety deposit box." Oliver slid his wallet back in his pocket. "I have something else I think you'll find interesting — and useful." His voice seemed to choke with emotion.

She couldn't help it. Her hand slid over his.

"After you called the first time, I sat rocking Amy, who's nearly two now. Anyway, I got to thinking about the commercial deals, the industrial warehouses, and the office crews I'd been on early in my construction career. My head went over all the systems that are a part of those kinds of buildings. Then it hit me."

"What hit you?" her father asked.

"Well, every outfit like Larimar Springs has an extensive security system. Especially when they're located in those out-of-the-way industrial areas." His eyes narrowed. "So, thoughts started running through my mind that there must be tapes from the system at Larimar. I did a little research, pulled the building permits, and found the security company that installed that system."

She lifted her head in surprise. Despite his worn cowboy look, this guy was no dummy. "And?"

"And I called them. Seems those boys keep records up to three years. So, I made a little trip into San Antonio and met with the owner of the company, who just so happened to be hoping to do a little residential work over here in this growing area." He smiled. "In the safety deposit box, along with that original report, is a video showing Greer Latham in Robin's office. He opened her cabinet drawer, removed a file, and pulled out a piece of paper, then shoved another in its place."

He leaned back, triumphant.

Her dad's finger tapped the paper on the table. "But that doesn't necessarily prove it was this report."

Oliver grinned. "True. But that dumb jack pulled out his phone and called Alexa and told her what he'd done. Confirmed loud and clear that he'd accomplished just what she'd told him to do."

Juliet's hand went to her mouth.

Her father shook his head, incredulous. "And you have the video?"

Oliver's face broke into a wide grin. "Yup, safe and sound. And the guy at the security place is willing to authenticate the document in court, if necessary."

As they walked from the restaurant, Juliet stopped just outside the door. She turned to Oliver Ford, her eyes brimming with grateful tears. Throwing professional propriety aside, she stepped forward and hugged him. "How can I ever thank you?"

His eyes grew moist as well. "Take them down — and make sure everybody knows what Robin did to try to protect the public."

She nodded. "I assure you, with God's help I will."

On the way to the car, she slipped her arm into her father's. The physical contact felt foreign, yet strangely natural. "Thank you, Dad. Your support meant everything."

His face drew into a satisfied smile. "Think nothing of it, Dr. Ryan. I'm here by your side because I love you."

49

Exhausted and exhilarated all at the same time, Juliet stepped off the elevator and moved briskly down the hall and toward her door, house keys in hand.

The meeting with Oliver Ford had been a stunning success. She now had everything needed to vindicate herself and her predecessor, who had been run out of the company for trying to keep the public safe. She would no longer face a ruined career or criminal charges.

There was still much to do ahead, but tonight she'd take a hot bath and slip into bed. With anxious thoughts no longer plaguing her mind, she'd finally get some long overdue sleep.

A noise caught her attention. Startled, she looked up — and stopped walking. What she saw at the door made her heart skip a beat.

Cyril Montavan.

"Hey," he said, a small smile playing at the corners of his mouth. "That was timed nicely."

A tiny part of her thrilled at seeing him again, but inside a yellow light flashed, and she told herself to proceed with extreme caution. "This is a huge surprise. What are you doing here?"

He stood in a pair of khaki slacks and an open-collared shirt, a jacket folded over his arm. "I wanted to talk to you — in person."

"And so you got on your jet and flew on over to San Antonio?" She unlocked the door, hating the edge in her voice. The guy could've just returned her emails.

"I wished you'd been able to reach me," he said, as if reading her mind. "I'm afraid I was in Africa, in a fairly remote area where communication is sometimes a little dicey."

She invited him in, recalling his philanthropic efforts in Angola and South Sudan. Her eyes went to her slippers on the floor, the unappetizing bowl of half-eaten cold cereal floating in a quarter inch of thickened milk. She quickly scooped up the bowl and moved to the kitchen. "Sorry, I wasn't expecting company. Uh, would you like some tea or something?"

He placed his jacket on the arm of her sofa. "Sure, that'd be nice."

She moved to the kitchen and grabbed the teapot. "So, I'm dying to hear what you flew thousands of miles to talk to me about." She held her breath.

On the surface, and from everything she'd discovered through her internet research, the guy was not cut from the same bolt of cloth as Alexa and that slimy Greer Latham. But if she'd learned anything over these past months, she now knew people could be the exact opposite of what they seemed.

She turned on the burner and faced him, leaning against the counter. "When you didn't answer my emails, I figured you'd heard."

Cyril joined her in the kitchen, smiling as if trying to put her at ease. "Yes, Alexa called me. Nothing I knew of you matched with the woman she described." He chanced placing a hand on her forearm. "Juliet, we've not known each other long — or all that well, for that matter — but in the small amount of time we spent together, I knew you would never purposely endanger consumers. You were torn up inside over your assistant and her little boy."

She took a deep breath and considered what he said. Could it be possible Cyril Montavan's interest in her was genuine — that she could count on his friendship?

"What did you say?"

His eyes twinkled. "Nothing much, really. Instead, I sent Alexa Carmichael a little gift."

She raised her eyebrows. "A gift? I don't understand."

He slid against the counter next to her and folded his arms. "I sent her a box of bugies with a note describing the Italian pastry's history — and a warning that liars always leave a trail."

"You didn't!"

He nodded, grinning. "Yes, I most certainly did. And right after, I had arrangements made to fly directly here. I would've called you first, but I assumed you might not take the call, mistakenly thinking I might be in on Alexa's plans to destroy you. I figured if I could talk to you in person, I could make you believe otherwise."

Juliet didn't have words for this. "Cyril, let's sit down. I have a lot to tell you."

After filling him in on the meeting with Oliver Ford and what she'd learned, she considered the implications and her mind filled with questions. "So, where do you go from here? You know what's ahead for Alexa and Greer, and what that means for the company. Seems to me Larimar Springs is sadly going down."

She hated the thought of Larimar Springs closing its doors and all those people unemployed. Good people. Like Malcolm Stanford and the staff in the lab. And Alva Jacobs, who'd taken a considerable risk to clue her in to the true nature of the people in charge at Larimar Springs.

And even Dale Frissom and Fred Macklin, members of the executive team who had been as clueless as she about what was going on behind the scenes. Disingenuous at times, but clueless just the same.

"What's ahead?" His eyes warmed, and he gave a casual lift of his shoulders. "Well, I'll let all this play out with the food safety officials, then I'll invoke the clause in the contract allowing me to buy out any shareholder found guilty of fraudulent acts of turpitude against the company. My legal team will be instructed to handle the restructuring."

"Restructuring?" She shot him a funny look.

His face filled with reassurance. Again Cyril seemed to know her thoughts. "I'll continue with Alexa's plans to take the company international. The bottled water market is thriving, and I stand behind the wisdom of my investment." He took her hand, and she felt the last vestiges of concern fade away.

"And one more thing," he said.

She wrinkled her face, puzzled. "What's that?"

"I'm naming you president."

50

After the truth broke, Juliet was exonerated of any wrongdoing. Larimar Springs had been closed temporarily, pending the restructure with Montavan International, giving her a lot of time to consider how perilously close she'd come to taking her entire life over a cliff.

In the weeks since the closure, she'd often spent her evenings in front of the television, watching the episodes of the last months of her life unfold like an HBO drama.

First, there were the images of the arrests — of Alexa being led from her posh Mediterranean-style home in handcuffs, followed by a stricken-looking husband and son, no longer the smiling family shown in the photos in her office.

Both she and her plastic surgeon husband agreed to relinquish the company to Cyril without a legal fight, in exchange for his promise not to sue for damages.

Greer didn't fold as easily.

Rumor had it that when Greer learned of the incriminating security tape, he'd come completely undone. He'd shouted at his attorneys, even shoving one to the ground after the guy had the nerve to tell his ruffled client that there was no viable way to keep the recording out of evidence.

In the end, Greer turned himself in to the authorities, and of course the media covered him leaving the arraignment, flanked by attorneys. While not a hair was out of place, no one but Juliet likely noticed that one of his cuff links was missing.

In one of many press conferences, Dr. Breslin stood in the parking lot of Children's Hospital and read a written statement that included an eloquent recitation of how the outbreak had affected government resources, the community, and taxpayer dollars. He expressed that no amount of government oversight was effective if people in key management positions wantonly disregarded public safety.

He pulled his reading glasses from his face and looked into the camera. "On behalf of the City of San Antonio, the Texas Department of Health Services, the US Department of Agriculture, and the US Centers for Disease Control, I hope the court will send a clear message that these types of blatant criminal acts placing people in medical danger will not be tolerated. I urge the court to send a strong warning to corporate officers across this country by rendering the strongest punishment possible in this case."

When Juliet learned that Alexa Carmichael and Greer Latham had later pled guilty to multiple counts of distribution of adulterated food product, as well as conspiracy and fraud related to the audits, she'd been relieved there would be no trial, yet saddened.

While no one could argue the former executives deserved to be brought to justice, she didn't relish knowing they'd likely be incarcerated, at least for a period of time.

Over the course of the past weeks, a lesson had been learned. She no longer held a fervent desire for meting out justice on her own. She'd leave punishing wrongdoers, including Alexa and Greer, to God and the proper authorities.

The Scripture her mother had underlined was spot-on. Juliet now could so easily see how God had indeed been right by her side the entire time, protecting and guiding her through the deep waters.

Sitting on the sofa, she reached across the

cushions and gently caressed the worn leather cover of her mother's Bible. "Mom, you were right. The better way is to forgive and let go."

She stood and headed into the kitchen, where she withdrew a pan from the cupboard, then moved to the refrigerator for the chicken she planned to fry for dinner. She'd worked hard to perfect her ability to make her mother's cream gravy and couldn't wait to show off her new skill to her father tonight when he came over for dinner, something that was a fairly frequent occurrence now that they were becoming friends.

Suddenly, she heard a familiar voice on the television.

"As recent as two months ago, forty people in Oklahoma were sickened with listeria linked to raw milk. And only weeks before that, in California, hundreds fell ill after eating romaine lettuce tainted with salmonella. I could name a dozen more such incidents, all in the last twelve months. No matter what happens within the justice system for the likes of Alexa Carmichael and Greer Latham, I hope health officials don't let down their guard, believing we've done even near enough to protect the public."

Smiling, she wiped her hands on a towel and quickly returned to the television.

Cameras flashed, and dozens of reporters scrambled to take notes, paying close attention to the man speaking, likely wondering who would be bold enough to make such assertions.

But Juliet knew.

EPILOGUE

Juliet stood alone in the green room, gazing in the mirror. The reflection looking back was still that of the educated, accomplished young woman she'd been nearly two years ago. But now her eyes held a certain wisdom she'd lacked before. The respect she'd earned since being hired at Larimar Springs had been hard won.

A slight rap at the door pulled her attention. "Yes, come in."

A perky young news intern peeked her head through the cracked opening. "Dr. Ryan? We're ready for you."

She took one final glance in the mirror. Her coral and turquoise jacket was perfect. Her lip color and hair, great. She was ready.

She followed the intern down a long hallway lined with photos — among them Matt Lauer, Katie Couric, Jane Pauley, and Al Roker. Despite fighting to appear calm, her insides fluttered. Especially when they arrived at a set of heavy double doors.

The intern turned and put her finger to her mouth, warning her to be quiet. She pointed to the red light flashing to the right of the door and shook her head, just in case her first signal to stay silent had been missed.

The doors opened to a massive interior with rivers of wires running over the floor. Men with headphones sat in tall, swiveling stools, perched next to cameras hanging from the ceiling, all directed at a brightly lit backdrop known as Studio 1A.

Natalie Morales smiled at Matt Lauer from behind the iconic anchor desk perched in front of windows looking over Rockefeller Plaza. "Matt, we have an interesting story coming up about a woman who exposed a company conspiracy — one that cost lives. Even those of several tiny children. She's authored a book about that experience and the extreme need for food safety in our country, and will be joining us to talk about it."

Matt raised his eyebrows. "Sounds like something viewers won't want to miss."

Juliet stood trembling, barely believing the famous morning news show hosts were talking about her in front of millions of viewers across America. For a flash second, she couldn't help but smile, oddly wondering if Ellen Shaffer was watching.

And Stinky Sam.

She followed the intern to an adjoining set with comfortable sofas and a coffee table. She positioned herself in her designated seat while another guy with headphones clipped on a microphone. "Testing, testing," he said.

Never in her wildest imagination would she have dreamed this is how her story would turn out. After a brief commercial break, she'd be reporting how she and her father had handed the evidence Oliver Ford provided over to Dr. Breslin, which led to criminal charges being brought against Alexa Carmichael and Greer Latham. How they'd pled guilty to avoid extended sentencing.

She'd tell America how Montavan International took control of Larimar Springs in the aftermath, and with her at the helm, they'd raised the bar in food safety. How she'd written *Up the Waterspout* and now traveled internationally speaking at food safety symposiums, warning about the dangers of foodborne illnesses and the destruction and havoc that could result from cutting corners.

Photos of the new Marquis DeAndre

Mosely Center for Children would be shown, built next to the expanded New Beginnings Birthing Center in San Antonio. She'd pay tribute to her mother and to the new director of both institutions, Tavina Mosely Jinks, who had married Leo Paternoster's paralegal. Pictures would flash on-screen of a very pregnant Tavina, locked in her new husband's arms, beaming.

Juliet's hand drifted to her own swollen belly. On camera, she'd smile across the studio at her husband, Cyril, a man of extraordinary integrity.

Her mother would be watching from heaven . . . pleased.

Lastly, and maybe most importantly, Juliet would look Matt Lauer in the eyes and express deep gratitude to the man who had stood by her side, a man she greatly admired and loved. The one who had taught her that without a heart and soul, she had nothing.

Her father.

AUTHOR NOTE

Like many of my novels, the idea for this story was sparked by a legal matter. In the midnineties, I was assigned to a case where a teenage girl left her high school during the lunch break and went to a nearby Jack in the Box restaurant. Like others in the car, she ordered a hamburger. After taking only a couple of bites, she opened the bun to discover the middle of the burger bloody rare and elected to toss the remaining sandwich aside, eating her fries instead.

A short time later, she fell violently ill — a victim of E. coli O157:H7.

Over the course of the deadly outbreak linked to Jack in the Box restaurants (and their parent corporation, Foodmaker, Inc.), many others became dangerously ill, and several young children died. During the time I was immersed in reviewing and cataloguing the massive amounts of evidence in this litigation, I developed a new appreciation for those charged with maintaining food safety.

One of those is my own husband, who has been in senior management in meat companies over the past two decades.

I knew I wanted to highlight this issue in a novel, and *Where Rivers Part* was born, so to speak. I will never forget sitting across a deposition table in San Diego and watching Foodmaker, Inc.'s quality control director tear up as he was questioned about his role. I saw the agony on his face as attorneys more than hinted he was a guilty party in the horrific event.

That prompted the question many novelists ask when starting a new story: *What if?*

While this story features what I learned while working on the Jack in the Box litigation, much of it is purely my imagination at work.

For instance, it is extremely rare for bottled water to contain deadly pathogens. Bottled water is highly regulated. The quality control processes include ultraviolet light disinfection as well as microfiltration and ozone disinfection. I chose to use a water company simply because it fit with the water theme I wanted to create in the book.

What I found particularly intriguing was how San Antonio fit surprisingly into the water theme. While this beautiful city is located in an arid environment, underneath is the Edwards Aquifer, a unique groundwater system and one of the most prolific artesian aquifers in the world, serving the diverse needs of almost two million users in south central Texas — and such an amazing picture of Jesus, who is often referred to in the Bible as our Living Water.

I've certainly found Jesus to be what satisfies the arid places in my life.

Kellie

ACKNOWLEDGMENTS

I extend my utmost gratitude to my publishing team at Revell. They not only help make these Texas Gold stories shine, but they support me as an author with their time, their ingenuity, and their marketing budget. Jen, Kelsey, Lindsay, Robin, Jessica, and so many other unnamed publishing champions at Revell — you deserve many more cupcakes!

My agent, Natasha Kern, is the best in the business. Joining arms with Natasha was one of the smartest decisions I ever made as an author. Her guidance and support mean the world to me.

Much gratitude goes to the retailers, bloggers, reviewers, and industry folks who support these Texas Gold novels. Thank you!

The time I spend with my writing partner on the phone each morning is simply a gift from God. Lynne Gentry is one of the finest word crafters I know. As a friend, she listens and points me to Jesus. A girl can't find better than that.

I also want to take this opportunity to acknowledge my prayer warrior, Diana Haibel, a woman who has prayed for me and my loved ones for years. May God pay you back, my friend.

The paralegal character in this book is named after a real young man, Seth Jinks. Sadly, Seth lost his battle with addiction last fall, leaving behind a devastated family. I met his mother at a book club, and she has become a friend. Vicki is a woman of incredible strength and dignity who now works tirelessly to support others affected by addiction. I admire her.

Big thanks go to the best hair designer in Texas, Shannon Morgan. Sitting in her chair once a month is so fun. The epilogue for this book was her idea. Thanks, Shannon!

I couldn't help but think of my husband when I wrote the character Cyril Montavan. Allen is such a hard worker and a man of integrity. We've been through a lot together in our thirty-plus years, and I am blessed.

Together, we raised two boys who are my heart's treasures. I am so stinking proud of the men Eric and Jordan have become. I may garner accolades for my novels, but my sons are by far my best work. I love them both more than can be adequately expressed. It was such a pleasure to dedicate this book to them.

Now a special note to my readers — thank you for purchasing my books, and for the reviews you post on Facebook, Amazon, Goodreads, and more. Your messages telling me how much you like these stories mean the world to me. You are always foremost in my mind when I write.

ABOUT THE AUTHOR

A former legal investigator and trial paralegal, **Kellie Coates Gilbert** writes with a sympathetic, intimate knowledge of how people react under pressure. She tells emotionally poignant stories about messy lives and eternal hope.

Find out more about Kellie and her books at **www.kelliecoates gilbert.com.** While you're there, don't forget to join Kellie's Reader's Club. As one of Kellie's VIP readers, you'll receive exclusive news about her books, exciting giveaways, and (shh!) maybe some special and exciting opportunities made available only to Kellie's Reader's Club members.